Praise for Rita Mae Brown's Sister Jane Series

"Cunning foxes, sensible hounds, and sweet-tempered horses are among the sparkling conversationalists in this charming series starring Jane (Sister) Arnold. . . . The biggest thrills are riding out with Sister and her chatty hounds on a cold, crisp morning."
—*The New York Times Book Review*

"[Brown] succeeds in conjuring a world in which prey are meant to survive the chase and foxes are knowing collaborators (with hunters and hounds) in the rarefied rituals that define the sport."
—*People*

"The rolling hills of the Virginia hunt country are beautiful, and all the gentility makes a perfect place to plop a dead body."
—*Toronto Globe and Mail*

"The fun of Brown's series is the wealth of foxhunting lore, the spot-on portrayal of Virginians . . . and the evocative descriptions of the Blue Ridge Mountains. . . . And then there's Sister, the seventy-three-year-old heroine who becomes even more appealing with each successive book. Brown has a winner in this memorable character."
—*Richmond Times Dispatch*

"[Brown's] foxhunting titles are great for readers who like gentility with a wicked little twist."
—*Library Journal*

"Readers will be charmed by Brown's endearing characters, animal and human, all of whom are given to philosophizing on the state of the world."
—*Publishers Weekly*

THRILL OF THE HUNT

THRILL OF
THE HUNT

A NOVEL

RITA MAE BROWN

ILLUSTRATED BY LEE GILDEA

BALLANTINE BOOKS

NEW YORK

2023 Ballantine Books Trade Paperback Edition

Copyright © 2022 by American Artists, Inc.

Illustrations copyright © 2022 by Lee Gildea, Jr.

Published in the United States by Ballantine Books, an imprint of Random House, a division of Penguin Random House LLC, New York.

Ballantine is a registered trademark and the colophon is a trademark of Penguin Random House LLC.

Originally published in hardcover in the United States by Ballantine Books, an imprint of Random House, a division of Penguin Random House LLC, in 2022.

ISBN 978-0-593-35762-0
Ebook ISBN 978-0-593-35761-3

Printed in the United States of America on acid-free paper

randomhousebooks.com

1st Printing

CAST OF CHARACTERS

THE HUMANS

Jane Arnold, MFH, "Sister," runs the Jefferson Hunt. *MFH* stands for "Master of Foxhounds," the individual who runs the hunt, deals with every crisis both on and off the field. She is strong, bold, loves her horses and her hounds. Decades ago, her fourteen-year-old son was killed in a tractor accident. That loss deepened her, taught her to cherish every minute. She's had lots of minutes, as she's in her early seventies, but she has no concept of age.

Shaker Crown, the huntsman, suffered a bad accident last season. He is hoping to recover, has seen specialists, but while he can ride he can't risk another fall.

Gray Lorillard isn't cautious in the hunt field, but he is cautious off it, as he was a partner in one of the most prestigious accounting firms in D.C. He knows how the world really works and, although retired, is often asked to solve problems at his former firm. He is smart, handsome, in his mid-sixties, and is African American.

Crawford Howard is best described by Aunt Daniella, who commented, "There's a great deal to be said about new money and Crawford means to say it all." He started an outlaw pack of hounds when Sister did not ask him to be her joint master. Slowly, he is realizing you can't push people around in this part of the world. Fundamentally, he is a decent and generous man.

Sam Lorillard is Gray's younger brother. He works at Crawford's stables. Crawford hired Sam when no one else would, so Sam is loyal. He blew a full scholarship to Harvard thanks to the bottle. He's good with horses. His brother saved him and he's clean, but so many people feel bad about what might have been. He focuses on the future.

Daniella Laprade is Gray and Sam's aunt. She is an extremely healthy nonagenarian who isn't above shaving a year or two off her age. She may even be older than her stated ninety-four. Her past is dotted with three husbands and numerous affairs, all carried out with discretion.

Wesley Blackford, "Weevil"—he's just tipped over thirty, is divinely handsome, loves hounds. He fills in for the injured Shaker Crown, whom he respects. Weevil has brilliance and the foundation of ballast.

Anne Harris, "Tootie," left Princeton in her freshman year, as she missed foxhunting in Virginia so very much. Her father had a cow, cut her out of his will. She takes classes at the University of Virginia and is now twenty-four and shockingly beautiful. She is African American.

Yvonne Harris, Tootie's mother, is a former model who has fled Chicago and her marriage. She divorced Victor Harris, a hard-driving businessman who built an African American media empire. She built it with him. She is trying to understand Tootie, feels she was not so much a bad mother as an absent one. Her experience has been different from her daughter's, and Tootie's freedoms were won by Yvonne's generation and those prior. Yvonne doesn't understand that Tootie doesn't get this.

Margaret DuCharme, M.D., is Alfred DuCharme's daughter and she's acted as a go-between for her father and her uncle, Binky DuCharme, since childhood. Her cousin, Binky's son Arthur, also acts as a go-between and both the cousins are just fed up with it. They are in their early forties, Margaret being more successful than Arthur, but he's happy enough.

Walter Lungren, M.D., JT-MFH, is a cardiologist who has hunted with Sister since his boyhood. He is the late Raymond Arnold's son, which Sister knows. No one talks about it and Walter's father always acted as though he were Walter's father. It's the way things are done around here. Let sleeping dogs lie.

Betty Franklin is an honorary whipper-in, which means she doesn't get paid. Whippers-in emit a glamorous sheen to other foxhunters and it is a daring task. One must know a great deal and be able to ride hard, jump high, think in a split second. She is Sister's best friend and in her mid-fifties. Everyone loves Betty.

Bobby Franklin especially loves Betty, as he is her husband. He leads Second Flight, those riders who may take modest jumps but not the big ones. He and Betty own a small printing press and nearly lost their shirts when computers started printing out stuff. But people have returned to true printing, fine papers, etc. They're doing okay.

Kasmir Barbhaiya made his money in India in pharmaceuticals. Educated in an English public school, thence on to Oxford, he is highly intelligent and tremendously wealthy. Widowed, he moved to Virginia to be close to an old Oxford classmate and his wife. He owns marvelous horses and rides them well. He thought he would forever be alone but the Fates thought otherwise. Love had found him in the form of Alida Dalzell.

Edward and Tedi Bancroft, in their eighties, are stalwarts of the Jefferson Hunt and dear friends of Sister's. Evangelista, Edward's deceased sister, had an affair with Weevil's grandfather; although hushed up, it caused uproar in the Bancroft family.

Ben Sidell is the county sheriff, who is learning to hunt and loves it. Nonni, his horse, takes good care of him. He learns far more about the county by hunting than if he just stayed in his squad car. He dates Margaret DuCharme, M.D., an unlikely pairing that works.

Cynthia Skiff Kane hunts Crawford's outlaw pack. Crawford has gone through three other huntsmen but Cynthia can handle him. Sam Lorillard helps, too.

Cindy Chandler owns Foxglove Farm, one of the Jefferson fixtures. She's a good friend and a good foxhunter.

Freddie Thomas has run her small accounting business for years and is a CPA in her early fifties. She is a good friend of Alida Dalzell. As the IRS grows insanely complex as well as being deeply unfair she has grown to hate her work, but she cares for her clients so she hangs in there. She rarely talks about her profession. She is a good rider, a very sensible person.

Greg Wilson is in his mid-fifties. He owns a large lumberyard. He is a newer foxhunter, catching up fast. He is generous.

Risë Wilson has been a good wife and a loving mother. She thought her life was perfect.

Arnold Synder owns and runs a successful semi-truck sales company. Covid has slowed business, but he is hanging in there.

Ransom Patrick, a resourceful slave who worked with Sophie Marquette, helped to raid British pay wagons during the War of 1812. He lived an eventful life from 1790 to 1853.

William Odegaard is not conspicuously successful. He is in his early thirties, semi-literate, and accused of theft and blackmail.

Gardner Thompkins is slightly more successful than William.

He at least owns a rust bucket truck. He is also accused of the above crimes.

Ryan Stokes has ambition. He is a videographer, has a video blog, which has a growing viewership. He wants to have a studio in Richmond and a much larger audience. He shoots ads for businesses to pump up income. He is good at it.

Ayanda Freedman assists Ryan. She excels at editing but helps shoot footage. She is quiet.

Sally Taliaferro, pronounced Tolliver, is the new Episcopal priest at Emmanuel Episcopal in Greenwood, Virginia. She, too, rides.

Kathleen Sixt Dunbar inherited the 1780 House, a high-end antiques store, last year. She's becoming part of the community. Her Welsh terrier, Abdul, helps at the store.

THE AMERICAN FOXHOUNDS

Lighter than the English foxhound, with a somewhat slimmer head, they have formidable powers of endurance and remarkable noses.

Cora is the head female. What she says goes.

Asa is the oldest hunting male hound, and he is wise.

Diana is steady, in the prime of her life, and brilliant. There's no other word for her but *brilliant*.

Dasher, Diana's littermate, is often overshadowed by his sister, but he sticks to business and is coming into his own.

Dragon is also a littermate of the above "D" hounds. He is arrogant, can lose his concentration, and tries to lord his intelligence over other hounds.

Dreamboat is of the same breeding as Diana, Dasher, and Dragon, but a few years younger.

Hounds take the first initial of their mother's name. Following are hounds ordered from older to younger. No unentered hounds are included in this list. An unentered hound is not yet on the Master of Foxhounds stud books and not yet hunting with the pack. They are in essence kindergartners. **Trinity, Tinsel, Trident, Ardent, Thimble, Twist, Tootsie, Trooper, Taz, Tattoo, Parker, Pickens, Zane, Zorro, Zandy, Giorgio, Pookah, Pansy, Audrey, Aero, Angle, Aces** are young but entered. The "B" line and the "J" line have been just entered, are just learning the ropes.

THE HORSES

Keepsake, TB/QH, Bay; **Lafayette,** TB, gray; **Rickyroo,** TB, Bay; **Aztec,** TB, Chestnut; **Matador,** TB, Flea-bitten gray. All are Sister's geldings.

Showboat, Hojo, Gunpowder, and **Kilowatt,** all TBs, are Shaker's horses.

Outlaw, QH, Buckskin, and **Magellan,** TB, Dark Bay (which is really black), are Betty's horses.

Wolsey, TB, Flaming Chestnut, is Gray's horse. His red coat gave him his name, for Cardinal Wolsey.

Iota, TB, Bay, is Tootie's horse.

Matchplay and **Midshipman** are young Thoroughbreds of Sister's that are being brought along. It takes good time to make a solid foxhunter. Sister never hurries a horse or a hound in its schooling.

Trocadero is young, smart, being trained by Sam Lorillard.

Old Buster has become a babysitter. Like **Trocadero,** he is owned by Crawford Howard. Sam uses him for Yvonne Harris.

THE FOXES

Reds

Aunt Netty, older, lives at Pattypan Forge. She is overly tidy and likes to give orders.

Uncle Yancy is Aunt Netty's husband but he can't stand her anymore. He lives at the Lorillard farm, has all manner of dens and cubbyholes, as well as a place in the mudroom.

Charlene lives at After All Farm. She comes and goes.

Target (a gray) is Charlene's mate but he stays at After All. The food supply is steady and he likes the other animals.

Earl has the restored stone stables at Old Paradise all to himself. He has a den in a stall but also makes use of the tack room. He likes the smell of the leather.

Sarge is young. He found a den in big boulders at Old Paradise thanks to help from a doe. It's cozy with straw, old clothing bits, and even a few toys.

James lives behind the mill at Mill Ruins. He is not very social but from time to time will give the hounds a good run.

Ewald is a youngster who was directed to a den in an outbuilding during a hunt. Poor fellow didn't know where he was. The outbuilding at Mill Ruins will be a wonderful home as long as he steers clear of James.

Mr. Nash, young, lives at Close Shave, a farm about six miles from Chapel Cross. Given the housing possibilities and the good food, he is drawn to Old Paradise, which is being restored by Crawford Howard.

Grays

Comet knows everybody and everything. He lives in the old stone foundation part of the rebuilt log-and-frame cottage at Roughneck Farm.

Inky is so dark she's black and she lives in the apple orchard across from the above cottage. She knows the hunt schedule and rarely gives hounds a run. They can just chase someone else.

Georgia moved to the old schoolhouse at Foxglove Farm.

Grenville lives at Mill Ruins, in the back in a big storage shed. This part of the estate is called Shootrough.

Gris lives at Tollbooth Farm in the Chapel Cross area. He's very clever and can slip hounds in the batting of an eye.

Hortensia also lives at Mill Ruins. She's in another outbuilding. All are well constructed and all but the big hay sheds have doors that close, which is wonderful in bad weather.

Vi, young, is the mate of Gris, also young. They live at Tollbooth Farm in pleasant circumstances.

THE BIRDS

Athena, the great horned owl, is two and a half feet tall with a four-foot wingspan. She has many places where she will hole up but her true nest is in Pattypan Forge. It really beats being in a tree hollow. She's gotten spoiled.

Bitsy is eight and a half inches tall with a twenty-inch wingspan. Her considerable lungs make up for her tiny size as she is a screech owl, aptly named. Like Athena, she'll never live in a tree again, because she's living in the rafters of Sister's stable. Mice come in to eat the fallen grain. Bitsy feels like she's living in a supermarket.

St. Just, a foot and a half in height with a surprising wingspan of three feet, is a jet-black crow. He hates foxes but is usually sociable with other birds.

SISTER'S HOUSE PETS

Raleigh, a sleek, highly intelligent Doberman, likes to be with Sister. He gets along with the hounds, walks out with them. He tries to get along with the cat, but she's such a snob.

Rooster is a Harrier bequeathed to Sister by a dear friend. He likes riding in the car, walking out with hounds, watching everybody and everything. The cat drives him crazy.

Golliwog, or "Golly," is a long-haired calico. All other creatures are lower life-forms. She knows Sister does her best, but still. Golly is Queen of All She Surveys.

USEFUL TERMS

Away. A fox has gone away when he has left the covert. Hounds are away when they have left the covert on the line of the fox.

Brush. The fox's tail.

Burning scent. Scent so strong or hot that hounds pursue the line without hesitation.

Bye day. A day not regularly on the fixture card.

Cap. The fee nonmembers pay to hunt for that day's sport.

Carry a good head. When hounds run well together to a good scent, a scent spread wide enough for the whole pack to feel it.

Carry a line. When hounds follow the scent. This is also called working a line.

Cast. Hounds spread out in search of scent. They may cast themselves or be cast by the huntsman.

Charlie. A term for a fox. A fox may also be called **Reynard.**

Check. When hounds lose the scent and stop. The field must wait quietly while the hounds search for the scent.

Colors. A distinguishing color, usually worn on the collar but sometimes on the facings of a coat, that identifies a hunt. Colors can be awarded only by the Master and can be worn only in the field.

Coop. A jump resembling a chicken coop.

Couple straps. Two-strap hound collars connected by a swivel link. Some members of staff will carry these on the right rear of the saddle. Since the days of the pharaohs in ancient Egypt, hounds have been brought to the meets coupled. Hounds are always spoken of and counted in couples. Today, hounds walk or are driven to the meets. Rarely, if ever, are they coupled, but a whipper-in still carries couple straps should a hound need assistance.

Covert. A patch of woods or bushes where a fox might hide. Pronounced "cover."

Cry. How one hound tells another what is happening. The sound will differ according to the various stages of the chase. It's also called giving tongue and should occur when a hound is working a line.

Cub hunting. The informal hunting of young foxes in the late summer and early fall, before formal hunting. The main purpose is to enter young hounds into the pack. Until recently only the most knowledgeable members were invited to cub hunt, since they would not interfere with young hounds.

Dog fox. The male fox.

Dog hound. The male hound.

Double. A series of short, sharp notes blown on the horn to alert all that a fox is afoot. The gone away series of notes is a form of doubling the horn.

Draft. To acquire hounds from another hunt is to accept a draft.

Draw. The plan by which a fox is hunted or searched for in a certain area, such as a covert.

Draw over the fox. Hounds go through a covert where the fox is but cannot pick up its scent. The only creature that understands how this is possible is the fox.

Drive. The desire to push the fox, to get up with the line. It's a very desirable trait in hounds, so long as they remain obedient.

Dually. A one-ton pickup truck with double wheels in back.

Dwell. To hunt without getting forward. A hound that dwells is a bit of a putterer.

Enter. Hounds are entered into the pack when they first hunt, usually during cubbing season.

Field. The group of people riding to hounds, exclusive of the Master and hunt staff.

Field Master. The person appointed by the Master to control the field. Often it is the Master him- or herself.

Fixture. A card sent to all dues-paying members, stating when and where the hounds will meet. A fixture card properly received is an invitation to hunt. This means the card would be mailed or handed to a member by the Master.

Flea-bitten. A gray horse with spots or ticking that can be black or chestnut.

Gone away. The call on the horn when the fox leaves the covert.

Gone to ground. A fox that has ducked into its den, or some other refuge, has gone to ground.

Good night. The traditional farewell to the Master after the hunt, regardless of the time of day.

Gyp. The female hound.

Hilltopper. A rider who follows the hunt but does not jump. Hilltoppers are also called the Second Flight. The jumpers are called the First Flight.

Hoick. The huntsman's cheer to the hounds. It is derived from the Latin *hic haec hoc*, which means "here."

Hold hard. To stop immediately.

Huntsman. The person in charge of the hounds, in the field and in the kennel.

Kennelman. A hunt staff member who feeds the hounds and cleans the kennels. In wealthy hunts there may be a number of kennelmen. In hunts with a modest budget, the huntsman or even the Master cleans the kennels and feeds the hounds.

Lark. To jump fences unnecessarily when hounds aren't running. Masters frown on this, since it is often an invitation to an accident.

Lieu in. Norman term for "go in."

Lift. To take the hounds from a lost scent in the hopes of finding a better scent farther on.

Line. The scent trail of the fox.

Livery. The uniform worn by the professional members of the hunt staff. Usually it is scarlet, but blue, yellow, brown, and gray are also used. The recent dominance of scarlet has to do with people buying coats off the rack as opposed to having tailors cut them. (When anything is mass-produced, the choices usually dwindle, and such is the case with livery.)

Mask. The fox's head.

Meet. The site where the day's hunting begins.

MFH. The Master of Foxhounds; the individual in charge of the hunt: hiring, firing, landowner relations, opening territory (in large hunts this is the job of the hunt secretary), developing the pack of hounds, and determining the first cast of each meet. As in any leadership position, the Master is also the lightning rod for criticism. The Master may hunt the hounds, although this is usually done by a professional huntsman, who is also responsible for the hounds in the field and at the kennels. A long relationship between a Master and a huntsman allows the hunt to develop and grow.

Nose. The scenting ability of a hound.

Override. To press hounds too closely.

Overrun. When hounds shoot past the line of a scent. Often the scent has been diverted or foiled by a clever fox.

Ratcatcher. Informal dress worn during cubbing season and bye days.

Stern. A hound's tail.

Stiff-necked fox. One that runs in a straight line.

Strike hounds. Those hounds that, through keenness, nose, and often higher intelligence, find the scent first and press it.

Tail hounds. Those hounds running at the rear of the pack. This is not necessarily because they aren't keen; they may be older hounds.

Tally-ho. The cheer when the fox is viewed. Derived from the Norman *ty a hillaut*, thus coming into the English language in 1066.

Tongue. To vocally pursue a fox.

View halloo (halloa). The cry given by a staff member who sees a fox. Staff may also say tally-ho or, should the fox turn back, tally-back. One reason a different cry may be used by staff, especially in territory where the huntsman can't see the staff, is that the field in their enthusiasm may cheer something other than a fox.

Vixen. The female fox.

Walk. Puppies are walked out in the summer and fall of their first year. It's part of their education and a delight for both puppies and staff.

Whippers-in. Also called whips, these are the staff members who assist the huntsman, who make sure the hounds "do right."

THRILL OF THE HUNT

CHAPTER 1

September 11, 2020, Friday

The bottom rim of the setting sun touched the spine of the Blue Ridge Mountains, the golden light, like a veil, slid down over the western side of the ancient mountains.

Jane Arnold, "Sister," drove slowly north toward Chapel Crossroads. Raleigh, her Doberman, and Rooster, her Harrier, looked out the back window, interested in all they passed.

To her left, commanding thousands of acres, reposed Old Paradise, an estate of uncommon beauty, begun in 1814. War, changes of fortune, Nature's good years and bad years, left their mark. Finally, the outbuildings and majestic home became a reduced treasure, rubble, really. The estate was being restored by Crawford Howard, a man of great wealth. At long last the house had walls, a roof, gorgeous marble steps up to the double doors. As so many drawings had been made of the impressive place, Crawford could revive Old Paradise close to its original state.

Stopping to admire the incredible palatial home, these slanting rays of the sun washed the Corinthian columns gold, then orange, lastly scarlet. The capital's acanthus leaves below the cornice now deepened from gold to scarlet, finally blood red. As the last of the light turned the capitals blood red, blood seemed to run down the tall, elegant, fluted columns.

Sister stopped, slightly shivered for a moment, then drove slowly toward the crossroads a quarter of a mile ahead. The simple church for which the crossroads was named at the beginning of the eighteenth century glowed in the sunset's aftermath, now a sugary blue fading to twilight's gray.

Old Paradise, once close to twenty thousand acres, now five thousand, remained impressive. The final touches to the interior were ongoing. All outbuildings had been restored. Crawford started there first, figuring his workers and the staff archaeologists could cut their teeth on these buildings, some as old as the house itself. The stable alone was extraordinary, as was the Carriage House, both finished in 1816. Apart from the wealth of Old Paradise, secure wealth for close to two centuries, finally frittered away, the estate displayed sensible layout, a true working farm with buildings intended to last centuries, which they did. Support beams, slate roofing, brick floors all held up. Wrought iron sagged off hinges for stalls, water troughs fell apart, but the core of those buildings stood firm. The DuCharmes, the family that owned it for those centuries, had a sense of elegance as well as pragmatism.

The founder of this extraordinary place was Sophie Marquette, a woman who stole from the British supply wagons during the War of 1812. As she was so divine-looking, officers babbled. She would show up in Maryland, or sometimes along the James River, ingratiating herself with the invaders. They had no idea, thinking the attacks on the supply wagons, the payroll, too, was the work of special army units among the Americans. Sophie was the mastermind of a small team. The woman made a howling fortune. After the war she put it to good use farming and endowing a private school for girls,

Custis Hall. Eventually she did marry, picking a man for brains as well as brawn, Widmore DuCharme.

If she could see it now, she would believe she was home, except for the fact that there were cars, tractors, equipment she would have never seen. Flexible, quick to learn, Sophie would have figured it out.

Sister could never pass Old Paradise or wind up on those lovely acres without thinking of this remarkable woman. As much as she and Crawford could butt heads, she was grateful to him.

His research team, using ground-penetrating radar, found the slave graveyard, totally overgrown. They also found a smaller, seemingly disorganized scattering of bodies. They believe these were Monacans, a native tribe of Virginia who lived in the area. All was done by Crawford and Marty, his wife, to honor the deceased, giving credit as best they knew it for the lives and contributions of the deceased to this shimmering estate.

Many of the slate tombstones, restored, displayed the name of the deceased, birthdate, death date. Often a carving accompanied this. A cross, a lamb, a palm, perhaps a key or even a sphinx decorated the marker.

Sometimes the chased fox would rip through the cemetery. Sister would glance at the tombstones, telling herself one day she would try to figure out the symbol's relationship to the deceased. Given the demands of being a Master of Foxhounds, she had not gotten to that yet. She told herself she would, as the living wanted to honor their dead. Of course, all were gone now.

At the crossroads, Sister turned right, passing the old train station, now restored by a hunt club member. The Northern and Southern trains stopped using the Victorian structure in the early 1950s. It, too, had been restored. Chapel Cross, surrounded by old estates, remained much as it had been even back to the early nineteenth century. Places sold rarely; often the inheritors of these historical relics hung on by their teeth, steadfastly refusing to sell for housing developments.

This made Chapel Crossroads perfect for foxhunting. As Sister was the Master of the Jefferson Hunt, she kept her eye on all the farms. Today she had visited every feeder box for her foxes in the area. This took two hours. The cubs were now half-grown, so she could again put a bit of wormer on the food. She was religious about cleaning out parasite loads. If she could, she trapped the young foxes, taking them to a vet cleared by the state to work on wildlife. Each disgruntled fox received a 7 in 1 shot plus a rabies shot, then she returned them home. Consequently, Chapel Crossroads hosted healthy, beautiful, saucy foxes, both red and gray.

The area burst with wildlife. Sometimes Sister, visiting a landowner, would sit with them, watching the black bears walk across the pasture, or a herd of deer gracefully leaping fences. She never tired of it, the birds always seem to be singing for her.

She stopped again, looking back at Old Paradise, the columns visible in the lingering twilight. A rumble followed by another, sounding like a loud cough, made her lower her window. She listened a moment then raised the window.

"A little earthquake," she informed her dogs, who had felt it before she did.

September air cooled quickly after sunset. She turned off the air conditioner, set at seventy-four, drove the twenty-five minutes home.

The gravel drive off the two-lane paved highway snaked through meadows and some old hardwoods for two miles until she passed her eight-stall stable, turned left to the house, passing the kennels, hounds dozing in their condos, others on their inside sleeping benches.

Across from the kennels rested a small log cabin that predated the brick house, the big house. This place, like Old Paradise, had stood the test of time, but with far less drama. A clapboard addition had been built in 1834 and was still tight as a tick.

Parking her car, she hopped out, opened the back door to release the dogs. Her husband's monstrous Land Cruiser was parked near the house's back door.

As she stepped through the mudroom and into the kitchen, the calico long-haired cat, Golliwog, lifted her head. *"I'm ready for supper."*

Sister stroked her for a moment, reached down to pet her dogs, then walked down the hall to the library. "Just a minute, you two, I'll get to you." She raised her voice, "Gray."

"You're home. Thought I heard the car." He came out of the library, gave her a big hug and a kiss.

"Any news?"

He shrugged. "The Commonwealth of Virginia is still confused about this bug. No more indoor gatherings, but we can have outdoor gatherings. I think people will show up for the first day of cubbing. Afterward we can social distance, keep it at six feet."

"I hope you're right." She looked down at the dogs. "Let me feed everyone."

"I'll feed you. I made my mother's famous pork chops. The ones you stand on end. And a little salad and fresh corn." Gray smiled.

They reached the kitchen, where he took over the stove. She grabbed the big electric can opener. "Honey, when is the last time you used a manual can opener?"

"I guess since the earth was cooling." He laughed, clicking on the gas stove.

"Hey!" The cat complained.

This exclamation was followed by fresh tuna . . . real tuna from the can, not cat food. Not another word from the cat, whose face was in her dish, her name on it in blue script.

"How were the feeders?" he asked.

"Well used. Filled every one then stopped at Yvonne's. She's poring over blueprints for the main house. She's been feeding her fox, so that saved me one job. Then I drove back to the crossroads as the sun was setting. Old Paradise glowed, first golden then scarlet, finally blood red. The columns looked painted by light."

The crackle of frying meat made her realize she was hungry. Sister often forgot to eat. "Crawford has done a remarkable job. I think he's into double digit millions now. When he first moved here I would never have thought he would try to rehabilitate Old Paradise."

"Me neither but he's learned a lot and truly seems interested in old architecture. Marty has been fabulous. One of the great things about living in one of the original thirteen colonies is the architecture. Marty could teach architecture history by now."

"Is there an old place in Virginia that hasn't seen destruction, suffering, murder even? Then you think of all the men who marched off to war, leaving the women behind to try and farm these places. I often think of my great-grandfather and then Dad going to war. I really am proud of them."

"Honey, they would be proud of you, too," Gray complimented her. "My grandfather, father, uncles all served. They weren't treated equally, but they served. They wanted to. Our ancestors put their lives on the line for our country even though our country treated them badly."

"Do you ever wonder when you pass Old Paradise what happened? How people managed with no refrigeration, fireplaces only? We are so spoiled. I think the women worked like dogs," Sister mentioned, then repeated, "We are truly spoiled."

"We are." He winked at her. "You spoil me."

They laughed, caught up, considered tomorrow's hunting as the animals plopped down, stomachs full, to fall asleep.

That night as Sister crawled into bed, the outside temperature was dropping to the low fifties; she got up and checked the thermostat. "I'm going to set it at seventy degrees. Sometimes this house can really cool off. I hate to get up to a cold room."

"Are you cold now?" Gray called, looking up from his book; he was rereading Adam Smith.

"No."

"Are you sure?"

She walked to the bed. "Sure."

"I'll keep you warm."

She laughed at him, snuggling up as he wrapped one arm around her, holding the book in his other hand. "You know, Gray, it was not exactly an optical illusion, but as I sat looking at Old Paradise and the Corinthian capitals turned blood red, it looked as though blood was running down the fluted columns."

CHAPTER 2

September 12, 2020, Saturday

A pileated woodpecker, wings at its side, wove through the trees like a rocket, one flap, wings back again, and it flew on. Sister, riding Aztec, observed the large bird with interest. Woodpeckers did not tell you where foxes were but they could tell you where pine beetles were, carpenter ants, all manner of insects delicious to the colorful fellow. The woodpecker was a fellow, as he had the white stripes on his cheeks.

Far ahead she heard her Huntsman, Weevil Blackford, toot just so his whippers-in and Sister, leading the field, knew where he was.

Cubbing, the beginning of foxhunting, takes place in Virginia and most of the Mid-Atlantic states right after Labor Day. The purpose is to bring your young hounds, usually one to two years old depending on birthday, out with the pack. She had three youngsters in the pack, this being their first hunt. Sister believed strongly in introducing the young hounds two maybe three at a time. If you put out all of them chaos might ensue, for even though she worked with them all summer, this was now The Big Time and a youngster could be overwhelmed. Also, if she took out all the young hounds, her whippers-in might wind up in the next county. You hope not, but why take a chance? It wouldn't be fun if a first-time hunter is being rated slow all the time, hearing their names sternly spoken. The point was that this should be exciting and great fun. It almost always was.

Aztec flicked his ears, as the woodpecker must have landed on a promising tree out of sight. The rap-rap-rap ricocheted off other trees. The pileated woodpecker's call was unique. Once heard it was rarely forgotten.

Sister smiled, for she trusted Aztec. They both tried to pay attention to wildlife when hunting. Other creatures gave you a lot of information if you knew what to see, literally.

Rap-rap-rap rang out. Other birds and groundlings could hear this call at least a quarter of a mile away if not more. That was the trick of cubbing in Virginia in early fall. The leaves on trees, bushes sagging with berries, so many forests loaded with oaks, hickories, sycamores, all manner of pines, created curtains of green. Virginia, being a lush state, meant foxhunters wouldn't see much until cold weather stripped the leaves off the deciduous trees. One hunted by ear. Staff worked harder during cubbing than the rest of the year. They surely had longer runs during formal hunting, but you could see more. Now what Sister heard was the rustle of deep green leaves, in a slight wind, two weeks from the first blush of color, the sound of Aztec's hooves as well as the sound of hooves behind her.

For all its difficulties, she loved cubbing. She lived to hunt, and of course they did not kill foxes. It pained her that so many people didn't know that.

It pained her that millions upon millions of Americans lived in cities or suburbs and no longer understood rural life or wildlife. So often their laws and attempts to protect the environment made it worse.

Rap Rap Rap.

She wondered if this was woodpecker Morse Code. Was that fellow with his thirty-inch wingspan talking to other birds, especially other pileated woodpeckers?

"Hey, dude, this is my territory, bug off. Don't you even look at my mate. She's the prettiest woodpecker in Virginia."

She laughed at the thought. Male behavior among warm-blooded animals seemed consistent. They protect the young and one's food supply. At other times, especially when there is a long drought or constant pelting rains, violence erupts. Birds can fight as well as humans.

But then birds rarely breed beyond the food and water supply, whereas humans do. That thought vanished, good thing, as it was dismal, and Sister wanted to love this first day of cubbing. Weevil blew "Gone Away." Aztec hit third gear, fast but not lightning speed.

Hounds opened at once, including the young ones whose voices had not all changed, kind of like the skinny kid in seventh grade who reads a passage and his voice cracks. That's what she heard.

Aztec knew the horn calls as well as she did. The trail narrowed. He had to slow to second gear.

"What are you waiting for?" Aztec wondered as the trail ahead widened.

This sounded like a snort to her but she knew what he meant and gave a light squeeze. Aztec never needed proddings. They galloped along the trail, ducking a few branches but most of the kennel trails had been cleared. They hit an open field.

The woods covered the western part of After All, the large, lovely estate bordering her own. The first day of cubbing was always from the kennels, and as luck would have it, in the wildflower field between Sister's place and the Bancrofts' they often picked up a fox. The hounds patiently worked at a fading line, very fading, for the last ten minutes.

Pansy, approaching her prime, spoke. *"Different fox."*

The other hounds fell in behind her now, working at an easy pace.

Sister waited. The hog's back jump between her wildflower field and After All, the Bancrofts' estate, sat probably a football field's length away. The two pups, a year old, Brexit and Bellhop, stayed in the middle of the group. A few second-year entries pushed ahead.

"Not so fast." Dasher, one of the steadier older hounds, counseled.

The fox circled once near the fence line then shot through the hog's back jump, as there was spacing between the thick railroad ties of the jump.

Weevil took the jump, more formidable-looking than it really was. Hounds were already over. Twenty yards behind them Sister and Aztec then cleared the jump, followed by a field of people hoping for a clear view.

The ground, harder than she would have liked, as it hadn't rained for two weeks, did allow for some speed. She needed it. The hounds were pulling away.

The trail veered to the right from the Old Pattypan Forge. She breathed a sigh of relief. Pattypan was a whistling bitch to get into and to get out of. The trail widening from a thirty-degree angle, began to straighten out. She could open up. Aztec was thrilled. He liked being in front. He was fast, which helped. No one would run up his butt.

Within five minutes, seemed like two seconds, Sister burst out on the farm road from After All to the Lorillard home place, where

Gray's brother, Sam, lived. The two brothers had restored the lovely clapboard home over four years, doing all the work themselves.

Wonderful to have a husband who can do things.

Across the farm road, Sister caught sight of Betty Franklin's horse's rear end as he vaulted over a fence, jumping the fence line between After All and the Lorillard place. Betty, her best friend and a good twenty-some years younger, proved a fabulous whipper-in. She had that instinct, plus she was quiet.

Sister turned left, for seeing Betty meant she didn't have to hesitate. She knew exactly where hounds were. They were suspiciously silent, as the singing cut off the minute Sister hit the farm road.

She galloped northward toward the house then held hard. Her Huntsman, a beautiful man if ever there was one, sat by the graveyard, watching intently. Hounds sniffed over the graves. Gray's family, generations of Lorillards and Laprades, rested therein, including his beloved cousin, Mercer, who was killed over a horse deal in the last decade.

Betty, emerging from the woods, pulled up also.

From behind Sister, on her left, came Tootie Harris, on one of Sister's horses, Matchplay, as Tootie's horse had an abscess. Tootie had had to negotiate miserable territory, hence the few minutes behind Betty. She pulled up closer to the house. Then stopped.

Brexit sniffed and sniffed.

"What happened?"

Trinity, an older hound by a few years, nose down, said, *"Scent vanished. This fox does this to us all the time."*

"How does he do that?" Brexit knew the fox was male, one could smell the gender.

Taz, another T line hound, laughed. *"If we knew that we'd be the greatest hounds of all time."* Hounds' names began with the first initial of their mother's name. Hence the "T" line for Mom, Thomasina.

Uncle Yancy, the red fox whom they had chased, built many dens on the Lorillard place. One was in the graveyard, which he rarely used. One was under the front porch which, when scent was fresh, drove the hounds crazy, for they couldn't reach the opening. A sumptuous den in the mudroom fooled everyone. Uncle Yancy would walk under the back step, crawl into the mudroom, for there was a small hole he had created in the floor. A pile of old clean towels and rags covered the hole. He'd push them aside, then pull them back over. He'd jump on a tack box then hop onto a lower shelf where Sam and Gray would toss their crops and gloves. From that shelf he'd leap over the hooks for coats, to reach a wide shelf, the length of the door. Some boxes provided cover. He would stretch on that shelf, his tail peeping from behind the boxes, as no one assumed a fox would be there, be that courageous; no one looked, even though they could smell him. The two humans believed the odor was his signature, as he wandered all over the place.

What Uncle Yancy was doing while the hounds sniffed and awaited orders from Weevil was looking down on these dreary domesticated canines. He had jumped into the graveyard, onto the top of a tombstone that was rectangular, and launched himself onto a very low branch of a tree at the edge of the graveyard. The leaves, thick, concealed him.

Ryan, from his truck, reached the farm and was shooting all this. Weevil motioned for Betty and Tootie to ride to him. "Heat's coming up but I think we can hunt back. If it gets too hot we'll walk. Maybe sixty-five degrees Fahrenheit, you think?"

Ryan Stokes, early thirties, had built a small business making videos for ads for other small businesses. He had the ambition to do more, make more money.

Betty nodded. "The only scent we'll get is red hot. Everything else will have lifted."

"It's a little farther but why don't we go down to After All and take the pack through the covered bridge? Be good for the pups and we can walk. Maybe an extra fifteen minutes?" Tootie suggested.

"That's a good idea. Be good for anyone on a green horse." Weevil looked down at the hounds, who were looking up. "Come along, children."

Ryan, anticipating the route, had gone on ahead to park on the other side of the bridge.

Diana, wise and now in late middle age, led the hounds. Still quite sleek and fast, she steadied everyone when needs be.

The pack fell in behind her, with Weevil up front, Betty on his right, Tootie on his left, Sister twenty yards behind.

Ben Sidell, the sheriff, rode Nonni, his tried-and-true horse. He was happy to be off this Saturday to go out on the first day of cubbing. With his schedule, he never quite knew.

Sister turned around to see the thirty people riding, chatting in low voices, for hounds weren't speaking.

A non-Covid first day might have fifty people. The hunt started at 7:30 AM. One could often manage a good run in that first hour when the mercury might be in the low sixties. By the last week in September the temperature at the early start was often now into the mid-fifties. Granted, it still warmed up fast, but that dew, a bit of chill, could send them flying.

Ryan turned around and slowly followed. He hoped for a bridge shot with the sounds of these horses echoing inside.

"Bobby," Sister called over her shoulder. "Come on up."

"Nice start." Betty's husband smiled at Sister.

"Was. We still might get a little run." She looked up at the sky. "Clear."

"High pressure. Never the best for scent."

"No, but Mother Nature does it her way. Some of the best hunts I've ever had have been during rotten conditions," Sister remembered.

"Did you think we'd get this many people?"

She shrugged. "I'm glad we did, but the media is working overtime to scare people. We're on horseback, outside, more than six feet away. I think we're safe."

"Hysteria sells." He smiled ruefully. "This isn't to say Covid isn't a problem. We should take care, but every day it's a different prediction and depending on your news outlet, really different."

"You know, I swear one of these days some of those media talking heads will get shot."

"Oh, Sister, all they shoot off is their mouths."

They both laughed.

"Thank you for helping put up the tables and chairs. Again the social distancing is what our governor decreed. Wonder who will wear masks? You know, I do think it prudent, but again we are pretty safe. All we need is a fight over this."

"Luckily, Ben is out today." She looked back over her shoulder to see the sheriff happily talking to Edward Bancroft and Tedi, his wife. They were now riding over Bancroft land, After All. "Good to see Edward out."

"He's eighty-six and I can't keep up with him." Bobby smiled.

"I'll be glad when this is over. Well, we all will but I think as the season goes on and more people become confident, the hunting numbers will rise." Sister added, "You know Edward is living proof that you have to keep moving."

"He is. Well, here's the bridge. Let's see what these reverberating hoofbeats do to any green horses, and I see that Greg Wilson is on a green horse," Bobby mentioned.

"Good-looking horse. Greg has been working on his riding."

"Looks like his business is booming, despite all. You might have slow days if you own a big sawmill but you'll never really run out of customers." Bobby, as a businessman, had interest in other businesses.

"Seems to be the case. Which reminds me, how are you and Betty doing for firewood? Cold nights will be here before you know it."

"Pretty good."

"Let me know. Gray cut and split all those downed tree limbs this summer. We have firewood out the wazoo."

"*Fox,*" Dreamboat called out, his melodious voice filling the covered bridge.

Diana, his littermate, both in their prime, opened as she touched the spot he had.

The run through the bridge gobbled ground. The fox, Target, a gray, swerved through brambles, emerging by the hog's back jump the field originally took to begin the hunt.

Sister easily cleared it; but then, Aztec could jump the moon. She looked up as she landed and noticed Ryan perched in a stout tree, shooting the jump. He was working hard today. She touched her crop to her cap, acknowledging him, then moved out.

Bobby had gone back to his second flight the minute Dreamboat opened so he was out of sight. Sister knew he could make up the ground as Bobby knew this fixture intimately.

The scent held through the wildflower field, ending at Tootie's log cabin with a newer, 1850 addition, lovely clapboard.

"*I hate this. He does this and you can't really crawl under the porch with all that latticework,*" Pansy moaned.

"*Tough,*" Target called from his opening.

All the foxes built good living quarters, close to water and food. Target by virtue of living under the cottage had the best of everything. He moved farther back into his den, invigorated by the brief run. Cubbing was beginning. Best to be alert and keep in shape.

Weevil stopped at the cottage. Sister rode up to him.

"Master."

"Pick them up, Huntsman. All in all, a fair beginning."

"Yes, M'am." He touched his hat with his crop, called to his hounds. All turned toward the kennel, a mere quarter of a mile away, clearly visible.

Parking was easy at Roughneck Farm. All was well thought out by Sister's first, late husband's uncle, who took over a scraggly pack from a hunt ending its days. Uncle Arnold had a gift for breeding. In three years, back in the 1920s, he created a good pack, and in seven, a great one. Those decades gleamed in hunt history. Railroads caused some adjustments but the highways that existed were two lane and twisty in the country. Most of the masters and huntsmen in Virginia, Maryland, and Pennsylvania knew one another. People could talk about bloodlines forever and did. How they loved it. Much of America had some familiarity with hunting. Men would take trains from Philadelphia, Baltimore, and Boston to hunt in the early morning then get back on and go to the office. This was a bit more difficult in New York but the wealthy had big estates on Long Island and they hunted, hunted fast, too. North Carolina and South Carolina were more in tune with each other than with the Mid-Atlantic but one could put one's horses on a train and rattle down to Middleton Place outside of Charleston for a hunt replete with hospitality beyond compare.

Sister often mused she had been born too late, but she made the best of it and hoped she showed good sport.

Alida Dalzell took charge of bringing out the food. Betty, Bobby, and Tootie, before the hunt, had set up the tables and chairs. People could distance if they desired. Given the situation it was well done.

Once hounds were in the kennel, checked, horses in the stable, and other horses tied to trailers with feed bags, the people sat at tables, plates full of food.

Ryan joined them after videoing the last hound stepping into the kennel, Weevil praising the happy hounds.

Everyone noted how fast time flies, who would think cubbing had begun?

Kasmir Barbhaiya, who owned Tattenhall Station, hosted as Sister saw to the horses while Weevil and Tootie saw to the hounds.

Betty, in the stables with Sister, hurriedly hoisted tack on tack hooks. "I'll get this after the breakfast."

"Sure." Sister nodded, sliding her saddle on a saddle rack. "Shouldn't take us long. How was your side of the hunt?"

"The trails were clear. Jumps repaired. These work parties did a good job."

They stepped out just as Greg Wilson carried a carton full of champagne, twelves bottles. Ryan got all this on film. Greg placed the champagne at the end of the food table. The champagne had been in a cooler in his trailer but this way it was easier to carry. He sprinted to the trailer, grabbed the cooler full of ice, brought it back, stuck the champagne into the ice. Then he retrieved a bottle, opened it with a pleasing pop.

"Ladies and gentlemen. To the start of a wonderful season." Greg visited every table, filling plastic cups. He'd go back for another bottle. By the time he had filled every cup he was down to four bottles. He then sat next to Bobby Franklin, six feet away.

"Greg, this is wonderful. I didn't recognize the label." Bobby held his cup, sipped again.

"You know who taught me about champagne? Kay Pflatz at Basic Necessities." He named a small shop in Nellysford in Nelson County. "She works for our vintners and I can't tell you her title. I'm not too good about that stuff but one day I was in the store to get a bottle for my wife and me to celebrate the equinox. Risé and I will celebrate anything. So I grabbed a big-name bottle off the shelf and Kay came alongside me, 'I can give you something better at one third the price.' As the price was two hundred and fifty, I was all ears. She went on to explain that the big French houses keep the best for themselves, which is no surprise. Often they make a blend. So, they sell us Cristal, a grand champagne, Veuve Clicquot La Grande Dame Brut, a sparkling white Dom Pérignon, Armand de Brignac Ace of Spades Rose, you name it. Big bucks. This is quite modestly priced compared to the big names. They keep the house blend for themselves. Have another sip."

"It really is fabulous."

"Call Kay when you need some cheer." He stood up and made the rounds again filling glasses for those with the capacity for two glasses of marvelous spirits.

He handed one to Ryan, they clinked cups.

Sister, not much of a drinker, swallowed half her cup. "Greg is nothing if not convivial."

Gray, next to her, said, "For which I am grateful." He called to Tootie, who was finally sitting down. "When is your mother going to ride?"

"She swears next hunt. She was nervous about riding with a big group her first time out."

"Okay. I'll hold her to it." Gray raised a glass to the young whipper-in, in her last year at UVA.

The merry mood meant people lingered. Many were happy to see one another, as the summer had most people sequestered and feeling lonely for their friends. The governor banned large groups but did allow outdoor activities. So a few trail rides gathered souls, but it wasn't the same. Everyone was so nervous except for Sister, Weevil, Betty, and Tootie. Even Gray had a touch of the circumspect; the hunt staff didn't, but they wore masks when getting groceries, stuff like that.

Finally, by ten in the morning, the last trailer pulled down the long drive.

After folding up the tables, Betty taking the oilcloth tablecloths home to wipe down and hang up, the small staff group bid one another goodbye until the next morning, when they would walk hounds. The next hunt would be Tuesday. Sister liked contact with her hounds so she would walk at least one day between hunts, which were Tuesday, Thursday, and Saturday; Saturday drawing the largest number of riders, of course.

Walking back to the house, Gray put his arm around her waist. "Happy?"

"You know, I am. I thought the three youngsters fairly composed. How was it back in first flight?"

"Well, you lead us on. Was fine. Greg Wilson had a few moments with his new horse. Nothing serious but I think Ryan Stokes may have gotten it on film. He'll tease him with it."

"No doubt. We may all live to regret hiring Ryan to video our season. He'll show pieces of it on his weekly video blog. So everyone sees a rider hit the dirt."

"You aren't going to hit the dirt." He smiled. "No worry."

CHAPTER 3

September 13, 2020, Sunday

As Sister, Betty, and Bobby walked down the aisle of the simple Episcopal church, the organ played in C major "A Mighty Fortress Is Our God." Sister loved the hymn, which was first played in 1527. Some say 1529, but no matter, as here it was 2020 and it was still beloved. While being an Episcopalian, she was more than willing to go into a Catholic church, a Lutheran church, any church that had a good organ. Listening to an old hymn or a gospel song, she would imagine the voices throughout the centuries singing, be it in Notre Dame or a simple plain church in Georgia. Standing at the end of the aisle was the priest, Sally Taliaferro, also a foxhunter.

"Sister, Betty, Bobby, it's always a joy to see you when I look down from the pulpit."

"We all need heavenly help." Bobby grinned.

"Hounds were blessed yesterday. A good run." Reverend Sally grinned.

After shaking hands, they stood outside, warm, chatting with the other parishioners.

Greg and Risé Wilson motioned for them to join in as they were talking to Crawford and Marty Howard.

"Interesting sermon." Crawford nodded as they joined in.

"This virus has taken over everything." Sister adjusted her mask. They were all masked.

"The media makes it ten times worse." Marty's glasses fogged up. "I don't know what to believe."

"Virginia has imposed stringent measures. The kids are home-schooling. We've been able to attend service only by sitting apart." Risé, possessing shiny black hair and petite, shrugged. "But for how long? Other churches are zooming."

Greg added, "Honey, it will come to that."

"What provokes me is, what happens when this is over? Some of the governors have assumed powers beyond their offices. Will they give that up?" Crawford frowned.

"Of course they will. Because you'll go down there and talk to the governor. You'll scare the devil out of him," his wife, Marty, teased him.

"She's right, Crawford. You can tell our governor that you have large burial grounds at Old Paradise. Grounds that probably predate the Revolutionary War and after for the enslaved, and maybe even the Monacans. If you stick him in there, who will know?" Greg grinned. "Actually, Crawford, you could get away with murder."

They all laughed.

Crawford could laugh at himself. "There have been times when I've been tempted."

"Haven't we all?" Betty laughed.

Rap Rap Rap.

Sister looked up. "Big one."

They followed her finger to see a full-grown pileated wood-pecker knocking away at an ancient hickory.

"He is big." Greg stared at the impressive bird. "Not too worried about us."

"Well, I don't want to eat tree bugs, do you?" Risé took his hand.

"My mother used to say that to me. 'You'll eat a bug if you don't clean your room,'" Greg joked.

"Did you?" Sister asked him.

"Once I pretended to eat a rubber one."

"Honey." Risé grimaced. "Your poor mother."

"My poor mother was a drill sergeant."

"Maybe our mothers went to the same school."

Bobby nodded as other parishioners walked by. "To change the subject, how is everyone's garden right now?"

"Winding down. Except for tomatoes. I have more tomatoes now than midsummer," Greg noted.

"Me, too. Gray and Sam always do a garden for Aunt Daniella. They said the corn won't quit."

Marty put her arm through her husband's arm. "Those two are so good to Aunt Dan. They take her to church every Sunday. They do her garden. They trim her lawn. Looks like a lawn service does it, it's so precise. And, of course, your husband has made it his life's work to get her a bottle of Blanton's bourbon once a week."

"One of these days she'll get Pappy Van Winkle." Crawford tilted his head. "Thousands of dollars, but can you imagine her face when she opens that package?"

They all nodded, smiling, for Aunt Daniella was wedded to her bourbon.

"The boys . . . her boys, she calls them . . . love her. When Mercer died they made sure she had what she needed. She loved her son but she is strong. She never gave way. Then again, if she did we would never see it," Betty pronounced with feeling.

"What will she be this year? Ninety-seven?" Bobby added.

"I hope so, Bobby. She's been ninety-four for the last three years." Sister raised an eyebrow.

"On that inspirational note, let me take you home, Mrs. Wilson."

"Oh, Greg." She sighed. "You just want your dinner." She looked at the others. "Fresh mussels."

They walked off. The Franklins, Howards, and Sister chatted a bit longer.

"Why don't you hunt Old Paradise this Saturday? I'll have Skip bring out my pack."

"Crawford, that's very generous. I'd love to hunt Old Paradise. I slowed on Chapel Cross Road a couple days ago to see the sunset illuminate those elegant columns."

He loved hearing this. "Interior is almost done. Marty has actually found some original pieces from the period. Kathleen Dunbar has been a godsend."

He named an antiques dealer fairly new to the area, who had become a good friend to Aunt Daniella, and Tootie's mother, Yvonne Harris. Kathleen often attended hunt club events although she herself did not ride. She and Sister hit it off.

"It has been a labor of love." Marty meant that. "What's odd . . . well maybe it isn't . . . is that with all the work we've done at Old Paradise, or restoring the Carriage House, the main stables, the outbuildings, the hay storage, and shoring up of the basement of the house, we never found one coin. Not one. Not one bracelet or earring. All those rumors about buried treasure. Poof!"

"Marty, every old house in Virginia is rumored to harbor pieces of eight." Bobby laughed.

"But given her life, I don't know. It seemed possible. She was a brigand, after all." Marty found the idea thrilling.

"Hey, there's still time. Who knows what else you'll find?" Sister leaned forward. "You found one huge burial ground and part of another. Maybe Sophie was like the pirate in *Treasure Island*. Maybe she buried it within the graveyard."

"I don't think she knew about the Monacan bodies. Our work discovered a few of them, and it was luck, pure luck." Crawford added, "We still don't know how old those bodies are. I wanted to get the bones carbon tested at least. People did know the Monacans once lived here. Sophie knew it. But she was a woman who kept her mouth shut."

"Your research on the people buried there was a special thing to do." Marty looked at Sister, Bobby, and Betty. "Crawford found old accounting books. Those had been stored at McGuire Woods. God knows how they got to a law firm. Had to be someone who moved things in the nineteenth century, because McGuire Woods was founded in 1834. Sophie was alive then. Maybe she started taking books there to be safe. I'm nattering on here, sorry."

Crawford continued the story. "Not only did those accounting books, some on vellum, have names, they had occupations and full descriptions of all the people here. Date of birth. Date of death. Sophie and her people certainly kept impeccable records. And she made sure each slave got a tombstone designed by the family. I doubt she thought she was an oppressor. Who does? When the house is open I will have copies of those records for people to read. Naturally, the originals will be in a vault. I'm not sure of the best place for the books. The Library of Virginia, Virginia Historical Society, or even University of Virginia."

"There is no hurry. Something will lead you to the right home. And you've seen the restored tombstones. Well, you've ridden by." Marty laughed.

Sister, Bobby, and Betty nodded.

Betty replied, "Each section has a brass plaque with the deceased's names, directing you to the burial site. It's moving."

"Funny, isn't it, how every society is most conservative when it comes to their dead?" Sister thought out loud. "Good, I think. Keeping to the old ways, using a service, centuries old."

"Well, ladies, let's be on our way. You're coming for breakfast, I hope?" Bobby allowed Sister on one side and his wife on the other, all arm in arm.

"Only if you let me do the dishes."

"What I want is you to make your scrambled eggs. Bobby will make hash browns. That's an invitation to work, but no one makes scrambled eggs as you do," Betty praised her.

They reached their cars, parked side by side, unlocked. No reason to lock your car out in the country. They opened the doors.

"I knew it!" Sister exclaimed.

Betty opened her passenger door. "The tomato gremlin strikes again."

Sister called over to her. "I should have known Greg was up to something when he talked about tomatoes."

They laughed and Betty added, "I bet he snuck tomatoes into every car here. He and Risé are the opposite of thieves. They dump the goods on you."

"Well," Sister held a fat red tomato, "how will this crime of giving end?"

"Oh, that's good. A crime of giving."

"Come on, girls. You can solve the tomato appearances in the kitchen."

CHAPTER 4

September 14, 2020, Monday

Light faded perhaps a minute a day from the summer solstice until the equinox, which was a week away. Country people notice such things as they worked outside. At 7:30 AM on a blessed low humidity morning, the temperature sixty-three degrees, Sister, Betty, Weevil, and Tootie walked hounds about a mile from the kennels. Mostly this got the kinks out from Saturday. Hounds had Sunday off like most people. A light walk loosened everyone up, plus the puppies became more and more accepted into the pack.

Gray, who often walked hounds, had left early that morning.

"Sweater morning." Betty inhaled the invigorating air.

"Don't you look forward to these days?" Sister asked. "First it's the mornings, but by October most of the days call for a sweater or a light jacket."

"I'm prepared for any weather," Diana informed them, although they had no idea what she said.

Ardent, an older hound, said, *"My undercoat is coming in. Helps."*

Pansy, a slender female approaching four years of age, a good age, remarked, *"Humans don't have undercoats. Must be awful."*

Dragon, egotistical, pushy, but possessed of a terrific nose, grumbled, *"Who cares? They can't smell either."*

"Not very well." Dreamboat agreed. *"But they have other gifts. And never forget, blowhard, Sister, Betty, Weevil, and Tootie feed you."*

A murmur followed the statement. Dew sparkled on the grass, the hay would be cut one more time, a real bonus.

Betty looked at the hay and said, "Been a fabulous year for hay."

"For everything; let's not forget the tomatoes." Sister laughed then told Weevil and Tootie about Greg sneaking bags of tomatoes into people's cars.

"Corn, squash, everything." Juno, now in her second year, stopped to watch a black swallowtail butterfly still here.

"Come on, sweetie," Betty said to her.

Juno glanced from the beautiful insect to Betty and walked on.

"Funny what you remember." Sister watched Aero, a three-year-old hound, gracefully move. "Maybe 1981 or '82, cool, low humidity, Ray and I got three hay cuttings. I always feel happy if I get two good ones. Well, this is a three-cutting year."

"Given that you're at a higher altitude than other places, you're up about one thousand feet, you do have a slightly different blooming and harvest time. I like coming from my place to yours. I'm only three miles away, lower altitude, but you are usually a week behind."

Sister's cellphone burped. She ignored it.

One minute later, Betty's cellphone beeped. She looked at hers. "It's Aunt Daniella." Clicking it on. "Hello, Aunt Dan, how are you?"

Betty's face suddenly changed. "That makes no sense. I'll tell her. Do you need anything?" A brief pause. "Okay. Thank you, Aunt Dan."

"May be the shortest phone call ever." Sister smiled at her.

"Sister, Greg Wilson shot himself."

"What?"

"Aunt Dan said Sam just called her. Greg was supposed to meet Crawford and Sam to look at a horse. You know Crawford can't stand tardiness, so he called Greg's cell. No response so he called the house. Ben Sidell picked up. He was there. All he said was Greg was gone. No signs of violence. He said if any of us can come to Risé, she's devastated. The kids can't get back to Virginia until tonight."

"Good Lord." Sister stopped for a moment.

Weevil volunteered, "Why don't you two go do what you have to do. Tootie and I will take in the hounds."

"Thank you, Weevil."

Once back at the kennel, Sister and Betty climbed into Sister's half-ton truck. "Betty, call Gray for me and hand me the phone."

Betty did just that. "Gray. Your wife needs to speak to you. She's driving."

"Honey," Sister said, "something terrible has happened. Greg Wilson has shot himself. Betty and I are going to the house, Risé is in a bad way."

"Sam just called me. I can come home."

"You stay in Washington. If we need you, we'll let you know. You might call Aunt Dan, as it was she who called Betty. We were on hound walk."

"Okay. If I don't come home early, I will see you tonight."

"Don't worry. Everyone will do whatever needs to be done."

As she drove, Sister tried to concentrate. "Betty, no one has said he's dead."

"I guess they don't have to. If he had been rushed to the hospital, we'd know that; I'm sure we would. So, we're talking about a suicide."

"It can't be true. He was a happy man, making plans as well as sneaking tomatoes into our cars. Someone had to have killed him and made it look like suicide."

"I hope so." Betty paused. "What am I saying? That I'd rather have my friend murdered than committing suicide?"

"Odd what goes through your mind. I cannot for one minute believe Greg would do such a thing."

By the time Sister and Betty arrived at the impressive home, gorgeous gardens, three other cars were there, all owned by hunt club women. In a situation of death or crisis the club pulled together. The women brought food, tended to whatever and whomever needed tending. Some had to act as doormen, too. The men took off work if possible, especially if whoever had passed left children.

It was felt that boys especially needed a strong male presence, hopefully one of their father's best friends. The women turned up to help daughters. While it might seem sexist to one never having lived through such a crisis, it often worked out this way. Sudden death devastated people, especially the children of the deceased.

Greg and Risé's two sons, successful, in their mid-thirties, lived out of state. Joe and his wife, Sheila, lived in Boston. Carl, thirty-two and still unmarried, lived in Atlanta.

Alida and Marty ushered people inside. Kasmir, Alida's partner, quietly allowed people to visit Risé briefly. Freddie Thomas had brought food. Other women would soon be bringing food. Freddie was in charge of putting it out, storing some in the refrigerator. Women and men in Virginia knew the "death drill," as Betty's mother used to call it. One flew on automatic pilot.

As Sister walked through the door, Alida grasped her hands.

THRILL OF THE HUNT

"Thank God, you're here." She then embraced Betty as she came through the door.

"Is she all right?" Betty asked.

"Walter is with her now," Alida informed Betty. "She needed to rest. She suddenly became exhausted."

Walter Lungren, Sister's JT-MFH and a cardiac specialist, was Greg's doctor. Risé wanted to see him. He dropped everything, arriving fifteen minutes ago.

Sitting with Risé, Walter held her hands in his. "His heart was strong."

"He just had his checkup with you. But if something was terribly wrong, you would tell me?" Her eyes pleaded with him.

"Risé, Greg was in perfect health, happy, looking to the future."

"My God, my God, that means my husband was murdered."

Walter didn't know what to say. "Would you like a sedative, a light one? Anything to help?"

She said to him, "No. He would be horrified if he thought I took drugs. People will come here and the boys are coming. The last thing they need is to see their mother stoned."

Walter nodded, his blond hair now darkening, as he was in his forties. "Risé, no one would ever think you're an addict. Look, I'll put this vial on your nightstand. If you should need it, take one. It's five milligrams, very mild. If you can't sleep, I do recommend it. Insomnia causes many problems."

She said nothing to that but then squeezed Walter's large hands. "Who would kill my husband?"

"I can't imagine. He was loved. You know Ben Sidell will work night and day on this."

She nodded. A light rap on the door lifted Risé's head.

Alida stuck her head in. "Risé, do you need anything?"

"No. People are coming. I can hear the cars."

"Yes, they are, but if you need to be alone or have someone with you, you do just that."

"No. I must do what is proper for Greg. I'll be out in a minute."

"Risé, if I may suggest something. Perhaps you could sit on the wing chair by the fireplace. That will make it easier on you should you need to leave and it will make it easier for people to speak to you. Everyone loves you, Risé, they loved Greg. People may fatigue you and they won't wish to do so."

"Yes." She paused. "I know I'm not exactly myself. That's why I came in here briefly."

Alida closed the door and told the others.

"God bless her," was all Sister could say.

As people swarmed through the door, Alida guided them to the living room. Risé was not yet there. Freddie took the food. Then flowers began arriving.

"Oh," was all Marty and Alida said, as they hadn't considered that. This was already becoming overwhelming.

Betty stepped toward the deliveryman. "Girls, don't worry, I'll handle this." She reached in her jeans and pulled out ones, all she had, and tipped him.

Sister joined her to carry the large arrangements. Somber but beautiful. They placed the largest one on the side table by the front door.

Ben Sidell walked across the front lawn. The ambulance had left. He was attended by two young law officers. Sister slipped outside to talk with him.

"Sister." He moved alongside her as they walked to his squad car, the two young officers falling behind them.

"Is there anything I can do for you?"

He smiled a tight smile. "No. We've fingerprinted the gun.

He's on his way to the morgue and from there to the medical examiner in Richmond."

"I cannot believe for one minute that Greg Wilson would commit suicide."

"Yes. I understand that. I can only give you the facts as I know them. At 6:35, Risé called to say her husband was shot on the back lawn. She thought he was dead. That was it. I wasn't the first person here. The team got here before I did, which is a good thing. They cordoned the area off and put up a blind so Risé couldn't see. It took a bit of persuading to get her into the house."

"On the back lawn. How dreadful for her."

"He lay faceup, the gun was near his right hand. Not in the hand. He died, we think, from a bullet wound to the temple. If there were drugs in him, something like that, the medical examiner will find it."

"Fingerprints?"

"They may tell us something. Many a murder is made to look like a suicide. This will take time. But a man we all knew, or thought we knew, is dead. I don't think this is going to be easy, whatever the truth."

"Yes," she quietly said while in her mind Ben's words *knew or thought we knew* swirled about.

C H A P T E R   5

September 15, 2020, Tuesday

Two ponds at different levels, a pipe sending water out of the upper pond into the lower, sounded restful. Between the two ponds a grass path big enough for a tractor allowed travel for horses in twos. An underground spring fed the flow. The sound really did provide an odd comfort.

Sister, relaxed on Matador, a flea-bitten gray Thoroughbred, watched the pack, two youngsters with them for the first time, crossing the path toward the woods bordering the long, lush pasture to the north. She took different youngsters cubbing each time until all had hunted once. After that the number might bump up to three or four.

Tuesday was a hunt day during formal season, which started on the day closest to St. Hubert's Day, November 3. She used St. Hubert's Day, as he was the patron saint of hunting, so each year she started the season on the Saturday closest to the Saint's Day. After opening hunt hounds were out with the field three days a week, the additional day being Thursday, but weather could scramble days. During cubbing Jefferson Hunt only went out twice a week. After that the start could be 7:30 AM sliding to 8:00 AM as the sun rose later and later in the month, same with the setting now earlier. Staff might go out alone Tuesdays for a tune-up during cubbing. Soon the fall equinox would announce equal light and equal darkness. After the special day, one lost about a minute of daylight each day until the spring equinox, when the process reversed. Like most country people Sister felt the light change, reacting to it.

This Tuesday was for staff only. Weevil cast hounds. The pack, always eager, put their noses down. He chose the walkway between the ponds, as moisture holds scent. The last two weeks had proved dry.

Hounds pushed along, moving toward the woods, then they turned right, climbing the rise in the pasture. Their sterns waved, a sign something had captured their attention. However, no hound opened.

Betty and Tootie whipped-in, as always. Sister enjoyed staff hunts. It helped the young hounds settle in, learn their trade, and it helped staff. Although each of her staff members had hunted all their life, as had she, which meant she'd hunted for over sixty years, having started as a child, they nevertheless began the season rusty. Good staff work ensures good hunting. No one can do anything about scent, but one can work well with other humans and hounds. The pack, led by Audrey, a steady girl, almost six years old, kept moving upward. Still no one opened. They reached the old, restored schoolhouse at the top of the hill. Not a peep.

Weevil waited while hounds circled the clapboard building. Tattoo stuck his nose in the den's opening on the south side of the building, at the foundation.

"*It's not fair,*" Tattoo complained.

The others joined him at the small dug hole by the side of the house, which was reeking with gray fox scent. Georgia, the fox, lived in the schoolhouse, having the run of it. She'd go in one of her many entrances. Georgia did things in a big way, on the first floor she had a pile of old blankets.

Cindy Chandler owned Foxglove, the farm on which they hunted. Being softhearted as well as a good rider, Cindy took blankets, toys, and a water bowl and food bowl for Georgia. The two had become friends. Georgia feasted on kibble topped with canned dog food. This made her lazy. She'd go outside for her constitutional but she rarely gave the hounds a run unless she strayed too far. However, during mating season, the vixen enticed many suitors. They always gave Jefferson Hunt a rip-roaring hunt. That time wouldn't begin until about mid-December.

Georgia was inside. Poor Audrey knew she wasn't going to come out.

"Audrey, don't worry. It's cubbing, which is spotty. We need some cold nights. Right now it's too warm and dry. It's morning and it's already warm," Taz, one of the T's, consoled her.

Audrey replied, *"I get anxious."*

Parker, a hound in his prime, called out, *"We all do."*

As hounds nosed around the schoolhouse, a raindrop fell, then another.

Sister liked hunting in a light rain but this quickly accelerated to a steady rain, which could soon drench her and the rest of the staff, wearing their light cubbing jackets.

"Weevil," she called out. "Let's go back."

"Yes, Master." He put his horn to his lips, calling hounds to him with three long blasts. "Come on, kids."

All trotted down the slope, not yet slippery. Within eight minutes the pack and humans reached the hound and horse trailers. They were soaked.

Tootie held Hojo's reins, the horse Weevil rode this morning, as he dismounted, opened the party-wagon door, and all the hounds obediently entered. Then Weevil walked Hojo to the four-horse

horse trailer, where Sister and Betty walked in their horses one by one. He led Hojo in and Tootie followed with a young Thoroughbred, Matchplay, equally wet.

Betty, face dripping, hopped in the driver's side while Sister climbed into the passenger seat. Weevil and Tootie drove the hound trailer, the party wagon. One had to drive all around Hangman's Ridge to reach a crossroad to Sister's farm. Only a few miles apart, Roughneck Farm and Foxglove were miles apart by vehicle. Once at the farm, Sister and Betty walked the horses down the trailer ramp into the stable, where they wiped them down. Weevil and Tootie opened the gates for the hounds to run into the non-roofed draw pen, where the rain fell. The humans then dashed inside and opened the door from the inside, allowing the animals to escape the rain as they stood in the wide hallway. The hounds were wiped down just like the horses then called to their quarters by name, girls to one side, boys to the other.

In the tack room, having put the horses in stalls, Sister peeled off her wet coat, as did Betty.

"Here it is, not really cold but that rain gave me the shivers." Sister reached for a towel. "Even my shirt is wet."

"Me, too." Betty grabbed an old frayed Levi's coat to slip on and she threw another one to Sister. The left arms of the worn-out coats had an embroidered Jefferson Hunt insignia.

"Feels better." Sister hung up her bridle on a tack hook as Betty did the same.

Cleaning, feeding horses, throwing on blankets, should the horses need them, then repairing to the tack room to clean tack always relaxed the two old friends. Something about simple chores drew them together. This routine was usually watched by Bitsy, a screech owl with a nest high in the rafters.

"Georgia will never come out of that schoolhouse," Sister remarked.

"You think she'd have her diploma by now." Betty laughed.

"You're right. Cindy spoiled her. Then again, look at those two gargantuan cows she has spoiled. Mean. Or, that Clymestra is mean."

"Aptly named." Betty smiled. "Joe and Carl got in last night. Alida called me this morning."

"Having the kids there will be a big help." Sister, like everyone else, knew the only thing you can do for someone suffering a terrible loss is to be available, pick up small chores. Listen.

"I still don't believe it." Betty washed the bit. "I just don't."

"I don't think anyone does. Greg Wilson wasn't the type to shoot himself," Sister affirmed.

"Does it make you wonder?"

"What do you mean?"

Betty said, "We think we know people. Maybe they are carrying around a deep pain, something they can't discuss."

Sister considered this. "Yes, yet I still think we have some inkling of a potential suicide. I'm probably wrong, but looking back over many of the people I have known in my life, some suicides, it now makes sense. You don't remember Ray's uncle's best friend, Henry Pollard. Liver cancer. He never spoke of it or complained. That's a painful death. He stopped eating. A slow suicide."

"Oh, Sister, how sad," Betty interjected.

"Well, you're right. Granted, he was born in the late 1880s and those men didn't complain. But you could see him deteriorate. I would not have thought Henry would starve himself to death. Back then there were fewer possibilities. Who is to say he was wrong?"

"Do you think we'll ever cure cancer?" Betty wondered.

Still wiping down her reins, Sister answered, "I don't know. There are different kinds of cancers. I kind of think there's something in us, some kind of trigger. I have nothing upon which to base this idea."

Betty, rubbing her hands on an old terry-cloth towel, nodded.

"I know what you mean. Back to Greg. Maybe he had cancer. Maybe he lost his money. Who knows?"

"He didn't lose his money. We'd all know. That lumberyard of his made a small fortune. Once on the other side of Covid, lumber will pick up again. He'll always make money. Plus Greg wouldn't kill himself over money. I can't see it."

Betty dropped into a director's chair. "Well, I can't either. I hate to think of Risé. What must be going through her mind?"

Finishing up her bridle, Sister sat in the director's chair near Betty. "Poor woman." She paused a minute. "Glad for this jacket. Still a little cold and clammy."

"If we go to the house, I'll make you tea in your own kitchen," Betty offered.

"Good idea."

The two women ran through the now pouring rain into the mudroom, stripped off coats, shirts, leaving their bras on, and walked into the kitchen. Betty ducked back into the mudroom, retrieving two jackets, warmer than the now soaked denim ones.

Jackets on, Sister made sandwiches while Betty boiled water for tea. Both loved tea.

"English breakfast, Irish, Lipton's, your cabinet beckons."

"English breakfast. Strong but not too strong."

"Okay." Betty opened the stocked cabinet, took down a black tin, and measured tea into a little tea ball made just for this purpose. They both liked loose tea, either in a tea ball or in a pot with a holder for loose tea.

Sitting down to eat and warm up from the inside, they demolished the sandwiches.

"I was hungry," Betty confessed.

"Me, too. Not on my cubbing schedule yet."

"Cubbing, for me anyway, is harder than formal hunting. I can't see much, the leaves are thick on the trees. They soak up sound, too. But I love being out with hounds no matter what." She savored her hot drink. "Thursday?"

"I'll call Kasmir. Tattenhall Station ought to be good. We'll take the two most settled youngsters. You know, I'll bet Crawford has a theory about Greg. If we see him Thursday we ought to ask . . . discreetly, of course. Hounds might cross over to Old Paradise."

"Old Paradise is coming to life. I wonder how many millions he has spent?"

"Betty, he'll never tell. Maybe that's a good thing."

"Think he'll move there?"

"I don't know. At some point he has to have special events where it's open to the public. There goes your privacy."

"Our privacy died with the Internet," Betty sarcastically said.

"Some, but we can still defend our physical privacy. You know those stories about buried treasure there? You'd think with all their reconstruction someone would have found it."

"Oh, every old house in Virginia is haunted and has buried treasure." Betty laughed. "I've said that hundreds of times. I'm right, too."

"That's the truth, but I am a little superstitious about the dead, and there are a lot of dead there." Sister tore off a little piece of meat from the small remains of her sandwich for Golly, who joined them. "Wonder where the dogs are?"

"On the couch in the library," Golly informed her.

"I have heard throughout the decades, but first from Ray's uncle Arnold, that wherever Monacans are buried, bad things happen. Fires. Windstorms. Earthquakes. Of course, no one knew at the time that Monacans were buried there. I doubt Sophie Marquette knew that. The tribe had left here before the War of 1812." Sister felt a nibble at her fingers.

"Funny how ceremonies tell you a lot about people, whether

they're weddings or funerals. Those events don't change much."
Betty was interested in people's ideas, customs.

"It's changing a little bit now. When I was young, a Christian wouldn't be cremated. Fires of hell."

Betty nodded. "You're right. We are running out of room. So it is more acceptable. Still, the ceremony stays pretty much the same."

A silence followed this. Then Sister blinked. "Just thinking. What if Greg found the treasure, or something strange like that? Or disturbed a grave?"

"Ah, come on, now, that's too much. He had about as much traffic with Old Paradise as the rest of us. He didn't find anything."

Sister smiled. "I know, but what if, just saying, what if he disturbed a grave or found where the long-talked-about treasure was? Would it be enough for someone to kill him?"

"I don't know. Well, maybe if that person was hoping to dig it up and make off with it later. I guess it's possible. A stretch though."

"Yeah, I know."

"But I believe we are looking at murder not suicide."

"It sounds terrible, but I hope you're right. I can't bear the thought of Greg shooting himself."

CHAPTER 6

September 16, 2020, Wednesday

"You're the first foxhunter I've interviewed." Ryan smiled from behind the small camera on a tripod.

Two tiny lights filled the room, the backdrop a simply unrolled large sheet of off-white paper. Sister sat in a high-backed but comfortable chair, looking at Ryan while Ayanda Freedman sat at a low desk, using the computer to edit. The whole operation utilized the latest equipment, all small.

"That's a dubious honor," Sister replied.

"First thing, I'll ask you questions but I'll be off camera. Viewers will hear my voice but they won't see me. You look at the camera. Okay?"

"Sure," she said dutifully and looked at the small camera. Ryan then introduced her as a master of Jefferson Hunt for over forty years. He provided a little history of the hunt, going back to Big Ray's uncle, but hurriedly reached today.

"Tell us why the title *master* is used?"

"Through our history, kings and the wealthy, whether in ancient times or feudal times, closer to us, had a person in charge of the hounds. Hunting with hounds is one of the oldest sports people pursue. The pharaohs did it. 'Master of Game' was the title usually bestowed on the man, always a man, in charge of the king's kennels. He hired the staff, looked after the welfare of the hounds, and usually hunted with them. This was a coveted position. It came with a good place to live, good food, proper clothing. The clothing proved important because if, say, the King of Portugal visited the King of France, the King of France needed to have everyone look perfect. How you dressed was critical in those days, for it was an indication of status, as was your title. A Master of Game, if he provided good sport, reflected glory on the king or whomever he served, thus securing the position, usually for life. As he aged, a successor would be selected, often trained by the master himself, who then would still live in his home, et cetera. Once we move beyond feudal times, get into the Renaissance, showing off became more luxurious. As the industrial age took over, men's fashions changed abruptly, Masters of Game still dressed if not all in green then with a green coat, high boots, cap. So the title stuck throughout the centuries, hence I am the Master of Jefferson Hounds. As a sidelight, to give you a sense of tradition and how important it is, the pharaohs had their sight hounds walked to the hunt on couple straps, two lead lines going to a circle, which was a handhold for the person walking the couple. Hounds are measured in couples to this day. The motto of foxhunting is 'If it works, let it be.'"

"I had no idea." Ryan was genuine in his interest.

"People tend to learn something about the sports that interest them. Like football. The forward pass was first tried in 1876. Most historians date it to September 5, 1906, by Saint Louis University."

"How did you remember all that?"

She grinned. "I'm a bit of a history buff, plus I love sports, including cricket. Just love them."

Ryan stopped the camera for a moment, Ayanda stopped, too. "Sister, don't worry about time period, we'll edit this. I should have told you that in the first place."

"Okay."

He started the camera again. "When did you first foxhunt?"

"Age seven. On a pony. When I was young, even city people had some familiarity with country sports. City people would take trains to foxhunt. The fixture might be perhaps fifteen or twenty miles away. Train service was reliable then. Or you'd hop on a train, stay in Philadelphia, and go to Baltimore for a baseball game. Well, I guess you can still do that, but when I was a child there were lots of passenger trains."

"Did your parents hunt?"

"A bit. But all of us played something. Not like now, when if a child has talent they specialize; we played football, baseball, ice-skated, rode, ran track. The girls, once out of school, all played with the boys. When we got bigger, the sports were divided by gender. I hated that. We played football, too."

"Really. You all played football?"

"We did everything. Fished. Shot skeet and clays. It was a different time. A good time if you liked the outdoors."

"Do you remember your first foxhunt?"

"Vividly." She broke into a huge smile. "I actually viewed. Even though my mother had taught me the rules, which is if you view you tell the field Master. If you can't get up to the field Master, you take your hat off, point your horse's nose in the direction the fox is traveling, and stretch out your arm. I wasn't to open my mouth. The field Master told us to count to twenty to give the fox a sporting chance and then bellow 'tally-ho.' Well, I was so excited. I stood in my stirrups and screamed, 'The fox!' My mother, mortified, was going to take me home but the old field master, a lovely fellow, a World War I vet, actually, said quietly, 'Mrs. Oberdorf, she has brought us luck.' Then he looked at me, winked, and said, 'Next time button your lip.' "

"Were you mortified?"

"I was too excited, but once back at the stables my mother let me have it. She did soften the blow by saying I had ridden well but I really had to shut up."

"What do you do if someone today bellows 'tally-ho'?"

"I hope they haven't viewed a cat."

The interview lasted forty-five minutes, with Ryan asking the standard questions and Sister not necessarily giving the standard answers.

Finally, they wrapped it up. He turned off the camera, Ayanda stayed at the computer but stopped selecting images. Ryan had introduced the two women; perhaps fifty years separated them.

Sister said to the young woman, "Ms. Freedman, thank you. I have no idea what you're doing."

Ayanda happily explained she selected images, changing tiny things if something was off. "What happens once we're done is we'll have a thumb drive. We saved our footage and if someone wants a show, for a small price we send it. Most people can simply copy our video with their equipment. Pretty simple to do. We'd prefer to sell it, obviously."

"I do know what that is." Sister sighed, glad she wasn't totally ignorant.

Ryan pulled up a director's chair to sit next to Sister for a moment. "What we'll do is shoot actual hunts, the big ones. I will interview your joint master, your huntsman, your whippers-in, members of the field. Then Ayanda and I will edit the whole thing and create a record of the hunt, which you can sell to your members. It's not for the general public, although your interview for the blog is. It ought to be a good fundraiser." He paused. "And I am also doing this for Keswick Hunt, plus I shoot most of small sports. You know, clays, rowing, the stuff that is ignored. This particular episode will be on my weekly show, Friday late afternoons. I have a viewership in central Virginia of 750,000 people."

"I had no idea social media and vlogs could generate such numbers."

"My hope is to eventually have a big Mid-Atlantic audience. I need a studio in Richmond or Washington. I'll have to travel more, but I like doing this. Then if I sell things, say a T-shirt or Beretta pays for an ad when I do a show on days, I'll make more money."

"I see." And she did. "Can you find more sponsors?"

"Yes. Beretta, as I mentioned, located in Maryland, sends me money to show off their shotguns. I don't make a lot but I make enough to keep going and pay bills. Even kayaking paddles are different. They can be marketed. Lots of stuff can."

"And if you expand, surely you will make more than enough."

"From your mouth to God's ear."

"I often hope for that myself." She stood up, stretched her legs, walked over to the desk.

"Ayanda, please come to a hunt. There will be someone who can drive you. You need not ride. Yvonne Harris often drives people. She will soon be riding, by the way."

The young woman's eyes widened. "The model Yvonne Harris, from the 1990s?"

"Yes, one of the first black runway models, and she still bedazzles a room." Sister smiled.

"I would love to meet her."

"Consider it done." Sister, wearing cubbing attire for the camera, reached in her chest pocket and pulled out a card. "You can call me anytime. You are always welcome."

Ryan, now standing next to Sister, stepped over to the desk, all of four steps, plucked a thumb drive from Ayanda's tray. "Here. This is the footage from the first day of cubbing. There's a great shot on there of Greg Wilson looking up at the tree and shaking his crop at me. It might help people to see him happy. And if I'm not shooting, Ayanda can ride in a truck. If I am shooting, she will be, too, so she'll be in my truck. You can never have enough footage."

"You can watch the thumb drive on your computer. Well, Gray can do it. I understand he's the computer whiz." Ayanda smiled.

Sister smiled back. "Gray can do anything. Well, thank you. I hope I gave you some good footage, as you say."

"You did."

LATER

"Isn't Tattoo, that whole T litter, wonderful movers." Sister could brag about her hounds with her husband.

She was circumspect with others. It's a bit like babbling about one's children.

"You have a knack for breeding. I can look at hounds, look at bloodlines, but I don't really have it." He put his arm around her shoulders as they sat in front of his gargantuan computer screen.

She had handed him the thumb drive with the video from the first day of cubbing, which he popped right into his computer. Gray could do anything with the computer, as could his Aunt Daniella, ninety-seven be damned. Sister lacked the affinity for modern technology. She did her best.

"That hog's back jump can cause problems for visitors when we hunt from here. You know, it's good to have different kinds of jumps. Foxhunters are too dependent on coops." She held up her hand. "I know why. Easier to build. Still, a rider and a horse need to look at different obstacles."

"It's the airiness of the hog's back jump," he noted, for this type of jump has space between the heavy logs or railroad ties used to create it. To many, it resembles a rounded hog's back.

"Sure. Something about daylight in a jump . . . well," she waved her hand, "it can set some horses off. They'll stop. Period. Dasher looks good. Solid, solid, solid. I'd rather have solid than brilliant. Fortunately I have both."

"Feel the same way about people. Some brilliant people are dependable. Some aren't. They get away with stuff because others are impressed. You know, honey, I'm beginning to think simple competence is revolutionary."

She laughed. "Me, too."

He smiled as the video kept going. "He's going to edit this, of course?"

"He wanted us to see the footage. He'll pare it down to a half hour for the whole season. Or maybe he said an hour. We were talking before filming. I didn't pay attention."

"Ryan is smart, focusing on the so-called 'small sports.' Tell you what, put any of us in a crew scull and it wouldn't seem like a small sport."

"I don't know how they do it. Oh, look at Alida. Took that jump a bit early."

"Airborne, but okay." He drew closer to the screen as the image of Greg Wilson appeared. "Saw Ryan in the tree." He shook his head. "Greg's happy. Did you ever notice that he always wore a boutonniere or a silk handkerchief?" He stopped the motion. "See? A white rosebud. He and Mercer should have been a pairs team." Gray mentioned his deceased cousin, a clotheshorse.

"Yes. I never saw Greg when he wasn't properly turned out, on or off a horse. It's hard to look at him. Hard to believe he's gone."

Gray started the video again. "Yeah, it is. The older I get, the more Aunt Dan makes sense. You know her famous exhortation: 'Do it now. You'll be dead a long time.'"

"She's right."

"How did you feel the interview went?"

"Oh, Gray, I blabbed on. Just wandered all over the map. He

better edit. Usually I can be concise but I talked about hunting with Mother, my first time in the hunt field. Then I wandered onto tradition, nomenclature, stuff that will bore the bejesus out of people. Thank God he didn't ask me about bloodlines. I'd still be there."

Gray laughed. "You don't even talk to me about bloodlines." He paused. "I don't know how you remember everything."

"You are the last person I wish to bore." She kissed him on the cheek.

"You never bore me. You might infuriate me sometimes, but I have never been bored. How many men can say that about the fabulous woman in their life?"

"Flattered. Don't let me stop you."

As the images rolled on they teased each other, watched, commented on hound work, the reverberations, and the covered bridge, little things they enjoyed.

"Want me to run it again?"

"No. I hope we made the right decision hiring Ryan to record a season's hunting. Thankfully we only pay him half price because we're allowing him to use the footage for his show. He'll make videos for other clubs. Especially after his first year. Keswick and we are the first to try this. He'll make money. Runs in the Stokes family."

"We won't know until the season is over, I guess. I think people will want to buy a copy of the season, most especially if they are in it." He leaned back in his chair, which was almost as expensive as the giant screen. Gray hated sitting for long times but this office chair, which cost over two thousand dollars, did make it easier. He'd stand up, stretch, and wasn't stiff.

"He even got Greg and his horse struggling inside the covered bridge. Was pretty funny."

"I don't know how he does what he does. He's in a tree. Then he's trailing us in his truck, driven by his assistant. How was she, by the way?" Gray asked.

"Quiet. Seems nice enough. Pretty. Young. Her name is Ayanda Freedman. I think they're an item. Just a hunch."

"Ayanda is a Zulu name." Gray thought for a moment. "When we were little, Mom and Aunt Dan would make us study the different tribes, popular names, stuff like that."

"You never told me that."

"Actually, I don't think of it much, but hearing that name brought it back to me. Mom said we'd never learn in school that there were civilizations in Africa and Asia, that history wasn't all Europe."

"Two smart sisters." Sister recalled Gray's mother, Graziella, who greatly resembled Daniella but was a far more subdued lady.

"The difficulty is, so little is written. So Mom said to pay attention to the art, lots of art, pay attention to what music survives. Every kind of people have a history. And, of course, wars, lots of wars. Doesn't matter where you live, someone is killing someone else."

"Mmm. Do you think we are born a violent species?"

"Oh, you and I have batted this around before. Sam has an interesting outlook. He thinks we are violent by nature but civilization means channeling that violence into sports, art, producing things. I don't know. But are we violent even now? The statistics certainly point to that." Gray leaned back in his chair.

"I keep returning to Greg. Was his death an act of violence against himself? Is that what suicide is? Or was it an act of violence by someone else, someone who hated him, although I can't remotely think why anyone would hate such an energetic, giving man?"

"I don't know." Gray exhaled. "If you think about it, both acts are murder . . . well, they can make sense once you know the particulars. You and I can't understand suicide. But for someone suffering, perhaps with a disease from which there is no cure, I think it makes sense. You and I have brushed against that darkness but we never went to that place. I will never know how you survived your son's death. But you did."

"Ah." She was quiet for a long time. "Yes, I did brush against the darkness. It was 1974, and some days it's as though that dreadful farm accident just happened. He'd be forty-six now." She reached for Gray's strong hand. "What saved me was love. My son loved me. If he thought I would give up on life, he would be horrified. Once the worst of the shock subsided I made a vow to do things he loved, like foxhunting, working with hounds, going to baseball games when possible, pushing myself. It took a few years, but his love carried me through. That's the thing, Gray. Someone dies. Their body is gone but the love remains. He's been dead since 1974 but my relationship with him has grown. Love."

Gray listened, remaining silent for a long time. "I never thought of it in those terms. But I can still hear Mother's voice. Mercer, he's never far. I guess it is love. Dad died while I was too young, but my memories of him are fond. But Mom . . . she's with me. Sounds kind of woo-woo, but she's near."

"I know exactly what you mean. And that's why I look at Greg and want to know. Was he in pain? Did someone have it in for him for reasons unknown? Then I think of Risé, Joe, and Carl. How they feel right now. I trust Greg's love will see them through. You know, when you're young, you don't think of these things unless something shocking happens, like your best friend drops dead on the football field. Mostly, for me anyway, this has come with age. I never thought I would like growing older, but I do. I am so grateful."

"Oh, that's easy for you to say. You look like the new Master I saw as a young man out of college before I trooped to Washington."

"I am hearing such good stuff today."

"It's true. You are a beautiful woman. Striking. Men can't help it. We are floored by beauty. Then if you have any brains at all, you look for ethics, kindness, focus, responsibility, and humor."

THRILL OF THE HUNT

"Same with us. We are more resistant to handsomeness, I think, because our mothers drum into our heads things like 'Will he take care of you?' 'Will he provide?' 'Will he be faithful?' There's more, but I did my best to resist Mother's laundry list."

"She was right, though, wasn't she?"

Sister nodded. "Is there a woman in the world who doesn't swear she will never be like her mother and then one day, what comes out of her mouth? Exactly what her mother said. And of course, Mother was right. I swear this happens to every woman." She laughed.

"Growing up and old is ever an adventure. Just so you know, Bobby, Kasmir, and I are rounding up some of the men in the club to go over and do whatever needs to be done at the Wilsons'. Mowing, weeding, anything that needs to be done. The boys and Risé have their hands full. The endless stream of visitors alone is exhausting. Greg was a popular guy."

"That's wonderful." She looked over at Golly, asleep on the back of the sofa, her tail swaying gently right over the dogs' noses. They weren't to get on the couch, but so what.

"Oh, Crawford volunteered to help, too. He was bombastic about the death. He swears it had to be murder. He believes that a detective should be hired."

"Well, I hope he keeps it to himself. Risé doesn't need to hear that now. And I trust Ben Sidell. He won't leave a stone unturned."

"We may be glad of that and we may not."

She switched subjects. "Tomorrow. Tattenhall Station. We need to get hounds out and I'll bring along two of the most advanced B line."

"Be good for people to go out. Always is but if something terrible has happened it helps. At least it does me. Anything to give you a lift, focus your mind elsewhere."

"Everything is changed but nothing perishes."

He looked at her. "What brought that on?"

"I don't know, it popped into my head. Ovid. I guess I'm thinking about Greg. Everything is changed. If nothing perishes apart from breathing, maybe there is something."

Gray, now standing, said, "Only you would think of that."

CHAPTER 7

By eight in the morning the mercury reached sixty-two degrees Fahrenheit. However, the haze didn't lift. Often the mornings of the changing seasons wrapped the mountains in fog, which then thinned to a haze or lifted upward to dissipate. This Thursday, while you could see a short distance in front of you, the white haze persisted.

Hounds worked southward from Tattenhall Station on revived pastures belonging to Kasmir Barbhaiya. He'd limed, fertilized, overseeded religiously over the last four years. The results showed. Hounds moved through but the field rode along pasture's edge. As the hay had not yet been cut, they would tromp it all down.

Cubbing presented scheduling difficulties for Sister. Since it was harvest time no one wished to upend an apple harvest, pumpkins, hay, whatever needed cutting, plucking, pruning. With the shift in climate, especially the longer summers, Sister dutifully called to check and double check. Kasmir, as always a gracious host, advised her to ride on the edges. He hoped to cut his hay if the rain held off. The weatherman, or weatherperson, could tell you the day would be clear and at four o'clock a deluge would engulf people, horses, cattle, you name it. Paid to be mindful even though forecasts often changed. No one ever wants to cut hay then have it rained on.

A blue jay's squawk answered by another blue jay, the conversation short-lived. Sister thought it was strangely silent. Some mornings you'd go out and it was avian gossip central. Today, not much. Nor did she see deer, but given the haze, hounds and the field would have to come right upon deer to see them, though they could smell them if nearby.

Hounds walked, noses down. American hounds possessed terrific drive.

"Nothing," Dragon crabbed.

His littermate growled, *"Shut up. If there is scent, we'll find it."*

Vain though he was, Dragon knew better than to cross his sister Diana. He put his nose down, pressed on.

Sister could hear the clop clop of her whipper-ins' hooves, especially Betty, who rode outside the fence on hard ground, occasionally stepping onto the old rutted farm road.

An hour passed. Not a peep.

"Well," Sister thought to herself. "Finding that not all oysters bear pearls is a lesson young entry must learn."

Jeeves, in his second year, walked next to Baylor, out for the first time. *"Don't worry. Sometimes we have blank days. It's no one's fault."*

"Okay," the handsome youngster replied, nose down, trying as hard as he could.

Up ahead, Weevil rode Gunpowder without saying a word. He didn't want to bring hounds' heads up, they were doing their best. He could just make out Tootie ahead on his left moving through the veil, popping over a stone fence, an old leftover from the original stone fence from the mid-eighteenth century. He knew the fence line loomed ahead.

He peered, squinting. A log jump, two logs over the sunken stone, had to be somewhere on his right.

"Hey," Pickens, a male in his prime, called out.

Giorgio was a gorgeous hound. Sister had asked for him from another hunt, as she wanted an outcross line. He was only a puppy then. Grown now into a truly spectacular specimen, he lacked the voice she so prized in her American hounds. He gave cry; however, it wasn't deep. He put his nose down where Pickens had spoken. *"He's right."*

In a flash all the pack, alert, moved forward. Aces picked up the line; his nose was just incredible. They were off.

The fox had doubled back, so the field stood still while hounds ran through them. Weevil could go around the people but he had to be extra careful lest he veer into the hay. The field was in a single line. The hounds could easily go through them. Weevil not so easy.

"Don't worry about turning around," the Huntsman called to them. "Let me slide by."

A few horses fussed a bit as Weevil literally slid by them, but most of these mounts knew the game and remained quiet. They wanted to turn around and follow hounds, which they couldn't do until the human with the horn had passed.

Weevil blew two short blasts. Tootie and Betty reversed as well but Tootie walked along the outside of the fence line toward the road. If the fox ran in a straight line she could take a corner jump there. If not, she would be ready to cross the road in case the fellow shifted over into Old Paradise.

The mist helped hold scent even as it blurred what one could see. Earl, a big red fellow that lived at Old Paradise, scooted through the pastures. He ran about seven minutes ahead of the pack. He tarried a bit in the hayfield when he should have moved on.

Putting on the afterburners, he tore through the meadows, headed toward the Carriage House, where he had a den. He had them all over the place. Ducking into an entrance alongside the back of the long stone building, he wiggled inside, no carriage in there yet. However, a few fancy tack trunks in Old Paradise colors, deep maroon and gold, lined the large tack room, folded blankets on top of the trunks. Crawford planned on buying carriages from the period of 1815 to the mid-nineteenth century. He hadn't time for that at the moment, but he did have a few tack trunks made to replicate the period, as well as a few more modern carriages he enjoyed driving. Crawford struggled to keep all in order, even with the people he had hired, apart from the construction workers.

Earl loved the Carriage House even more than his den in the main stables. Too many people now came in and out of the stables. He liked his solitude.

The hounds reached the den entrance. They howled, they dug. Earl heard Weevil's voice telling them not to dig. This added one more thing for hunt staff to do after the chase, make sure no damage done.

The small field, most had been put off by the early fog, listened. Sister smiled, for the hounds did well, especially Baylor and Peanut, other young entries.

"Master, shall I cast back to Tattenhall Station?"

"Weevil, why don't we walk back? If they pick anything up, we'll follow. We've been out almost two hours, that's enough for cubbing. They're in great health but I wouldn't say hounds or horses are a hundred percent hunting fit."

"Yes, M'am."

Sister studied the beautiful Carriage House. She could see the main stable beyond, hazy. Old Paradise had witnessed many deaths, most natural, but a few pure murder. A day like today would be perfect for murder.

Sophie Marquette broke ground in 1814, living in a few rooms off the temporary stable. The real work began once she was truly settled. No point in flashing money around during a war, but when Jackson won at New Orleans she knew she was at last safe. She broke ground and began what would be one of the most spectacular estates in the Original Thirteen. During that long time it wasn't surprising that some people would be killed.

As the haze intensified scent, it also seemed to magnify sound. Sister thought she heard talk behind the main stable but she couldn't see anything. Then again, maybe she didn't hear it. This was followed by what sounded like someone being hurt. As she was leading the field, she couldn't investigate. It didn't sound like much. She soon forgot it.

CHAPTER 8

September 18, 2020, Friday

"Can you feel fall coming?" Sister asked Cynthia Skiff Kane, Crawford's Huntsman for his farmer pack.

"Not quite yet," the slender woman, in early middle age, replied.

"A hint. Just a hint." Sister smiled, watching Betty on the right of all the hounds, Tootie on the left, and Weevil walking behind them instead of in front.

Skiff had called Sister, asking her to bring her pack to Old Paradise, where they could walk them together. As Crawford had finally become a farmer pack after years of wanting nothing to do with the Master of Foxhounds Association of America, all breathed a sigh of relief. His stubbornness stemmed from the fact, easy to understand, that he didn't want anyone telling him what to do. But because of that, he had been considered an outlaw pack and people could not hunt with him without jeopardizing their membership in a recognized hunt. A mess. Sister, usually obedient to MFHA rules, as she thought them sensible, occasionally hunted her pack with Crawford's at his invitation. No master wants to get sideways with a huge, powerful landowner who has their own hounds, recognized or not. Losing Old Paradise, which she nearly did because of all this, would have badly affected her hunting. After years of wheedling and wooing, Sister, Marty, and Skiff finally brought him around.

Marty's response was that all men need to be propped up, to think any idea is really theirs.

While Sister, too, had a very male husband, she never needed to pull feminine wiles on Gray. She considered herself lucky. Fortunately, so did Gray. They were meant for each other.

Skiff, now living with Jefferson Hunt's former Huntsman, Shaker Crown, agreed to an extent but merely nodded. Shaker had sustained a serious injury to his neck during a hunt. After expensive rehab, numerous stays at the big clinic in Cleveland, he had finally accepted the inevitable. The emotional pain of not hunting hounds outweighed the physical pain of doing so. But he bowed to wisdom. Skiff learned a great deal from him, so even though Shaker wasn't hunting the Jefferson pack, he felt useful. She was hunting a very different type of hound. He really did help. And she loved him. Soothing his frustration came naturally to her.

Shaker slowly drove behind the joint pack in his battered Ford F-150. Seated next to him was Aunt Daniella, literally along for the ride. She was excellent company and much as he tried to concentrate on the blended pack, he kept erupting in laughter. So did Aunt Dan.

"Are you sure you don't want to walk up with Weevil?" Sister asked Skiff.

"No. Better hounds learn to hunt for him and then I'll walk them back and he can keep you company." Skiff smiled.

"What might be your reasoning?"

A short silence followed, then Skiff began. "When we have a

joint meet we hunt them together up front. He blows the horn to start and I blow the horn to return. But thinking about it, should anything happen to either Huntsman I'd like hounds to feel all right about following only one of us. Pretty much they will follow the horn, but why add confusion?"

"Never thought of that." Sister smiled.

Hounds reached the southernmost boundary of Old Paradise. The roadside, Chapel Cross Road, was set off with a hand-laid stone fence. One could jump any part of it. But then you reached the boundary, a cross fence that was a three-board one with two coops in its long length. You would jump the stone fence then immediately turn to jump the coop, a nice trick. The other coop was at the western end. One needed good balance, tight in the saddle.

Weevil stopped. Hounds stopped. He fetched some cookies from his cookie bag and fed hounds. Skiff left Sister and walked to him. She also wore a big cookie bag and she fed hounds, too. Her pack, Dumfreishire, big black and tan, flipped those tails. Cookies motivated them. Any food motivated them. Sister's American pack also loved food but were less pushy.

"Ready?" Weevil asked.

"Yes." She glanced up. "Looks like some rain. We can use it but I bet we make it back to the stables." He left her to lead the pack and reached Sister, with whom he walked.

"Takes a few weeks when cubbing starts for me to get the kinks out."

"I know what you mean." She agreed with Weevil. "However, what kinks do you mean?"

"Hound kinks, my body kinks." He smiled.

"Ah, with me it's my back." Sister shrugged. "My theory is if you stop moving you're dead."

"I think you're right. You know, Shaker has helped so much with this pack. All they used to do was riot before Skiff came."

"They never had a chance, really, but now there's consistency plus a lot of affection. Hounds need affection. They need to know they are doing a good job. They can read you even if you say nothing."

"That's the truth." Weevil pointed with his crop to a large outcropping. "Think our young red is in there?"

"Perfect place unless he goes to the Carriage House or the stables. So much game here. Well, Old Paradise is right at the base of the Blue Ridge Mountains. Those mountains and ravines are filled with game. Some you want to see and some you don't."

He laughed. "Rather see the game than the moonshiners."

"Now, Weevil, in these parts we call that country waters. Not that I'm a big drinker, but I do believe our county and Nelson County make some of the best waters on the East Coast," Sister bragged.

"The government will want their revenue."

"Yes. And if any revenue man is foolish enough to go into those ravines, he'll never come out. That's why you'll see the government trucks parked on the roadside and usually two men taking pictures. They then go back to the big boss and declare they have investigated the area." Sister laughed.

"So those moonshiners . . . sorry, distillers . . . really kill people?"

"I have never seen them do it but I know they have protected themselves since the Depression, and even earlier I expect."

"So why don't the Feds hide and wait for the distillers to truck their product out? They'd see and hear them come down the mountain."

A big smile crossed her lips. "Indeed, they would. And that is why, Weevil, those men pack their mules and go over the mountains to come out on the Augusta County side; once there, on the back roads, the stuff is loaded onto innocuous trucks like, say, a potato chip delivery truck. Never underestimate the ingenuity of an American breaking the law."

A Canadian smiled back at her. "I'll remember that."

"Then again, some laws are made to be broken. Everyone likes to feel they're getting away with something, don't you think?"

"Ah." He pondered this. "I suppose it's human nature."

By now they had reached the main stables, completely restored. The hounds walked in. Skiff opened one stall door, the Dumfreishires walked in. Weevil opened another and in went the Jefferson pack.

"Come into the tack room. I've set up a table and Marty made her usual great chicken sandwiches, plus BLTs."

Skiff was right. The tack room smelled terrific. Sister, Weevil, Betty, and Tootie admired the table while Skiff pushed them forward. Aunt Daniella and Shaker walked in.

"Isn't this lovely?" Aunt Dan immediately looked for the bourbon.

Skiff, knowing Aunt Daniella would be along thanks to Shaker telling her, produced from under a saddle pad an unopened bottle of Woodford Reserve, which she handed to Shaker to open. Then she handed a bottle of Blanton's to Tootie and told her to open it.

"Aunt Dan, we thought you'd like to sample and make a judgment." With that, Skiff poured two tumblers half-full with Kentucky's best.

"Sit here, Madam." Shaker pulled out a chair for the nonagenarian.

"Thank you."

Everyone grabbed food. Weevil first filled a plate for the older woman, handing it to her along with a napkin. Her chair had arms, so she could place her bourbon on one.

Marty was a good cook and sandwich maker. The long walk,

about two miles, had spiked everyone's appetite. They left early this morning without much breakfast.

"Oh, we used to have such dances at the big house." Aunt Dan knocked off her Woodford Reserve, as well as what was on her sandwich plate. "Did I ever tell you about Dick and Bea Williams?"

Sister and Betty, having heard the tale many times, remained silent.

Scanning her audience, Aunt Dan began. "Well, you must first know that Dick Williams was a triple air ace in the Pacific theater in World War II. His father was an air ace in World War I and his brother was a double air ace in the German theater. His brother was killed in the war. The Williams men proved fearless, and Dick was also fearless on a horse once home. He met, in the hunt field, Bea, tall, stately, a terrific rider. Alluring. One thing led to another. They married, hunting usually with the Essex Hunt in New Jersey. Sister Parish, whom you must know, the great decorator, redecorated the Essex Hunt Club, and met her. Marvelous woman. Knew what she wanted. Well, I digress, a pleasure of age, I think. Anyway, for the most part it was a happy marriage, producing children, who also hunted. The one fly in the ointment was Dick noticed other women. They in turn noticed him. Bea became vigilant. A bit of liquor and Dick could wax amorous. If you watched too much, Bea rose to the heights of amorous recrimination. Well, one hunt ball at Deep Run, ever so perfect . . . but then, Deep Run always is . . . and the place was jammed with people north of the Mason-Dixon line who craved Virginia hospitality and hunting. The dance band packed the floor after the dinner itself. Everyone shimmied in evening scarlet, white tie, and we ladies wore black or white. I, of course, wore white. It always amused me and once I heard a Deep Run member whisper just loud enough for me to hear, 'Mixed blood, you know.' What I was was far better-looking than that fat cow, but that's another story. So there we were, whirling and twirling. My date, divine, truly divine, was a whipper-in at Green Spring Valley, I was in good hands, to which I can attest . . . but then, again, that's another story. Where was I? Oh yes. Dick's wandering. Well, Bea had retired for a few moments to sit at the table and refresh herself with a drink. Dick tapped the shoulder of another gentleman, who relinquished an exquisite creature into his arms. Bea, downing her drink, looked for her husband. I note she carried a small purse in which she usually carried a small gun. Bea was often armed, even in the hunt field. Quite surreptitious about it. You would think it would be Dick who was armed, but no, it was his wife. She noticed he was holding the gorgeous young lady close, too close, making her laugh, which of course made her sumptuous bosom heave. Dick noticed. So did Bea. She ran out onto the dance floor, uttering exhortations to stop staring at the lady's tits. Yes, I am afraid she did utter vulgarities, but they were splendid upright mammary glands. Bea swung her purse, hit Dick on the side of the head, and he sank like a stone. Then she took aim at the milk white bosoms. The young lady had the sense to retreat at top speed. Fearing she had killed her husband, Bea fell to her knees, purse still in hand to slap Dick's face. His eyes fluttered. Another fellow helped him sit up. We all heard him say, for the band had stopped to admire Bea's aim, 'That hurt more than getting shot down by a Zero.' "

They all laughed. Aunt Dan could entertain people for hours, as hers was not a boring life.

"Whatever happened to the well-built young lady?" Shaker laughed.

"Married the head of Reynolds Tobacco." Aunt Dan grinned then added, "Oh, those were the days and the nights."

More stories, more hound talk, finally the little group of hound walkers broke up. Sister and Betty walked to Betty's Bronco.

"You covered the right side yesterday," Sister said to her friend.

"Did. Not a bad day. Not a great day but it was good for all."

"Did you hear anything behind the main stable as we rode toward it?"

"Actually I did. Sounded like a moan."

"Yes, I heard it, too, and then I heard footsteps."

Betty nodded. "Me, too. It was far away. Whoever it was, if it was people, did not want to be seen."

"I thought I heard talk, not loud," Sister remembered.

Someone was back there. "Want to take a minute and walk near the graveyard?"

"Sure."

The two women walked behind the stable, twelve stalls on one side, twelve on the other. Huge. Soon they were in the slave graveyard, which was on flat land but higher than the stable below.

"Crawford has done a lovely job here. He says he has copied the information of who is buried here, and the year they died, at the county courthouse should anyone wish to trace their ancestors. The original documents are in his safe. There must be a lot of people descended from those who sleep here."

"One must honor the dead." Betty placed her hands in her jacket pockets.

"He says once all is finished here, those descendants can plan a remembrance. Could be special." Sister continued to walk, now more northwest.

"Is this the tribal graveyard?"

"They don't know much yet but maybe. I hope he doesn't go around digging people up to discover when they were buried. There won't be any records for the Monacans."

"The old wives' tale is that if you disturb a Monacan grave, something bad will happen. Kind of like the curses on Egyptian tombs."

Sister stopped. "I don't think you should disturb any tomb. I don't care who it was. Your friend. Your enemy. Let the dead alone."

"Hey." Betty pointed to grass just ahead of them.

The grass swept in one direction as though something was pulled over it or someone had dragged their feet.

The two women followed this.

"Blood. A trickle, I would say." Sister knelt down.

They followed the trail, which abruptly disappeared.

Betty, next to her, thought out loud. "It could have been a deer we heard."

"Bigger trail. We would've heard more thrashing about. Just poof."

Betty stood up, looking around her. "Is there any idea how many dead are here?"

"No. This is going to take some work and since whoever is in here is known, Crawford can ask for help, for historical protection. I guess that's what you'd call it."

"He almost has to dig up bones," Betty sensibly remarked.

"I know. I know. I wish there were another way." A raindrop pattered on a leaf, as trees dotted the supposed graveyard. "Come on. Maybe we can outrun it."

They trotted, passing a lovely large stone tombstone: *Ransom Patrick, Born 1790, Died 1853.* A bee and an acorn were carved on the stone. Patricks rested everywhere in this section.

The heavens opened. Sister and Betty hauled ass. Still got wet.

The two sped down the slight rise, dashed for the Bronco. Charlotte Abruzza drove out the back way, passing the stable. The yellow Bronco was visible even in the heavy weather. She drove on as the two women were running to the car.

"Perfect timing." Betty applauded them both as they opened the doors and slid inside.

As she uttered those words the car shook, made a rumble . . . not loud, but a rumble filled the air.

The two women looked at each other.

"Just a tumbler. Happens here." Sister had become used to the tiny earthquakes in the mountain range. "When I drove by before cubbing started, there was a little earthquake."

Betty started the motor and the windshield wipers. "That old wives' tale about disturbing the dead." She then reached for Sister's hand and gave it a squeeze. "Maybe we should remember that and stay out of there."

CHAPTER 9

September 19, 2020, Saturday

People turned out for Greg Wilson's funeral. He had grown up in the county, the Wilson family being an old one. Most of the hunt club members attended the gracious church, as did Greg's high school class, as many had stayed in Albemarle County. The men from his college fraternity at University of Nebraska showed up. As a high school graduate Greg had wanted off the East Coast, was admitted to Nebraska, the school known for its football but also quite good academically. He came home after graduation.

Risé, Joe, Sheila, and Carl sat in the front. The service, one most people in the church knew, as by now their parents had died, a few friends. The service for the dead offered consolation for many.

Sister listened, Gray next to her, Sam on the other side of his brother.

Reverend Sally Taliaferro hit the right balance. It's difficult for a priest to lead a service for a potential suicide. One has to be careful, given canon thinking regarding taking your own life.

Sister noticed Ryan Stokes, unobtrusively filming. She had noticed Ayanda outside filming. Took her some time to realize this was a record for the family. A gesture of friendship and consolation, she thought. Such things did not exist when RayRay died, nor Big Ray. She wondered if it had, would she watch later.

As the service ended, the family walked down the aisle first. Everyone stood. Most people there knew the worst part of this for Risé would come later when things calmed down, visitors returned home. Then it would hit her.

After the family left the church it emptied row by row as ushers came to the end of each row and gestured for the folks in the next pew to rise and walk down the center aisle. The two aisles on each side, narrow, helped some who didn't want to slide the whole way to the center, but most people wished to walk in the wide center aisle. The organ played but didn't blast anyone.

Once outside, the overcast day seemed to reinforce the sadness of the occasion.

Aunt Daniella joined her family outside. Crawford and Marty had asked her to sit with them. While this was unusual Aunt Daniella accepted, for Crawford, even though he had lived in the area for close to a decade, had offended so many people in the beginning, no one exactly welcomed his presence. Aunt Daniella gave notice to people that if she accepted Crawford and Marty, so should they. Few people would cross the grand old lady. She was right. He'd learned. Granted, he learned the hard way, but he did learn you can't just push your way into society in Virginia. You can't really buy your way either, and he'd brazenly tried to do both. He did give generously and was thanked for that but no one asked the two to their homes . . . perhaps to a fundraiser, a not intimate gathering, but he was otherwise frozen out.

His restoration of Old Paradise, cleaning up the forgotten slave graves, hiring Charlotte Abruzza, a historian, to research and publish the histories, helped his reputation. Aunt Daniella was the final step. She liked him. Who knew Virginia ways better than Aunt Dan?

People mixed outside; cars began to leave for the reception at Farmington Country Club. The number of people would have crammed the house uncomfortably, so Risé and the boys, as Sister thought of them, used the grand old club. The views were spectacular. So was the food.

Once there, you could almost hear a sigh of relief. It wasn't that the funeral was intense but the disbelief that Greg would take his own life had made the service critical. A suicide is not to be buried in consecrated ground. Reverend Taliaferro did not adhere to that old rule, but the memory remained. Few people there believed Greg killed himself, as nothing was noted of same, and that helped. Still.

Freddie Thomas with Jamison Metzinger, a new member, greeted Sister and Gray. Sam had joined Aunt Daniella with Crawford and Marty.

"The family picked a wonderful reading," Freddie noted as Jamison stood next to her.

"They did," Sister agreed. "I don't know how the family pulled this together in such a short time."

Gray added, "There's so much to do, in a way it's a help. You can't focus on your grief. At least most people can't."

"A sudden death really takes time." Jamison had only known Greg from hunting last season and the beginning of cubbing.

Ryan and Ayanda filmed the gathering, she from one vantage point, he from another.

Betty, talking to Kathleen Sixt Dunbar, the antiques dealer, said, "Do they have to get everyone's face? I don't know. This is . . . well, I guess this is now accepted."

Kathleen, an elegant woman, almost whispered, "It is. I can't get used to it."

Neither continued that conversation, as they were in sync. They didn't want anyone to overhear. It wasn't that they were criticizing but someone could take it that way.

Aunt Daniella motioned for the head of the University of Virginia Library to join them. She introduced him to Crawford and Marty. Crawford could make small talk but Marty was better at it. She invited the gentleman to come to Old Paradise when convenient.

The reception lasted for two hours. Many people walked outdoors with their drinks to sit in chairs facing the Blue Ridge. Sister stayed inside. As a master she knew most of the attendees and they knew her. Sooner or later the conversation would steer to fox and hounds. That evening, back at the farm, wrapped in her silk robe that Gray bought her, she sank into the sofa in the library. He sat opposite her in the big wing chair.

"How good of Yvonne to come," Sister said.

"Kathleen picked her up. Those two have become good friends." Gray thought a moment. "How about my Aunt Dan shepherding Crawford?"

"She has an unerring political sense. He needs her."

"What surprised me is that he knows it."

Sister put her feet on the coffee table as Raleigh and Rooster edged closer to her on the sofa. "All right, you two. You'll push me off of here."

Gray smiled. "They don't know how big they are. Snugglers."

She sighed. "I guess." Then she added, "No one spoke of Greg's circumstances. Wise, but usually someone mucks it up."

"It's possible something may turn up, but so far nothing. I'm like everyone else. Why would he kill himself? Doesn't seem likely."

"No. Did I tell you Betty and I walked through part of the slave graveyard and where the Monacans may be buried, at least some of them? Crawford has more work to do there. He has to be careful."

"You said you thought you heard someone running after the hunt."

"We did find a bit of blood, a narrow trail. Could have been anything. I don't know what's wrong with me. Greg's death has me seeing boogeymen. I think the worst. It could have been nothing."

"Could. Would we know if Greg was in financial difficulty?"

"Well, Freddie was his accountant. She has a lot of small businessmen as clients. I don't think their businesses are small, but they aren't General Motors. Not that she would ever expose a client, but if that were the case, she would have talked to Ben Sidell. As far as I know Greg was making pots of money. Once a month he'd fly to business meetings, often with large named timber companies. He kept his eye on projects."

Gray changed the subject. "This virus is affecting business. Some wore masks at the reception. Some not. We were lucky to be able to have a reception. People did their best."

"Gray, if they didn't it would show up in the newspaper and a woman facing desperate sorrow would be dragged through the mud. Did everyone socially distance? No. But most did. I know it's for the best. I hate all this."

"The death or the conflicting information about Covid?"

"All of it." Sister rubbed Rooster's head. "I wonder if this could in some way have impacted Greg?"

Gray considered that. "I don't think so. The lumber business is taking a hit but it will bounce back. He was a good businessman. He looked ahead. I think there's a murderer out there, among us, really. Greg hit a trip wire. And whoever killed him was smart enough to leave not a trace."

"Someone in law enforcement?"

—76—

"Mmm, no. But if you want to commit murder, you can now read all about how on the Internet."

"Gray, that's awful."

"Honey, you know what I mean."

"I do. I'm being peevish. I don't want to think there's a killer among us. Someone we know."

"And someone we probably trust."

CHAPTER 10

September 21, 2020, Monday

The high double doors of Old Paradise's main entrance stood wide open. Workmen climbed the long marble steps, carrying furniture, paintings, cartons. The interior, at last finished, was about to be clothed in splendor.

While his main office was at his home, Crawford kept a small office in the house. Next to it, small, was the office of Charlotte Abruzza, the main historical researcher. She was proving invaluable.

Charlotte stood in the main hall, wide, floor gleaming, as the heart pine had been replaced with heart pine salvaged from other buildings. The damage from the weather had ruined the gorgeous floors but the "new" floors were beautiful. Everything that Crawford restored came to life. All the wealth, aesthetic glory, and echoes of a checkered history filled one's senses.

Crawford sat at his computer, as big as Gray's; both were technical wizards. He double-checked delivery schedules, especially for the paintings. Sotheby's had been a great help, steering him to items that would not be auctioned or had failed to meet their reserve.

Fortunately, he, Marty, and Charlotte knew what had been on the walls. So many people had visited Old Paradise over the centuries and wrote about it, a decent record survived. When the DuCharme brothers, not speaking, sold off paintings in the sixties and seventies of the twentieth century, records were kept as to where the items went. Many of those purchasers did not wish to part with something from Frederick Church, but others needed cash. Times change and finances so often change with them.

Church, known for the Hudson School of Art, painted a marvelous view of the Blue Ridge behind Old Paradise. As with any artist, a commission paid promptly was a blessing.

Other lesser-known painters also benefited from the DuCharme's wealth throughout the centuries. Given the family's equine pursuits, they brought over British painters, which may have helped spur Americans to look for equine painters in their own country. Whether the DuCharmes were responsible for the growth of art in America was up for debate, but they certainly didn't hurt it. The nonspeaking brothers used some of what was left of their once vast inheritance to fly over Jim Meads, the famous British photographer, who did them proud with pictures of the family and friends in hunt gear. This, too, pushed some American photographers to seek employment, which they secured. Really good work once hung on the walls of Old Paradise. The photographs were in the library, cypress, unusual but illustrative of Sophie Marquette's wide-ranging taste. It also led to questions of did she raid the British in South Carolina? She never revealed her past. After all, she never knew if in the future she would need to do business with the former enemy. Sophie outsmarted most everyone she ever met.

As they researched, poked around, made calls, traveled to other elaborate estates, Crawford, his wife, and Charlotte absorbed a great deal. Colonials we may once have been, but we were not unsophisticated when it came to garden design and interior decorating. If anything, early Americans craved beauty, felt slighted by Europeans, and were damn sure determined to prove them wrong. Even a simple cabin often had lovely flowers around it, whether a freeborn person's cabin or a slave's. People cared about where they lived. Home needed to feel like home. It was where women could execute their influence and creativity.

Those early citizens realized how extraordinary Old Paradise was. How it lured other wealthy people to Chapel Cross. Once the road came, so did the people.

But Crawford couldn't understand why the photographs stayed in the library. Why not something in the hall? Charlotte taught him, discreetly, as you never pointed out that Crawford might be on the wrong track, that in the beginning photography was not considered an art form. For that matter, neither were motion pictures. So no pictures escaped from the library.

He would stare at the photo of the great Ellie Wood Keith Baxter floating over a four-foot fence, wearing her proper bowler, her hands perfect, her seat perfect, at one with a stunning Thoroughbred. Whoever took that photograph knew what they were doing. No name in the corner.

On a whim, Crawford thought he'd pull up more pictures of Ellie Wood Baxter. Then he strayed toward Virginia Olympians. Then he lingered over a terrific photo of the late Sallie Wheeler, wearing a subdued fabulous evening gown, driving a fine harness horse.

While Crawford was losing himself at his computer, a common enough vice, an interruption popped up. He started to remove it then he saw the image of a drop of blood on the screen, a teaser. He pulled it up.

"You have twenty-four hours to place a bag of fifty thousand dollars in unmarked bills in the church graveyard at Chapel Cross. Hang the waterproof sack on the large monument of the Bland family. Hang it on the corner of the base of the statue of Mary Magdalene. If it is not there by sundown, the following video will be released to Channel 6 in Richmond."

"What the hell?" He scrolled. A shrouded image in heavy mist was digging in the slave graveyard, tombstones knocked over. A pit could be seen. Human bones piled next to it.

More copy appeared, accusing Crawford Howard of desecrating the remains of slaves and Native Americans. The list, fanciful, called up one sin after another. Tossing about bones to make way for a carriage drive around the estate was used as the provocation for this dark deed by an impossibly rich man.

"Charlotte," he called.

She hurried into his office. "Yes, Mr. Howard."

"Look at this."

She leaned over his shoulder, reading every word, studying the images. "Twenty-four hours?"

"Who has been in the graveyard?"

"No one. You can see the stable behind the mist. They shot from above. You can't really tell when this has been shot. Maybe we'd better go up there and look."

"No. Let me call Sheriff Sidell. We might destroy evidence. But twenty-four hours."

"Would you like me to call the sheriff?"

"No. I'll do it."

Within the hour the sheriff arrived in his squad car. He sent his three young assistants, Jude Hevener, Jackie Fugate, and Carson Blanton, to the spot that might have been filmed. As Ben hunted Old Paradise, he knew the area very well. His three officers in training had worked at the Chapel Cross intersection last year dealing with hunt protestors. He told them to go slow. He'd be up shortly.

Sitting next to Crawford, Charlotte standing, Ben reviewed the threat.

"What I find curious is why would they tell you to put the bag on the Bland monument? Whoever this is can't be stupid enough to know we won't have cameras there."

"Should I stuff the bag with, I don't know, rags?" Crawford was confused.

"We'll get to that in a minute. Can you think of who might have it in for you who would use the graveyard?"

"No. I've asked for help. For honoring the slave graveyard as well as the undetermined Monacan graveyard."

"All right. What about someone who wants to use this for political gain? Can you think of anyone?"

"At this point in our political history? Hell, Sheriff, I could fill a book."

Charlotte said, "Excuse me. Sheriff, we have to do something. If we ignore this, it could unravel two years of hard work plus the years before that when Mr. Howard began rehabilitation of the stables. We'll be put on hold. Someone in the House of Delegates will love to be protective of the environment, the history, you know the type. And then we'll get the protestors."

Ben rubbed his chin. "I understand. Crawford, I know you have great wealth. No one, rich or not, wants to be robbed like this. What I can do is put up cameras, stake Jude and Carson hidden around the church. I'll put Jackie at the old Gulf station. Don't put actual cash in a bag. Would you consider making fake stacks then placing a hundred-dollar bill on the top of each stack, tied with twine or ribbon? Pack them in a bag . . . something waterproof, just in case. Put it on the Bland grave."

"This is absurd. It's blackmail." Charlotte tried to remain calm.

"They'll snatch the bag and discover it's a ruse." Crawford's anger mounted.

"If whoever this is snatches the bag, we'll have them," Ben replied.

Crawford thought about this. "All right."

Ben Sidell then walked to the graveyard.

"Anything?" he asked Jackie.

"Yes. Look at these probes. Someone pushed a long knife, something, into the earth. If you notice, tossed down the rise there are deer bones. They were not dug up. That would be obvious. But someone, not a country person, could think they were human graves desecrated."

Ben looked, walked, looked more. "Damn. I'd feel better if this were the work of an organized gang."

"Why?" Jude's eyebrows rose.

"Dealing with amateurs is always dangerous."

Four hours later, the sun setting, Crawford, alone, placed a bag on the corner of the Bland monument base, near the feet of Mary Magdalene. It was a canvas bag, waxed, with a sturdy shoulder strap.

Ben sat at Tattenhall Station's parking lot with Kasmir, who'd allowed him to use it. Kasmir had binoculars. Ben had his cellphone. His three assistants were in place, as were all the cameras. They'd worked at a feverish pace to get it all in order.

Darkness came. The only cars that moved through the crossroads either turned left or right to their homes, and there were few of those. No one stopped near the crossroads. No human activity was observed.

Jude, in the church, could see Mary Magdalene's figure clearly. Carson, the night having grown cool, was bundled up, squeezed between two large hay-bale rolls at the corner of Tollbooth Farm and the church.

Suddenly both men focused. Something was moving through the dark graveyard. Jude quietly reached for the doorknob, gun in hand. Before he could open the door, a medium-sized dog, an Australian shepherd, sped through the graveyard, reached the Bland grave, snatched the bag's hanging strap, and rushed toward the woods above the church on North Chapel Cross Road.

"Sheriff," Ben answered his phone, listened. "Dammit."

Kasmir started to speak but Carson called in.

"Sheriff, the dog ran up toward Crackenthorpe. It disappeared into the woods. It stole the bag." Carson stepped out from between the hay bales as Jude walked out of the church.

Ben called Jackie. "Meet me at Tattenhall." Then he reached Jude. "Go north on the road." Then he got Carson. "Walk toward Crackenthorpe."

"Want company?" Kasmir asked.

"Sure."

After an hour of listening, searching, nothing. Jackie sat in the back of her car, with Ben and Kasmir. Jude picked up Carson on the road as he emerged from the woods.

They gathered at their SUV with no sheriff's department markings.

"Nothing," Jude told him.

"Well, this is a first." Ben sighed. "Go home. See you in the morning."

Puzzled, angry, Ben drove Kasmir back to the station, thanked him, then drove Jackie to her car parked inside the old garage.

Finally, he called Crawford.

"Crawford."

"Yes," came the eager reply.

"Your bag was stolen by a dog."

"What?"

Ben filled him in on what they knew, advised him to sit tight, he'd be back tomorrow, then drove home thinking this really was a first.

CHAPTER 11

September 22, 2020, Tuesday

Fresh cardboard boxes put together sat on the bedroom floor. Sister, Betty, Freddie Thomas, and Risé finished up the chest of drawers in the big closet that had been Greg's. Half of the boxes contained carefully folded sweaters, shirts, some shorts.

Risé struggled with such personal items, but she was determined to get a difficult job done. The boys took some sweaters. "Most of Greg's clothing doesn't fit them. As you know, he'd put on weight."

Freddie, not raised in this area, rolled up a belt. "Joe and Carl are tall men. Greg was, what, about five ten? Your boys are basketball material."

Risé smiled. "We sometimes wondered, were they really ours?" Then she laughed. "I knew they were mine."

Sister smiled, too. "Odd isn't it, how some children resemble one side of the family or the other and some look as though the stork dropped them. I don't know if we'll ever really understand genetics."

"Coming from you, our hound breeder, that's interesting." Betty started moving the filled boxes out to the main hall.

"Betty, I'll help you," Risé called out.

"I wanted to make a little more room. Big though this closet is, it's getting crowded. Now, Risé, what do you want to do about these Paul Stuart shirts? Expensive. Bobby guards his for fear I'll borrow one."

Betty pulled out a lovely lined shirt, a touch of silk, on the hanger. Risé fingered the fabric.

Sister read the label. "Forty-six. What would you say? Thirty-eight is slim. I mean, no man's shirt will ever say small. This isn't a tent. You could wear it as a light jacket almost."

"Is there anyone in the hunt club this size?" Risé asked. "I don't think I could wear Greg's shirt."

"I don't know." Sister then added, "That doesn't mean you have to give any of these clothes away."

"No. No." Risé was firm. "I have to do this. I have rings and his watch. I'll keep his ties; God knows why, but I love his ties."

Risé smiled as best she could. The girls helped. Just being there helped. They cared about her. They knew nothing could wipe out the pain of a sudden, strange death. The more normal they were, the better she felt. She knew them all well enough to bawl her eyes out if the tears came.

"Did I tell you Ryan dropped off the DVD from the funeral? He does good work. I thought this would take weeks," Risé mentioned.

"Didn't Ryan shoot footage of the sawmill for Greg? Greg mentioned advertising. He thought Ryan could help." Freddie then asked, "Did anything surprise you? If you had time to see it?"

"No. So many people. I showed it to the boys before they left. I more or less pushed them to go home. There is nothing they can do. Made them promise to come back for Christmas and stay a week."

"Good idea." Freddie thought it was, too.

"We've got this closet pretty well cleaned out," Betty noted. "I can run this down to Goodwill for you."

"Oh, thank you, Betty. I don't know how much I want to be in public for a bit. I think I'm okay and then I'll cry. Out of the blue."

Sister put her arm around Risé's shoulders. "Honey, it's not out of the blue. You've endured a dreadful shock, a grievous loss."

Risé, knowing Sister had lost her son and then some years later her first husband, felt comforted.

Freddie picked up a box, carrying it to the hall. She then tip-toed into Greg's office, came back out. "We're making progress. Risé, do you want to go through the office?"

"I think I'll wait. The clothing is more pressing. Most of his files will go to you, Freddie. His books and DVDs, that stuff can wait, too. I think eventually I'll make that my office. There's so much to do before then. Do you know the head broker from Fine Estates Realty called me to see if I was interested in selling? How tacky is that?"

"Pretty tacky." Betty curled her lip.

"Once upon a time people had manners." Sister allowed herself a peeved moment.

"Oh, Sister, they still do. The rude and vulgar have always been rude and vulgar. They breed more of the same." Betty laughed.

"I hope you're right, Betty. Let me pop my head in Greg's office for a minute." She slipped into the room, a large partner's desk, dark wood, maroon leather on top with gold pinstriping along the edges. His computer screen, large but not enormous, sat on the desk's clutter. His DVDs, lined up neatly, took up one shelf underneath the screen. She did not open desk drawers. That was up to

Risé. But she did wonder how Risé would transform this typical masculine office into something not exactly feminine but not so dark. She walked back into the bedroom.

Her cell rang. "Excuse me."

As she chatted in the hall, the other three tidied up the room, brought the last of the filled boxes into the hall.

"You aren't going to believe this." Sister informed them of the details of Ben Sidell's call. "Betty, Ben wonders if we can go to Old Paradise this afternoon, say at four?"

"Sure."

"A dog. A dog stole the money bag?" Freddie's mouth hung open.

"That's what Ben says and he asked for Betty and me as we hunted there Thursday. None of this is public yet but he didn't tell me to keep quiet."

"A new form of blackmail. Very political," Freddie shrewdly surmised.

"There's little sympathy for the rich and we all know Crawford is rich, rich, rich." Risé sat in a chair in the living room for a minute.

Freddie followed as Sister and Betty stood.

"Rich and highly intelligent, if not so emotionally intelligent," Sister replied. "Crawford has called the Historical Society for Descendants of the Enslaved and the leadership of the Monacan tribe. A false charge may alert people to issues they have avoided, but in the long run will undermine those issues. Accusations of financial gain infuriate most people."

"The times in which we live." Freddie nodded. "Crawford and Marty as well as their historian, Charlotte, have done everything by the book."

"Which is why we have to wonder why hold them up? Well,

Crawford. Whoever did it assumed Crawford had a safe with ready cash, which of course he does."

"Thinking that someone in Crawford's position has cash on hand is reasonable." Betty now sat down, and Sister followed.

"Greg would know what to do. He was good in a crisis." Risé tightly smiled.

"One expects that the culprit will be furious when he finds out the bills are fake. Only the top bill is genuine," Sister mused.

"Whoever this is probably knew he would not get the money that fast. Crawford would try to flush him out," Freddie thought out loud. "Perhaps this is a prelude to something bigger."

"Think the dog will be part of it?" Betty couldn't help but laugh.

CHAPTER 12

September 22, 2020, Tuesday

LATER

"The heavy mist obscured their features," Crawford pointed out to Sister and Betty, who strained to see more.

"You can see digging," Betty mentioned.

Sheriff Sidell stood with Charlotte a bit behind the two women to whom Crawford showed the images on the screen plus the threat.

"How did you know we were back there? We heard a car but the rain came down at once and we weren't sure who drove past Betty's yellow bomb." Sister put her hands on her hips, again studying the images.

"Was me. Betty's car is infamous." Charlotte smiled. "I didn't think anything of it until Mr. Howard called me back on my cellphone."

"We heard what sounded like a fall, some talk as hounds came back from their joint walk. The mist got heavier and Betty, on the right, heard it better than I did. Nothing dramatic but odd. It nagged at us so we walked up to look." Sister continued, "The grass was bent one direction, you could barely make out footsteps and a bit of blood."

"Would you know where that is now?" Crawford asked a foolish question of women who had an unerring sense of direction and a memory for topography. Hard to be hunt staff without it.

"Sure. We can take you up there. The rains will have washed most everything away but both Betty and I remember the spot."

Pulling on rain boots, all trooped behind the stables as Sister and Betty led them up the rise. The two women stopped to look back to be certain of their bearings then walked on. Was slippery. The hard rain had soaked everything.

The two stopped just over the rise.

"Here," Betty said.

Sister pointed to the ground. "The grass bent in this direction. A bit of blood led to this point. Well, look, you can still see the marks into the earth. Like something hard had been stuck in, but no digging."

"That means what we saw on the screen may have been a composite." Crawford didn't know film terms.

Ben knelt down. "From the distance where this was shot, actions could be somewhat obscured by the roll of the land. No tombstones are knocked over."

As he stood up Sister focused on the spot. "Someone could have edited this. Gotten footage when Crawford was restoring everything. It was unkempt then, markers knocked over. Why risk being caught here? It has to be added footage. The same with the bones."

"Well . . ." Crawford was confused.

Charlotte, younger, was more familiar with cellphone videos, visual stuff. "Anyone who is under forty and has a cellphone could work this out. I'm not saying that's what happened here but it can be done. Young people can do anything with phones, computers, you name it."

"The point is to have skeletal remains, make it look . . . well, like graverobbing, for lack of a better word. Desecration. Could this be done in a studio?"

"Sure. If one has footage, it could be done at home. You don't need a studio as much as you need editing." Charlotte folded her arms over her chest.

"You could do it." Crawford didn't mean to sound accusatory.

"Well, I am just under forty, if that's what you mean," she agreed.

"I didn't mean it that way," he quickly said.

Ben walked toward the back, returned. "These days, the changes are so fast even teenagers can't keep track of them. But Charlotte, you have a point. There are so many workmen here, and there was a joint walk of hounds. Our culprit must know schedules. Why risk being seen?"

"True, but whoever this is, they were bold enough to come up here, thick as the mist was."

"You know, maybe we don't want to know. Maybe that had nothing to do with this threat to Crawford," Sister posited.

"It appears to be the same spot, or did until the rains. Given what we saw on his screen." Betty held on to her idea.

"Crawford, I'd like to bring my team up here. We'll cover this area. It's possible we missed something. I'll have Jude, Jackie, and Carson walk over quadrants." Ben looked up at Crawford.

"Of course, of course," he readily agreed as they turned to walk back down to the stables, then to Old Paradise itself.

By habit, Crawford went to his office, clicked on the computer. "Sheriff."

Ben hurried in, looked at the screen.

"Dammit. Dammit," Crawford cursed "Girls, come in here."

Sister whispered to Betty and Charlotte, "It's wonderful to be called a girl in your seventies."

They smiled, walked in, stood behind Crawford to read.

You failed the test. You have one more chance before I release the footage of desecrating graves. This time the price is one hundred thousand dollars. Set the bag on the front step of Bishop's Court at the end of South Chapel Cross Road. As for the hundred-dollar bills you put on the so-called stacks of money, clever but not clever enough. Unmarked bills.

"He knows the territory." Sister exhaled.

"Well, anyone who lives in the Chapel Cross area knows." Crawford twirled around in his chair. "But I grant you, Bishop's Court is a little off the beaten track."

Bishop's Court was the first Catholic church in the county, founded immediately after the Revolutionary War. Catholics were not encouraged anywhere but Maryland in the Original Thirteen; they struggled to build a church, to worship as they believed, and to avoid the censure of their fellow citizens. It was hard for a Catholic to find a job. Not as hard as in England itself, but the colonies, former colonies, reflected the Mother Country's prejudices thanks to Cromwell and, worse, Henry VIII. Those early Irish settlers kept their heads down, worked hard. As time rolled on, more churches appeared in Albemarle County and up and down the East Coast. However, it was never to one's political or social advantage to be a Catholic. Even the magically beautiful Grace Kelly faced prejudice in Philadelphia in the 1930s. Her father's wealth could not pry open Philadelphia society. Her siblings were as beautiful as the movie star herself. The prejudice against Catholics ran deep. While perhaps not as severe now, it has never vanished.

Sister's mind filled with that as she thought of the simple church. It was small, clapboard, at the end of Chapel Cross Road, where the road turned into a track over the Blue Ridge Mountains. When one turned right, a quarter of a mile down the road, the once neglected, somewhat restored church was nestled among tall trees.

Ample places to hide as well as escape.

"Let me send someone to help you put together a bag," Ben suggested.

"I need time to think this through. Is it worth one hundred thousand dollars?" Crawford's practicality came to the fore.

"That's a difficult decision." Charlotte wanted to be supportive of her boss.

"Pay and he may well come back. But you'll be attacked through the media until the truth comes out." Betty folded her hands in front of her. "This is an easy time to turn people against one another and it's vicious. Crawford, you have given us a wonderful gift restoring Old Paradise. Archeologists, historians, architecture students, and more can come here, and step back in time. See how hard life could be even for the rich. One can only imagine the trials of the poor. But you really have given our state . . . well, anyone . . . a great gift."

He blinked slightly. "Thank you, Betty."

"We don't show our appreciation enough."

"She's right," Sister chimed in. "We don't, but once it is open to the public, I do hope that changes."

"I'll stay here. The team will get here in an hour at the latest. If you don't mind, Crawford, I want to go through every structure here," Ben asked.

"No, not at all."

Sister sat as Betty drove the yellow bomb home. "What do you make of this?"

"Very clever. Doesn't think he'll be caught. I think it's a he."

"Why, because women don't commit big crimes, you know, like armed robbery?" Sister noticed a blush of color at the tops of some maples.

"I could be wrong but if a woman commits a big money crime it tends to be embezzlement," Betty mentioned.

"Think you're right. Then again, Betty, criminals of any gender don't think they'll get caught," Sister agreed.

"All those TV shows with instant solutions. How many murders are unsolved in our country? I don't know, but I am willing to bet it's not an insignificant number." Betty shrugged.

"Well, let's hope this doesn't wind up in murder." Sister tapped her armrest.

CHAPTER 13

September 23, 2020, Wednesday

A line of large diesel trucks, sparkling clean, sat in front of Synder's Trucking Service.

Ryan and Ayanda, both in his Ram truck, slowly drove in front of the new trucks.

"Okay, go around these," Ryan directed Ayanda, who was driving.

Once this was accomplished they stopped the truck, got out, and Ryan opened the back of the big rig.

"Wow," Ayanda noted.

"Oh. Let's shoot the interior."

She climbed up on the big metal step, opened the door, inhaled the fresh new-truck odor, and stepped down.

Ryan climbed up, stayed on the step, carefully filmed the interior with a close-up of the multi-gear box in the middle. He also leaned forward a bit to shoot through the driver's window. Satisfied, he stepped down.

"You don't realize how huge these things are until you're in them." Ayanda appreciated the size.

"Thirty thousand, used, to two hundred thousand, brand new." Ryan sat on the step for a minute to clench his high-end Canon, which itself cost two thousand five hundred dollars.

Ayanda's eyes widened. "That's a fortune."

"Mr. Synder makes a lot of money. These here are about eighty-five thousand apiece. The only reason I know that is he told me when he hired me for the ad, and they aren't even considered the biggest of commercial trucks."

She looked at the cameras. "Good shot of the front of the building."

"Okay, let's go in the back. Best to have it, even if we don't need it. Shots of the trucks now in use."

They drove through the open gate, Ryan filming the back lot. The used trucks were clean. All Peterbilt trucks. Different sizes.

Ryan talked as he kept shooting. "He rents trucks long term. For some businesses that's cheaper than buying these babies, especially if you're starting out."

"He must do a great business." Ayanda admired the cleanliness of the trucks.

"All up and down the East Coast. It's not just individuals and small companies. The refrigerated trucks are really expensive. Big companies rent them annually."

"Smart man." She drove him to the last row, older trucks, but all tidy.

As they drove by one, doors closed, they heard what sounded like talking inside.

Ryan ignored it.

"Is someone in there?" Ayanda asked.

"Maybe. Maybe not. That's why this place is surrounded by

chain-link fencing with barbed wire on top. To keep out the home-less. Sometimes if you drive by late, lights are on in Synder's office, cars parked outside. But the chain link is locked up even if he and his people are at work late. There are a lot of desperate people out there."

Back in the front of the small, clapboard office, once a home, Ryan hopped out.

Ayanda parked the Ram in front, handing him the keys to the truck where they shot the interior.

Ryan opened the office door, walked in to hang the keys on the key rack by the front door. He knew where to put them.

Arnold Synder's office door was open. "What'd you think?"

"Beautiful." Ryan moved to the opened door. "Someone is in the back now. Door closed."

Arnold nodded. "I'll take care of it."

"You know, you could sell the old trucks. People could refur-bish them and live in them."

Arnold smiled, he was an attractive man in his mid-fifties. "When the engines start to go, that's not a bad idea. By the time I close up, if anyone's been in an old truck, they're gone. Usually leaving it clean."

"I'll have this ready for you in two days. Have been filming hunts, making a little money, I hope. People now want DVDs in-stead of yearbooks."

"Good. Still want a studio?"

"Do. Then I can hire other people to shoot. On camera is where the money is."

"Should I get a facelift?" Arnold paused.

"Nah. Okay, see you."

Arnold waved him off, so to speak. He did make a bit of money off the older trucks in the rear now, but maybe it was time to retire them.

CHAPTER 14

September 26, 2020, Saturday

Thirty-three people showed up early in the morning to hunt from Mill Ruins, a favorite fixture. The old mill, huge, the water wheel turning as it had for two centuries, fascinated most people who saw it and heard it. The slap of the wheel, the water flying off the paddles, was once a sound familiar to people in both the New World and the Old. Grain needed to be ground, the waterwheel proved perfect, durable, and serviceable even today.

Hounds had moved past the beautiful large stone mill. Ryan Stokes, shooting footage of the mill itself, was now videoing the field riding past it. Hounds had moved ahead. He'd sent Ayanda up ahead in his truck. She stood in the back, catching the riders coming straight at her. She knew to go no farther without Ryan taking over the wheel. She had no idea about foxhunting nor did she know the territory. The pageantry of it was not lost on her though.

Weevil walked with hounds.

"He could cast us now." Jingle, a youngster, wondered why they weren't searching.

"He will. Best to get a little beyond the mill," Aero counseled. *"James lives behind the mill and he's crabby. He'll waste our time."*

"He's old. Can't stand anyone, not even other foxes. Never gives a run. But we can pick up his scent around the house, because he goes straight for the food tossed out the back door by Walter. Dr. Walter. He's the tall man riding at the back of First Flight," Cora, one of the pack leaders, told the ready-to-roll Jingle.

"Don't worry. There are lots of foxes here. We'll get something. You just put your nose down when Weevil tells you to," Thimble advised.

They walked on the farm road, fences weed-whacked clean, jumps also perfect. Ryan sprinted behind the riders toward his truck. When they passed, he slid into the driver's seat as Ayanda scooted to the passenger side. He slowly followed the field.

"Get Betty over there. She'll take the coop at the end of this field. Will look good. She's a strong rider."

"Okay." The young woman held her Canon DSLR.

Both Ryan and Ayanda used this camera, which looked like a still camera but wasn't. Light, easy to focus, great color, the camera also had an interchangeable lens. So if needed, you could take stills as well as video. The best part of the camera to Ayanda was how light it was.

Betty indeed soared over the jump in style on Magellan, a rangy Thoroughbred she had inherited from a deceased hunt club member years ago. She forgot how old Magellan was getting to be . . . but then, she forgot about herself, too. If your mother never told you your birth date, no one would know how old they were. Not a bad idea.

"There's a car behind us." Ayanda looked around.

"Yvonne Harris, Aunt Daniella, and Kathleen Dunbar, who owns that high-end antiques store on Route 250. They often follow. Don't worry. If they want to go around us, they'll do it when the field pulls away," Ryan informed her. "If there's time after the hunt you can meet Yvonne."

"Get 'em up," Weevil called to his pack.

Noses down, they eagerly did as they were told. A hound lives to hunt, and so do most of the people following.

Rabbit scent, fragile, lifted into noses. Nothing doing.

"What's this?" Bellhop was confused.

Dasher walked over, took a big inhale. *"Raven. Big blackbird, really pretty big. Distinctive odor. They are smart. Hate foxes. Sometimes they'll tip us off."*

Hounds moved from a walk to a trot, not brisk but enough to cover more ground. Those forward hounds wanted to hit a line.

Weevil glided over the coop, three feet six inches, on Kilowatt, a talented Thoroughbred given to the club by Kasmir.

If members give solid horses for the hunt club staff, it's a big help to the club. Having to buy suitable hunters is costly. That was one of the reasons Sister bought young untrained Thoroughbreds. They were affordable. She didn't mind putting the years into them.

Sister waited until Weevil pulled away by thirty yards, then she popped over on Rickyroo, her twelve-year-old Thoroughbred. He was a glorious horse with a goofy sense of humor.

One by one the field took the jump with an "Oomph" here and an "Uh" there.

As they bumped along, Ayanda leaned out the window to focus on the field ahead, especially the jumping.

Behind them, Yvonne's SUV crawled. Kathleen had picked up Aunt Daniella to drive to Yvonne's, who lived at Beveridge Hundred, the farm south of Tattenhall Station, abutting its southernmost border.

Tattoo, a large doghound, nose down, swerved to the right just as Diana, an excellent hound, shot into the woods on the other side of the jump, a thirty-foot cleared strip between the fence line and the woods.

Diana noticed, slowed.

"The line is over here," Tattoo called out.

Diana carefully retraced her steps, nose down. Indeed, Grenville, the fox, had hooked right.

"Overran the line." Her littermate grimaced.

"Then let's shut up and get back on it." Diana loathed Dragon, her brother.

The pack stopped, emerged back onto the strip, crossed the road in front of Ryan and Ayanda, reaching Tattoo, who plunged into the woods.

"If she leans out any more, that girl will fall right out of the truck." Aunt Dan lifted an eyebrow.

"They are determined to get footage. This is a new idea for the club. Not cheap either," Yvonne noted.

"I suppose everyone likes to see themselves flying along," Kathleen sensibly observed.

"It's the involuntary dismounts that humiliate you." Aunt Dan grinned. "Like that famous Marshall Hawkins picture of Jackie Kennedy parting company with her horse."

"She was a good rider, that's what people who rode with Orange Hunt say. A lot still left, as they were younger than the First Lady." Yvonne thought Mrs. Kennedy a good example of athletic ability allied to tedious political duties.

"Yes, that's what they say. You know, we've had quite a few presidents and first ladies who rode, and rode to the hounds." Aunt Dan continued, "Back then there were fewer amusements. You either rode, perhaps hiked, someone played the piano. People made their own fun. Shooting clays was a big sport. Well, still is. Ever try it?" she asked the other two.

"No," came the reply.

"Try it sometime. My sister and I used to shoot clays. I really like it. Was also quite social. Most of us girls went without our husbands because, being husbands, they all felt compelled to tell us how to shoot. I could outshoot my husband, so he did not natter on to me . . . but then again, he didn't want to be shown up, so I went with the girls."

"Your sister never remarried, did she, after her husband died?" Kathleen, fairly new to the area, asked.

Aunt Dan shook her head. "She devoted herself to the boys. She always said she wasn't going to take care of another man. I found it easy. Tell them what they want to hear, keep them happy in bed, look good in public, and tell everyone how fabulous they are. I got more jewelry that way."

"I should have known you when young." Yvonne hated her ex.

"Well, now, my pretty, you resolved your divorce and did get half of your media company money. You didn't want to run the damn thing anyway. I mean, you helped build it, but life is more exciting here. Trust me on this."

They laughed because with Aunt Dan around if it didn't start exciting, it often ended up so.

"Well, hounds are heading down to Shootrough." Yvonne named the back end of the farm, which had been used for hunting for years. Walter abandoned the grouse hunting, putting much of it in hay. The farm roads were terrible. The big storage building was in great shape but it was only forty years old. New in these parts.

"Think he'll make it in that big ass new Ram?" Aunt Dan watched the impressive truck, heavy and big, start the downward drive to the flatlands below. The ruts in the road cut deep as they did once down at Shootrough itself. Seemed foolish to take a new truck there.

"Had to cost seventy thousand dollars if a penny." Kathleen kept her eye on the dollar. "I guess his business is good for such a young person. He's thirty, maybe?"

"All he has to do is pay over time. That's how we all got into debt, be it personal or political." Yvonne had an almost instinctive reaction against blowing money if you didn't truly need something. She fought with her ex over this constantly.

Size helped Tattoo push through some of the underbrush choking parts of the woods. The woods at the back of the farm were a good mix of pine reaching the end of its lifespan and hardwoods, which could go on for centuries.

Ayanda nearly bumped her head as Ryan hit a pothole then hit the gas to escape it.

"Damn." She clutched her camera.

"Put on your seatbelt," Ryan told her. "It gets worse."

As they reached the bottom of the hill, Tattoo and the pack sped through the cut hay, easy to do, crossed the rutted road, which revealed the hill road. Two rows of round bales, perhaps fourteen bales, seven to a row, beckoned them, scent heavy.

Dragon leapt to the top of the bales. Audrey and Aero, A line, followed; as the other hounds squeezed through the middle of the bales, still others walked carefully around it.

"Why are these outside?" Baker, another young entry, wondered.

"Not good enough for horses," Taz simply answered as he stopped. *"Baker, see if you can squeeze in there."*

The youngster, thrilled to be given a special task, wriggled and wiggled between the bales to get into the line in the middle.

"Fox." Baker didn't hesitate.

Pookah, a small hound, slid toward Baker. *"Is."*

Before Pookah could speak again, Aero dropped down. *"Yes. Heading back."*

Ryan crouched near the bales, good footage, and Ayanda, in

the bed of the truck again, caught the hounds on the hay bales. That would be fun for viewers.

Hounds roared across the farm road, heading toward the storage building. Grenville had popped into his den and was now inside the spacious building, listening to the bitching and moaning outside. Made him laugh.

"He always does this. We never get a great run out of him," Pansy, Pookah's littermate, loudly complained.

"Well, we got something," Cora wisely replied.

A long run once youngsters have the drill is wonderful. The young entries were learning, fitting in nicely, but shorter runs helped them settle in, and more than anything having to search for scent helped make a good hound. Weevil encouraged his youngsters.

Sister and the field waited close to the large shed. Doors closed. Walter had lined old hay bales on the north side of the sixty-by-thirty-foot building. This helped keep it warmer in the winter. The large shed used to contain tractors, but all the mechanical equipment was moved to sheds by the mill. Getting down that hill in bad weather to retrieve a tractor with a blade on the front to push snow became harder and harder as the road deteriorated. He would fix the road but so many other needs preceded that one.

"All right, let's find your fox." Weevil smiled at the pack as he cast them toward the second creek, crossing farther away from the storage shed.

Hounds made good the ground, but nothing. Weevil turned to head back up the steep hill. Ryan pulled the truck off the road and Yvonne backed up until she was on the other side of the muddy intersection . . . or usually muddy. Today it was dry.

"You're good at backing this thing up. Even with the backup cameras, I'm awful." Kathleen sighed.

"They help but I still do better if I turn around and look out the back window." Yvonne did not say that sometimes it was difficult to twist that much.

Slowly Ryan followed the field.

Ayanda asked, "Is there a reason we're far behind?"

"Yes, some horses get nervous and the people in the back of the field are the ones who don't jump. Depending on the fixture, sometimes I can park and wait for them to ride toward me. I am determined to get footage of the fox watching them, foxes running. Seeing the fox gets people crazy."

"They're beautiful," Ayanda said. "I didn't want to do this but when you told me they don't kill them I thought, 'okay.' But didn't they used to kill foxes?"

"Sister would know the time frame better than I do, but I think that started to phase out in the 1970s. And in territory like this, chances of killing a fox are slim. They are highly intelligent animals."

Hounds filtered into the woods, began climbing upwards. Ryan again told Ayanda, "Fasten your seatbelt. I don't know which is worse. Going down or going up."

As if to confirm this statement, the right front tire dropped in a rut. Took a bit of work to get the big truck on more solid ground. It was only a half ton, but it was big, almost unyielding.

"A brand-new truck," Kathleen noted. "I'd bring something less new. Then again, you don't have any trouble."

Yvonne replied, "I can pretty much drive anything. In high school I'd drive the boys' cars in empty parking lots. They'd dare me, I'd make a bet and win."

"One way to pick up pin money." Aunt Dan smiled. "I can't hear anything, can you?"

Windows down, the women strained.

"No. All I can hear is the engine in that new Ram." Kathleen listened intently.

Once hounds reached the top, Weevil jumped into the fenced pasture across the farm road, opposite the pasture the hounds had moved through to start. Betty and Tootie were visible riding along the fence lines.

The sun peeped in and out of clouds. Rain scent promised wet skies later.

Slowly hounds drew back toward the mill.

Sister walked along, watching the pack. This would be a so-so day. She enjoyed watching the young entry grow more confident. She still brought out two or three at a time. By the beginning of October she should be able to put more in the pack. She had twelve first-year entries to work with. Five youngsters remained at the kennels. They were too young. They'd be ready next year. It was a late litter. She really had to breed the female before she was a bit too old. Sister never liked to take a chance with an older female. Birthing was hard enough in your prime, hound or human. She tried to think of her pack three years in advance. Sounded easy. Wasn't.

A little warble from Dragon alerted everyone. He shut up soon enough. Not much.

Ryan, on the road, drove ahead to the mill, where he turned the truck so it was facing the road, the horse trailers behind him. Would be a good shot getting the pack coming in, light filtering through the clouds and the trees still full of leaves. Behind him as he and Ayanda set up, water sprayed off the paddles, the sun hitting the spray creating tiny rainbows.

Yvonne, Aunt Daniella, and Kathleen slowly followed.

A ding rang on Aunt Daniella's phone. "Drat. Sam." She named her nephew, Gray's brother.

Reading the text, she breathed deeply then clicked it off.

"Okay?" Kathleen asked.

"No. Arnold Synder killed himself. Sam said Arnold's brother called him. Crawford had been promised a truckload of heavy oak.

Which Arnold was to bring on one of his older trucks. Incredible fellow. Would drive stuff himself if needs be. It was the last oak Greg had at the sawmill. They did business together. Odd."

Yvonne stopped the car. "I didn't know him. But I'd see Synder's Trucking Service trucks."

"I didn't know him either."

"Well, this Covid disruption of supply lines hit him pretty hard. That's what I heard. He lost a lot of money. Then, too, he'd been through a bad divorce last year before all this Covid stuff." Aunt Daniella thought a bit. "But he didn't seem like the type, not at all."

"Neither did Greg Wilson," Kathleen added.

"I still don't believe he killed himself." Yvonne started the car again.

"Sometimes suicides go in waves. One sets off another." Kathleen considered this. "Maybe Greg Wilson was murdered. Either way, his end is terrible, and it could be that Arnold believed Greg killed himself."

"I think those fellows shared a lot of information." Aunt Dan paused. "Forgot. He also shot himself."

Yvonne replied to Aunt Daniella's thoughts. "Covid has somewhat forced the government to consider small business." She thought a moment. "Maybe he didn't really shoot himself either."

Kathleen, in the back, leaned forward. "Small business hires more people in America than the giant companies, plus we are part of the community. Don't get me started. Then again, I'm not even small, I'm tiny, but I have a dog in this fight."

"We all do," Aunt Daniella wisely replied. "Look, girls, let's keep this bad news to ourselves. No point telling anyone at the tailgate, six feet apart, remember?"

"Okay," the other two agreed.

"Good idea. If someone else is called, let them be the bearer of bad news. Everyone will have a theory," Yvonne prophesied.

"They can have all the theories they want. Two men are now dead by their own hand. One seems impossible. Arnold may be easier to understand but no one yet knows the facts. Something doesn't add up," Aunt Daniella firmly stated.

CHAPTER 15

September 27, 2020, Sunday

St. Paul, the golden rooster atop the stable, glowed in the morning light. Sister, standing with her cup of tea in her hand, smiled at the pretty sight then walked back to sit down at the kitchen table.

"Feel good about cheating?" Gray looked up from the weekend edition of the *Wall Street Journal* to smile at her.

"A tiny bit guilty, but yes. I really wanted to sleep late today. Both of us. You and Sam are dutiful, taking Aunt Daniella to church every Sunday."

"He was happy to take her without me. Every now and then one has to shrug off a duty; it's a little duty, and why passing on it makes me feel free, I don't know. I actually like going to church with my aunt and my brother, but last night I was like you— dragging."

"I think Arnold's suicide right after Greg's affected me more than I realized. It's not like I was close to Arnold, but when the news popped up on Freddie Thomas's phone and everyone had a theory, it got to me. You know what really surprised me? Aunt Dan, Kathleen, and Yvonne knew but didn't say anything. Aunt Dan was right, why be the bearer of bad news at an occasion that should be happy? And of course, I do miss Greg in the hunt field. You could rely on him."

"You could also rely on Arnold the few times we needed a big truck to move equipment or even trees. If he didn't have what we needed he found a temporary rental at a good price."

"Greg knew that people who succeed in business provide first-rate service. Everyone else provides excuses."

Gray nodded in agreement. "Sometimes driving home from Washington I'd go past his lot on 250." He named Route 250, which ran east to west. "The lights would be on in the office. Cars parked there. Some in the back. He put in the time. Every now and then I'd go that way as opposed to the back way. Little by little, more businesses are opening from the 250/240 intersection to Crozet. More and more people are moving west of Charlottesville," Gray noted.

"East, too. Louisa County is becoming chic," Sister replied.

"Eventually it will be a neon rash from Richmond to Staunton, from Richmond to Boston. I am not enthusiastic."

Gray neatly folded the paper lengthwise, then in half, putting it on the empty seat next to him as Sister sat across from him.

No sooner did the paper land on the seat with an enticing crinkle than Golly jumped up on it, her face peering hopefully over the kitchen tabletop.

"Golly." Sister chided her with her tone of voice.

"There's bacon left on the plate."

As if to torment the long-haired beauty, Sister picked up a piece, eating it with relish. She then saved an end, which she placed in front of the cat, who daintily hooked it with a claw, bringing it to her mouth.

"Not fair," Rooster complained from the floor.

"See what you've started?" Gray sighed but gave in to the Harrier, adding another piece for Raleigh. Both dogs laid under the table, sliding out once Golly ate the bacon, which they could hear. Nothing like the smell of bacon to arouse humans and animals.

"Yes, I can see you are as disciplined as I am." Sister laughed at him then changed the subject. "Well, tonight is the night for Bishop's Court. I don't think Crawford would mind if sometimes you offered to read the threats on his computer. You often have a way of looking at things that the rest of us don't."

"Thank you, honey, but if Crawford wanted my opinion, he'd ask." Gray reached for a small apple tart, a sweet taste for breakfast.

"You're right." The phone rang, she rose, walked to the counter, and picked up the wall phone, ancient but easy to hold. "Good morning."

"There's a black star by your name in heaven," Betty teased her. "And you missed a good sermon."

"Sally always gives a good sermon. She doesn't harangue."

"This morning she talked about translations. Jesus spoke Aramaic. The Old Testament was written in Hebrew, the New Testament in Greek. Not everyone agrees with that, but the New Testament wasn't written until about forty years after Christ's death. Anyways, there's a lot of argument about that and Sally says no matter about the exact start, what wasn't written in Aramaic would have been translated into Greek because that was the language of educated Romans. But what made her sermon so good was taking certain words like *teacher, rabbi,* and looking at different meanings. She said that one word in Greek can have a variety of meanings, inflections, as the word pool is so small. So was Jesus considered a teacher? It was really good."

"Well, sounds good. I am grateful we don't have to hear about hellfire and brimstone . . . but then, Episcopalians rarely do."

They laughed.

"Sally gave a good sermon." Sister raised her voice a bit so Gray could hear better. "Okay. Did everyone miss us?" Sister said with a smile in her voice.

"That followed the sermon. Where is Sister and Gray?" Betty couldn't resist more teasing.

"You were all devastated, I'm sure," Sister fired back.

"Funny you should use that word, quite a few people are upset about Arnold Synder. Risé was there so no one talked about it with her, obviously. The fact that he shot himself made it worse."

Sister replied. "Don't psychologists say that people who really want to die either hang themselves or shoot themselves? Gruesome thought."

"I don't understand. I have never once considered suicide," Betty honestly stated.

"Me neither, but murder I sure understand."

A silence followed this. "Me, too. There's an unease. I don't think it will be minimized until we know for sure about Greg. As for Arnold, yes, he did it, but no one really knows why. A lot of people think it was that he lost so much money due to the supply lines drying up, the Covid things."

"Hold on a minute." Sister called out to Gray, "Honey, from what you know of Arnold Synder's business, could it have bounced back?"

"If the debt wasn't an avalanche, I think he could have come back. He had brand-new Peterbilt semis on the lot. Something was moving."

Sister relayed this to Betty.

Betty replied, "What's an avalanche in business?"

Sister asked this of Gray. "That depends on your business. For instance, years ago the rule of thumb for buying commercial property was you could pay up to eight times its value. Anything less was a bargain. Part of the incentive was you could write so much off. It's not the same today."

Sister relayed this.

Betty thought a bit. "Given these times, you see small businesses closing right and left. I don't know how long anything will take to open and even if we do get back to business, stores open, people not needing to stand six feet apart, I don't think there will be a clear sense of what anything is worth. Too much confusion. Then again, people have learned to live without shopping in person."

"What are house prices worth? Building materials tripling. It's crazy." Sister shifted the phone to her other hand. "Prices are insane."

"Yes, they are, but it has to fall back sooner or later. If people can hang on."

"Maybe Arnold couldn't. Maybe he hid his stress, the money stuff. He sure got beat up in the divorce. Who's to say? If this farm weren't paid off, I don't know if I could manage it. Ray made wise investments and I'll tell you, thanks to him, I turn to the stock prices each day in the paper. One day the market is booming and the next day it's in the gutter. Like housing, it's just crazy."

"Bobby says the same thing. It is crazy. He says don't give in to your emotions. Wait it out."

"He's right, but Betty, we can wait it out. There are millions who can't. I have no answers."

"It's one thing if you have no answers, it's another if our government has no answers."

"Betty, that's a whole other subject."

Gray, listening to Sister's side of the conversation, put his hand on the paper but didn't pick it up. "I can sometimes hear a little bit of what she's saying."

"The government has no answers."

He leaned back in his chair. "It does, but millions don't like them. Remember, this is an election year, whatever the Republicans say the Democrats will declare it will destroy democracy. The people will suffer. In the reverse, the Republicans swear that whatever the Democrats propose will destroy the economy. The people will suffer. Bad theater."

"Did you hear him?"

Betty said, "That deep voice, I did. Well, to change the subject, do you think Crawford will put out the money?"

"I do. Ben will have people everywhere. How can they not grab whoever it is?"

"The dog." Betty laughed.

"I'm sure they have fresh bones everywhere." Sister laughed, too.

Sheriff Ben Sidell, thanks to foxhunting, knew Bishop's Court's topography. Fifty yards behind the old simple church the woods rolled down from the Blue Ridge Mountains. Dressed in black, Jude had been posted in the woods, Carson hid in the small foyer, and Jackie was hidden behind a woodpile at the rear door of the church in case anyone came down from the mountainside.

Ben knew that whoever this was must have been watching where his officers were posted. But the department might be able to fool them with Jackie, flat against the tall woodpile next to the back door. It was the best Ben could do. No point in blocking the single driveway, the small parking spaces, too, were watched, but no human form was visible. Ben even toyed with the idea of using one of the department's German shepherds to be on the alert for the dog. After careful thought he nixed that. What if the thieving dog, smelling the police dog, backed off?

Each officer carried a gun, along with a high-powered flashlight. Ben sat quietly behind the pulpit. He doubted the perp, as one thought of these people, would come inside. It would be too easy to be trapped.

Crawford followed instructions, placing a canvas bag, strap not affixed to the door, on the front door to the church.

Fall, around the corner, gave notice, for when the sun set the temperature dropped. Central Virginia was about three weeks from the first frost, although one could be fooled. Bearing that in mind, each officer wore a black jacket, sweating originally but glad of it an hour later. Two hours passed. Nothing.

Three hours. Staying alert tired Jackie. She would doze off, pinch herself.

Twilight had long faded. Darkness blanketed Bishop's Court.

Jude slowly stood up as an odd sound alerted him. Jackie, too, heard a small motor. Carson, in the foyer, a small window just cracked, also heard the tiny whirring.

The sound grew a bit louder, Jude shouted but it was too late. A drone dropped right down, picked up the canvas bag, shot straight upward, and sped away up over the mountain.

Ben, on his feet, rushed out the front door, as did Carson.

"Jude! Jackie!"

They ran to him, Jude tripping in the darkness.

"A drone," Jackie sputtered. "I could only make it out when it dropped down."

"Dammit. Dammit to hell. Who is this guy?" Ben cursed.

"Someone who understands technology." Carson stated the obvious.

Jude nodded. "You can buy these things in hardware stores."

Ben, exasperated, said, "Could someone make one?"

"Yes." Jude replied. "But it's just as easy to buy one. You can buy various sizes, speeds. A lot of realtors use them to put footage of properties on their websites. You can program them to follow boundaries."

"So a lot of people in this area, realtors anyways, would know how to operate one?" Ben leaned against the door, now closed.

"Excavators, putting in a culvert on a farm, need to examine the ground of the culvert. They might need to know the condition of the farm roads. A lot of people have these, including someone who wants to have fun like kids with planes."

"Dear God." Ben exhaled.

He did not consider himself a technical wizard but he thought he was relatively current. He was not.

"Let's walk out. Jackie, call Eddie to come pick us up."

Eddie Meister, an older officer nearing retirement, was parked three miles down the road in the Beveridge Hundred driveway. If anyone drove past he would know.

Walking in silence, it seemed every footfall crunched. The night air turned a bit cooler, a slight wind added to the feeling of a dropping mercury.

"How big would you say the drone was?"

Jackie said, "Smaller than a garbage can lid."

Ben nodded. "Well, let's go to Old Paradise and deliver the blow to Crawford."

No one said a word.

CHAPTER 16

September 29, 2020, Tuesday

A mud fence still standing after two and a half centuries loomed up ahead. Sister felt Rickyroo, her trusty Thoroughbred, lengthen his stride a bit as hounds sped away on the other side of the fence. Ricky was not to be left behind. Fortunately, the ground, red clay, wasn't rock hard thanks to sprinkles over the last few days. Weight on her stirrups, eyes ahead, the two flew over the obstacle, landing softly on the other side. She was glad she brought him out again today, even though he had hunted Saturday.

Four youngsters joined the pack today, and as luck would have it Jeeves found the scent. That was a half hour ago. Tuesday was turning into a hell of a run. Sweat slid down Sister's back as well as between her breasts, which always irritated her. A trickle of sweat zigged down from her hard hat, so old the fabric inside had long ago deteriorated. This was a reminder to line the cap with terry cloth. Well, too late now.

The temperature had nudged right over sixty degrees, about right for a late September morning, given how warmth lasted longer in the season these days. Still, the first frost wasn't too far ahead. Not that that would do her any good now.

The pack ran together, a huntsman's dream and a master's pride. Music filled the air from the basso profundo of her old "A" line to the higher pitched excited calls of the youngsters. Sister thought of them as countertenors.

Ricky's ears swept forward and back. Trusting her boy, Sister slowed the pace. Hearing hoofbeats charging up behind her she stayed still for a moment. Walter Lungren tried to slow Clemson, his mount. He'd run up her butt if he couldn't slow the normally paced horse. One assumes people can control their mounts. Most times they can, but every now and then a horse takes a notion or the rider isn't paying attention. A pileup can occur.

The hounds grew quiet. She saw Weevil's cap over the rise ahead, all she could see of her young Huntsman. He wasn't moving either. Behind her, things settled down.

The blush of fall colored a few maples. Willows were turning yellow down by the large, swift-running creek. Soon. Soon that magical season beloved of hunters, hikers, and most everyone, fall, would drape them in coolness, color and birds migrating overhead.

"Well?" Baylor, a young entry, asked.

Diana, in no mood to indulge a first-year entry, snapped, *"That's why you have a nose. Put it down and shut up."*

The pack, spread out in a large circle, searched for scent. They covered a lush pasture, still green, abutting the stream. Scent should have been a snap here. It wasn't.

Weevil looked around. No deer. No birds. Quiet.

On his right, Betty also scanned the territory about one hundred yards away. Fortunately, the woods were maybe another fifty yards to her right, so she could see quite a bit.

So could Tootie on the left. The rich, moist earth odor assailed her nostrils. Nothing else, and even though her nose was but a human one, if the fox crossed recently sometimes a human could discern the distinctive off-sweet odor that in conditions such as these would be rising. By the time it reached a human nose, scent was over hound noses. A huntsman knows he is going to have to try to find a place where it may still be on the ground. But nothing gave evidence of scent, and it wasn't above hound noses, at least not yet.

Patiently hounds made good the ground. Trinity and Zorro, working near each other, drifted toward the woods to Betty's right. Sterns aloft but not really wagging, they persevered.

Betty heard a squeak. A blue jay flew out of the woods past her.

Edging into the cooler hickories, oaks, evergreens, some of advanced mighty age, Zorro flipped his tail a bit. Then Trinity, too, picked up the scent.

"Fresh." Zorro made ready to open.

Trinity advised, *"Hold on one minute."*

The larger, slightly older hound trotted ahead on the line then he stopped. *"Come here."*

"Here." Both studied the fading scent then opened.

The pack rushed to the speakers; they, too, spoke. They followed the line, which again abruptly stopped. Logs, large, blocked easy traffic.

Betty threaded her way through the fallen logs, victims of high winds. The owners of Mud Fence didn't clear trails on their property and Jefferson Hunt was behind on clearing and building jumps. During the sweltering summers, enthusiasm for outdoor work waned. Now that it was cool, Betty realized she, Sister, Weevil, Tootie, and the hunt club stalwarts needed to organize some work parties. The chiggers were gone. The stinging bugs were slowing down, spending more time in their nests. It was now or never.

Weevil slid by her to hurry up to where the pack milled around a large fallen log.

Tootie remained out in the pasture but closer.

"Dicey," Weevil remarked to Betty.

Hounds nosed into the log. They were too big to wriggle in there. They were screaming.

"He's in there. And he's not budging. My hunch is he has a den opening inside the log. He had to go in to get to it, so it's cleverly hidden. If we cast about I'm sure we'll find openings outside by the log. He's dug tunnels," Betty noted.

"I'm sure he's not going to bolt for us." Weevil half smiled. "Clever buggers."

"Indeed." Betty nodded.

Touching his horn to his lips Weevil blew a simple toot then moved deeper into the woods. Hounds followed.

As the sun rose higher in the sky, the shadows stretched across the broad path through the woods. Broad enough for a tractor, this was a shortcut to the large pasture on the other side. The original owners of the Mud Fence had no tractor, as it was immediately after the War of Independence, but they were wise enough to know one might need to drive a team of heavy horses through the woods. Make it easy for them. The farm was named for the mud fences they built, as they lacked the money for wood fencing.

Sister watched the woodpeckers, a few flashy varieties, dart about overhead. The nuthatches would hang on a tree trunk then waddle around it, peering at the riders. The hounds cast at seven-thirty. It was now 9:00 AM, so the warmth would soon be a problem. However, the stinking, suffocating heat of summer was over. You never know. Didn't mean hounds couldn't catch a hot line. She observed tree trunks where stags rubbed their growing antlers. Finding shed antlers throughout the year pleased her.

Weevil, now out of the woods, felt a whisper of wind on his cheeks. Oddly it came from the south. He steered the hounds into it.

Pickens, a steady fellow in the prime of life, bounded forward, stopped nose down. *"Gray."*

Off they tore, back through the woods but closer to the old farm roads. Hounds headed for the Tollbooth Farm, on the northeast side of Chapel Cross Road. Those farms, more modest than the ones on the southwest side of the road, persevered throughout the centuries, as had the richer ones.

Another mud fence, all the original mud fences were covered in grass, stood up ahead, the last barrier before Tollbooth Farm. Hounds easily roared over it, as did Weevil and his whippers-in. Jumping an unusual obstacle perked everyone up. You had to use your judgment. If you did part company with your horse you hit the turf, not stone or wood.

Sister followed, heard a distant whirr, looked to her left, and saw Ryan Stokes, far enough away not to scare the horses, videoing the scene.

The pace notched up to a full gallop. Hounds screamed, ducked under scattered bushes, veered back into the woods, then ran through the woods far above the wide path they had traversed. Now it was a matter of ducking low branches.

Sister slowed, looked for anything, a deer path, found one. She rode on that. No point knocking someone's head off, a brisk trot covers ground efficiently.

When she emerged from the woods she had fallen about a quarter mile behind the pack but she could clearly see. Hounds now vaulted over the freshly painted coop between Mud Fence and Tollbooth. So did she when she got to it. The pack slowed, then picked up speed again, finally stopping at the old hay barn, the one farthest from the main house.

Gris, the gray being chased, had tarried over on Mud Fence. He really put on the afterburners to make it home. He slid down into his den, coming up on the other side in the old barn, huge hand-hewn beams overhead. He trotted to the remaining hay bales stacked high.

His mate, Vi, having heard the commotion, popped out behind the hay bales. *"Long run?"*

"Yes, I was over at Mud Fence. They've left corn for fodder. Wasted time."

"Come on out," Aero, a younger hound, shouted.

Gris walked to the inside opening on the other side of where Aero shouted down the outside opening.

"Get lost, you worm."

Aero, young enough not to have had many direct conversations with a fox, sat down, eyes blinking. *"He called me a worm."*

Gris added, *"Useless worm."*

Thimble, a good girl just approaching her prime, also sat down but she was laughing. *"You'll get used to it. Wait until you hear what James calls us if we disturb him at Mill Ruins."*

As Weevil called the hounds, headed back toward where the trailers parked at Mud Fence, Vi chided her mate. *"Why do you have to go so far? There's plenty here. These humans eat good and they don't put on their garbage lids very tight."*

"You're right. Can't help myself. I want to see what's going on. And that corn at Mud Fence is sweet."

"Stick closer to home." She jumped up on a hay bale, her tail hanging over it.

As the two grays settled down, the hounds reached the trailers parked near the entrance to Mud Fence.

Tuesday, usually a small day but especially during cubbing, had fifteen people out this morning. Sister decided to open it to the club. Up until now she'd used it for staff hunts only. It's easier to get the kinks out if people aren't around. Everyone tied their horse to the trailer, removed tack, most of them threw on a sweat sheet then put out a tie bag of hay. The humans gathered around food, which Betty placed on the back of Walter's Chevy Silverado. People brought folding chairs and sat gratefully eating muffins. Sister drank hot tea that she'd brought in a thermos, a big thermos, a gift from Betty for the first day of cubbing.

Hounds had an upper deck inside the trailer with a ramp. Half stayed on the ground floor. The others were on the deck. All had fresh water to drink, which would be removed once the trailer pulled out. They reviewed the hunt, as did the humans.

Kasmir Barbhaiya, nibbling a fresh piece of corn bread, remarked, "Good run. A bit of a surprise."

Betty, also eating corn bread, agreed. "I love those earth jumps. Makes chasing foxes even more fun."

"Does," Walter agreed.

Gray and Sam, who had brought up the rear, downed strong coffee. Both had been up since four o'clock. Sam had to finish his chores before hunting even though he was hunting a green horse for Crawford, a handsome fellow named Ranger.

Ryan's big Ram drove in, parked at the end of the trailer line. He and Ayanda walked up.

"Please, help yourself. It's a meager repast, but the weekends are good." Sister smiled.

They did so, then dropped into the folding chairs. Everyone brought folding chairs.

"This is good." Ryan smiled.

"Mother's corn bread." Betty smiled back.

"Wanted to get footage of the mud fences . . . well, grass fences. They are so unusual." Ryan swallowed his corn bread. "Said I'd not see you all again until Opening Hunt, but I couldn't resist. Got good footage, too."

Ayanda chewed corn bread. "This is good. My mother never made corn bread. She used to make rice patties. Sounds odd, but they were good."

"Where were you raised?" Kasmir asked the young woman.

"Milwaukee. I went to the University of Wisconsin. And I wound up here." She laughed. "Why Mom stuck to rice, I don't know. That and green vegetables were her staple."

"Wisconsin is a terrific school," Sam chimed in.

"It is. I wanted to see the East Coast. First went to New York and realized I could never live there. I met some friends from Charlottesville, and they invited me to have a look. Did." She smiled an inviting smile.

"Bet you didn't foxhunt in Wisconsin." Betty laughed.

"Cross-country skiing," she replied.

"Good legs." Sister smiled. "Helps you ride. If you have any interest at all, we'll help you."

"Thank you. I think I'll have to work up to it," Ayanda shyly replied.

Ryan grabbed another piece of corn bread. "I can't help it. This is awesome."

"How's work coming?" Bobby asked.

"Good. It's fun but Covid is getting some people to rethink their business. Realtors now show properties on their website. The stuff needs to be professional. I'm getting work. Arnold Synder started using me about a year ago to shoot trucks, some individually." He paused. "Poor guy. Ayanda and I shot a new line he got in. He seemed fine."

Betty quietly said, "You never know. It's interesting that Covid has helped your business. Good for you."

"Thursday. Let's try Prior's Woods, on the opposite side of the end of the road where Bishop's Court is." Sister then added, "Will take four young entries. I'm adding some but keeping the numbers low."

They broke camp, packed up, grabbed the Jesus strap inside the doors, above the windows, and hauled themselves into the trucks. Walter, tall enough so he made getting up that high look easy, aroused envy in the short people.

Betty and Sister drove back, following Weevil and Tootie driving the hound trailer. In front of that, Gray and Sam led the way.

"Haven't heard any more about Greg or Arnold." Betty leaned back while Sister drove.

"Me neither. Don't especially want those subjects bandied about. Best to keep our mouths shut."

"Tell me why you are going to hunt Prior's Woods?"

"Well, I figure that would give us a chance to see if there's anything dropped on that side of the road. I'll call Ben. Be good if he could hunt that day. Gives him a break but also he can look for anything disturbed, different."

"You and I, along with Ben and his deputies, are the only ones to know about the drone. Well, I told Bobby."

"I told Gray. The only thing in the paper was that Old Paradise is a tricky crime. The hope is our crook will get fat, so to speak. Best to keep the blackmail part under wraps."

"Maybe the drone was sent off from Prior's Woods?" Betty wondered.

"Could be. A dog steals the first bag and a drone takes the second. Pretty clever." Sister nodded. "No one has identified this dog."

"It is. And we still don't know what is or was going on in the Old Paradise graveyard. Maybe just curiosity?"

"What could possibly be in burial grounds from before the Revolutionary War? What would Crawford need to do to find out? Would he need not to disturb graves? Well, Crawford is smart and rich. He'll do what he has to." Sister turned down the long drive to the kennels. "It's becoming a dark time. I have no idea why."

"I always feel things go in cycles." Betty offered an explanation. "Threes."

"We've had the three, Greg, Arnold, and the threats to Crawford. Three."

"No. Won't be three until we have a third death."

"Betty, don't say that." Sister shivered slightly.

"Oh, it's an old wives' tale."

"Well, this old wife believes it."

CHAPTER 17

September 30, 2020, Wednesday

Heavy clouds obscured the full moon, the Corn Moon. Next month would be the Harvest Moon, a name most people remembered. Recalling the name or not, mammals felt the tug of the moon whether on two feet or four.

Earl, the large red fox who formerly lived in the main stable but had moved to the Carriage House to avoid all the activity in the large main stable, popped outside.

His main living quarters were in the southeast corner stall, a huge size for the big four-in-hand carriage, a Brewster coach worth a fortune, which Crawford had just purchased after intense searching. It was the only red carriage there. A pony cart was in another stall. Crawford had moved his newer, less expensive carriage to a small stall farther away.

Earl liked the stall. In one corner an old-fashioned large wooden tack trunk stood. In the other corner a few hay bales were stacked. It was behind these bales that he had an entrance. He had bolt holes through the building, including the roof peak, lined with paned windows as a small spine. One could walk along these, crank them open in the summer. The architects of Old Paradise proved practical, solid people, as their buildings stood the test of time, even neglect. To walk along the main aisle of the Carriage House now, no one would ever dream it had been neglected.

Thick blankets, placed in the four-in-hand as well as the pony cart, ensured that anyone venturing out in cold weather would be warm. The four-in-hand had a closed cab. The pony cart was open, like a pre-convertible.

A chill made Earl fluff his coat. He hopped into the seat of the open pony cart, looked out the windows. Not much to see but being a curious fellow he returned to his large den, slid down, emerging outside of the Carriage House.

Crawford kept no cattle yet. His horses remained at Beasley Hall, his private estate. Earl had no one to chat with unless Sarge, who lived in a big bouldered den to the west of the Carriage House, came over for a visit. Sometimes Gris from Tollbooth Farm would come over. Gris burst with curiosity. Earl liked him well enough, although he had a habit of snatching old tack or towels. Gris also liked leather. Chewing it made him nod off. Sitting outside listening, Earl heard a rustle directly over his head. Athena, the great horned owl, far from her nest, swooped low. Neither spoke. While not enemies, one wouldn't classify them as friends.

A light footfall made the glossy red turn and he saw the young Sarge, in good coat although a bit thinner than Earl, walking his way, his tail held straight out.

"Evening." The younger fox approached him.

"Be a lot of hunting tonight." Earl believed full moons lured everyone outside.

"Well. I went over to Beveridge Hundred before coming here. The dog box was full of cookies and even little bread sticks. Yvonne leaves good food. She even leaves steak pieces. However, that useless Norfolk terrier of hers

barks each time I visit. Unless he's asleep. The most spoiled dog. Ever."
Sarge curled his lip slightly.

"*Norfolk terriers are. People think they're cute.*" Earl shared Sarge's
disdain.

A distant clank diverted their attention to the graveyard one
hundred yards plus to the west. The clouds, low, hugged the mountains.

"*Sounded like metal.*" Sarge's ears swept forward.

"*Does.*" Earl headed in the direction.

The two foxes, loping silently, reached the flattened land
guarded by trees, large evergreens, the lower branches sweeping
the ground. They ducked their heads between branches.

Neither fox uttered a sound as they watched two humans,
dressed in black from head to toe, with black masks on like skiers,
masks covering the whole face.

The humans each carried a long metal stick with a circle on
the end of it as they swept the ground. This was a metal detector,
but all the foxes surmised were two people ridiculously swinging
something.

Neither human spoke.

Below them a light flicked on at the main house. While far
away it spooked the humans. Crawford didn't live at Old Paradise
but some of his research staff did, as well as his main stable man.
For now anyway.

The taller one touched the shorter one on the shoulder. They
quickly headed toward deeper woods. The foxes followed. After
twenty minutes the humans emerged on a farm road hugging the
southernmost border of Old Paradise. A half-ton beat-up Chevy
truck sat there. The two placed their metal detectors in the bed, got
into the cab of the truck. Keeping their masks on they drove off.

"*There's nothing up there,*" Earl commented.

"Who knows. Maybe humans like dirt. I couldn't catch their scent, could you?" Sarge asked.

"No. Whoever they are they don't want the Old Paradise people to know they've been up there. Nothing there but dead people that I know."

Sarge thought a moment. "Not far back some of the humans went up there. Sister and Betty." He knew the foxhunters.

Earl looked up, a raindrop fell, then another.

"I'm heading back. Sometime let's go over to the chapel. The sexton leaves stuff tossed about everywhere. He's a drunk, you see. Seems nice enough but not quite together."

"Sure."

"I'm looking for a work jacket with fleece lining or heavy plaid," Earl informed him. "You can really curl up in one of those."

"Come with me to the little house by Beveridge Hundred. The one the pretty, tall lady lives in. She folds jackets, scarves, all kinds of stuff, and leaves it on the covered porch until she puts it away. Sometimes that takes days. Has coats in the car, too. Bet we could lift one. It's a long way to carry but worth looking at anyway."

Earl thanked Sarge as he headed back to the Carriage House. Sarge headed to his boulder den, well protected from wind and rain, full of straw, old blankets, and toys, very warm.

Coming up behind the straw, his old blanket there, too, Earl circled then dropped down. A little wet but not too awful, he liked the odor of the straw and hay. Thinking on clothing, he decided to sneak into the big house when the humans were busy and distracted. Had to be all kinds of warm items, even coats, there. He could always snatch a saddle pad, a sheepskin one from the main barn, but that would set them in a tizz more than a coat. Humans could be forgetful, they'd blame it on themselves. Even though horses were not stabled there right now, Crawford wanted everything perfect in the main stable. Saddle pads, heavy saddle pads, were luxurious. Well, he'd get in the house if he could figure a way out if anyone sniffed him. Sometimes humans could smell a fox. They could fool you.

The rain drummed on the tin roof. Earl was happy to be curled up. The activity at the estate fortunately was confined to the big house and the Carriage House but he recognized the sheriff's squad car and the county sheriff SUVs. They'd been around. Human affairs interested him little unless they impacted his activities. But he knew enough about human life to know law enforcement vehicles are rarely good. And there had been something up there. When the ladies returned after a hunt he heard what they had heard. He watched the day the small group walked up there with Crawford, who he recognized. Whatever might be there was well hidden. He couldn't imagine what would be important.

CHAPTER 18

October 1, 2020, Thursday

"Things pile up." Sister folded a repaired winter horse blanket, which was heavy.

Betty also folded a blanket, lighter weight, letting it hang over her arm. "Where do you want to put these things?"

"Those that are specific to a horse, marked on top of the blanket, put in the tack box by their stall. Everyone has two tack boxes, so there should be room."

"Okay. What about the spares?"

Sister stopped, stared at the growing pile of professionally cleaned spares. "There isn't room for one more tack trunk in the tack room. We need them here. I don't want to walk to the kennel or some other building to fetch them."

"Me neither, because it will be cold and maybe snowing. Why not wrap them all in plastic and put them up in the hayloft?"

"Don't we need something heavier?"

"Yes, but until that time just wrap them up, and that way we can easily carry them. Then we can throw a heavy tarp over them. Until something better occurs to us."

"Betty, you are so smart."

That task took another forty-five minutes. Neither woman wanted to climb the ladder affixed to the wall to the hayloft, lean down, and try to grab a wrapped blanket handed up from below. So Betty tied rope around each blanket, tossed the end up to the Master, who then hauled it up hand over hand. Once the blanket was in the hay loft, Sister untied the rope, dropped it back down, and put the blankets in a corner that had been cleaned out.

Done, Sister climbed down the ladder. Both women repaired to the tack room, dropping in chairs.

"Glad that's done." Sister sighed. "Want tea?"

"I'll make it." Betty rose, walked to the small hotplate in the spacious tack room. "Won't take but a minute. Feels raw, like rain's coming. I need something warm even with the heat turned on."

"This time of year you never know. It can be seventy one day and forty the next, but you're right that rain is raw." Sister glanced at the large thermometer on the wall, advertising horse feed. "Says fifty-four. Feels like forties."

"Does." Betty poured the hot water on the tea bags.

A rumble from the motor of a big Ram truck alerted them just as rain began to fall. The motor cut off, a light rap on the door revealed Ryan Stokes.

"Come on in." Sister motioned for him to open the door.

"Starting to really come down out there." Ryan brushed off his jacket.

"Tea?" Betty inquired.

"No thanks. Thought I'd drop off more footage. See what you like." He pulled a DVD out of his pocket, handing it to Sister.

"Sit down, Ryan, and thank you."

He sat in a director's chair, stretched his feet out, the soles of his boots wet.

"You surprised me at Mud Fence Farm." Sister smiled.

"I should have called you. It was a last-minute decision. I looked at the weather, saw rain in the forecast with a question mark, and thought, 'Well, I'll shoot Mud Fence.' The history of the place, the big earthen fences are cool."

"Every fixture has a story but the grass-covered mud fences are unique. Think you got some good footage?" Betty asked.

"Hope so. It's all on there. There are a few cubbing fixtures you haven't visited. I'll be at those but during formal hunting. So you won't see too much of me until then. The other reason is that I want this year's video to reflect the three seasons of hunting."

"Good idea." Sister smiled. "I hope this works. I really hope people buy the video. More exciting than still photographs."

"Interesting way to put it." Ryan turned to look outside the window as the rain intensified. "Well, let me get going. Just wanted you to have this and also not worry if you don't see too much of me until Opening Hunt."

"Fine," Sister replied.

As he left, when the door opened, the two women could really hear the rain, sounded like BBs.

"Great day." Sister sighed.

"Well, wait a bit. Maybe you won't have to make a run for it to get to the house."

"Maybe. Say, have you heard anything from Risé?"

"I call every other day. Highs and lows. She did mention that their accountant told her she was well provided for. The will leaves everything to her."

"Wonder if either of the boys will come back?"

"Be nice for Risé if they did, but she's more than capable of running the lumberyard. Greg trusted her, as would I. Very capable person."

"Mmm." Sister crossed her feet at the ankles. "I never asked Ray about our money. I suppose I should have but I was raised that was the husband's job. If we had been in business together like you and Bobby, I would have asked."

"I'm just enough younger than you that while that remained the prevailing idea of marriage and money, times were changing. Bobby never minded. I think it's a relief for him that we both go over the books."

"I'm sure it is." Sister crossed her ankles in the other direction. "The truth is, I was never much interested in money. When I taught at Mary Baldwin I paid my bills. If I had anything left over I was happy. I just didn't think about it."

"You know, our whole society is wrapped up in money, in things. Do I think one should know what's in the bank, what the possibilities for the future hold? I do. But I wouldn't want my life to revolve around it."

"Do you think Americans were always money hungry?"

"I do," Betty quickly answered. "You know history. Pompeii was rolling in money. Crassus. Those old Roman families were shrewd. The nobles under King Edward I were obsessed with money. Everybody was and is obsessed, but some lucky few, who perhaps have enough to eat and keep warm, walk away from it and just live, take what comes."

"Maybe that's it, we're taught to take control of our lives. A delusion, I think. Think of the wars. Upended everyone. The Spanish flu. Control really is a delusion."

"I guess." Betty found the rat ta tat tat of the rain comforting, making her a little sleepy.

"Knowing that the Wilsons' account is in order, the business profitable, that has to be a relief, and it more or less shuts down the idea that he killed himself. Men really will kill themselves over money. I don't know if women do it or not, but if we do, we do it in much smaller numbers."

"Think you're right," Betty agreed. "But I haven't heard anything to contradict the suicide. I mean, no possible killers or motives."

"I know." Sister sighed. "Just seems to be a strange time. Crawford's blackmail. That's what it is. Then Greg. Then Arnold. Crazy. Crazy stuff."

"This is looney but I always find more disturbances during the changing seasons."

"Never thought of that," Sister truthfully said as she stood up. "Come on, grab my old raincoat on the peg. I've got my Barbour here. Let's run to the house and I will make you a proper cup of tea."

"What was wrong with my tea?" Betty's eyebrows rose.

"Nothing. It was adequate."

"It's the hotplate, not me."

"Yes. Now, let's go."

"You are being awful. I love tea."

"I didn't say you didn't. I can make better tea in the house. No matter what, I love you. Great tea or not."

As the two friends bolted for the kitchen, Gray Lorillard sat across from Freddie Thomas. She was surrounded by papers, a large business checkbook, and a personal checkbook.

"Thank you for going over this with me, Gray. Your eyes are a big help. No one knows more than you. I was afraid I missed something."

"You didn't miss anything. It is more than possible records are missing."

"Shocks me. Arnold was flat broke. I balanced his books two

weeks before he died. Rental monies were due, plus he had thirty-two thousand dollars in his account."

"When you paid the bills, they were the usual monthly bills?"

"Yes. Electric. Filling the huge gas tanks for the trucks. He had, as you know, his own tanks. Big underground tanks. He had advertising bills. By the way, a lot of that television footage was shot by Ryan. Reasonable rates. Arnold's ex-wife kept bugging him for money. God knows, she got enough from him. Covid, supply lines, difficulty getting parts, servicing the rigs. He was under a lot of pressure."

"True, true. You never know. Maybe he just got tired. If someone doesn't ask for help, is a pretty good actor, how could you know? And Freddie, you had just done the books."

"What I want to know is where did the thirty-two thousand go? What I have on record," she turned the deposit and withdrawal slips around for him to see again, "is he made three withdrawals of nine thousand dollars each and one of five thousand, each day of the week before he killed himself. Any amount under ten thousand dollars cash was spared scrutiny. The government, as you know, tells us this will stop drug money. Big withdrawals that can't be justified."

"Doesn't work." Gray shook his head. "So he had the cash?"

"Someone had the cash."

"Have you told Ben Sidell?"

"I called him the minute I had combed through everything. And I told him I was asking you to go over my work."

"This last year, did Arnold buy anything new, expensive?"

Freddie shrugged. "No. Well, most all the money went to the ex-wife. But he kept the business going, or I thought he did. He made payroll."

"I figure that's the key, too." Gray nodded.

They sat there in silence for a bit then Freddie spoke softly. "I feel so guilty. If only I had noticed something."

"Don't. The best you could have done was try to gently steer him toward a therapist. My experience is, many men won't go. It's not butch." He half smiled.

CHAPTER 19

October 3, 2020, Saturday

By eight in the morning the long rays of the sun swept the lower meadows of Old Paradise. The house and most of the buildings rested on an east-west axis, given that facing north would have been windy and cold. Also the Blue Ridge backed up the western part of the huge estate. The wind flowing down from the northwest began to bite usually by mid-fall.

Hounds had crossed the road from Tattenhall Station to Old Paradise. The fox evaded them. The vixen circled around the closed Gulf station, the orange and blue sign swinging, then crossed over to Old Paradise, where she shot into the restored main stables. No one was there. It didn't take her long to find Earl's old dens, especially the lush one in the tack room, cleverly hidden behind an old tack trunk from the mid-nineteenth century. It was so big and heavy, the humans wouldn't move it nor would they pull it out enough to see the entrance to the part of the den allowing a fox to scoot out and down. Mostly one could live in the tack room in a royal manner.

Weevil blew the pack away from the stable to walk down the old farm road to the other side of the majestic Carriage House, where he again cast.

Matchplay, ears flicking with each horn call, carried Sister at a leisurely pace. He was getting time on the target, as he had been slowly, carefully brought along to learn hunting. Young but solid, he glided under Sister. If one has to be out there for hours, best to ride a horse with smooth gaits.

Young entry now joined the pack in two couples, four hounds. This was progress, especially since the pack accepted them. Those long walks on foot in the summer paid off in the friendships, and younger hounds learning they needed to obey older hounds. The older hounds provided far more discipline than Weevil, Sister, Betty, or Tootie.

Given the open land for much of Old Paradise, Sister could watch her hounds closely. Eventually they'd wind up in the woods or the beginning incline to a mountain. Good. The more a hound, human, or horse negotiates, the better they get.

Saturday's field numbered about twenty-two. Each week the field grew thanks to cooler weather, soft sunlight, and wildlife preparing for winter. All creatures proved busy. Nature does not reward lazy animals; only people do that.

The mercury nudged into the mid-fifties. The day, clear, brilliant, proved pleasant although the scent dissipated much faster in high pressure systems than low pressure, especially if low-hanging clouds accompanied it.

Wearing ratcatcher, the field displayed delightful individuality but correctly so. A few wore colored stock ties. Others wore regular ties, the colors vibrant, but no red. A few liked Churchill's tie, navy blue with little dots. People looked fabulous and felt same. How could you not feel vital, excited, on such a morning among friends?

Sister snagged one of Gray's ties that she liked, promising herself she would call Ben Silver in Charleston and replace it at a healthy price. Her husband could wear anything thanks to his beautiful coloring, café au lait.

Riding in the field, Gray laughed with his brother about Sister. They wondered, did she harbor cross-dressing impulses? Gray decided no, but she favored his silk ties with embroidered running foxes. The brothers attributed attire vanity to women, ignoring the fact that they were picture perfect. This wasn't so much criticism but an embrace of a lady they loved.

The fox cared nothing for human vanity. No one looked as good as a fox anyway. This particular fox left a fading scent.

Parker and Pickens, littermates in their prime, drifted to the right. Noses down. Sister studied the two brothers, sleek tricolors. She noted that often hounds from the same litter thought alike.

"Couple of hours, what do you think?" Parker commented on the diminishing scent.

Pickens inhaled deeply. *"Better than nothing. Might heat up."*

With that they sang in unison, moving at a trot.

Matchplay tensed. Sister let out his reins lightly but didn't squeeze. Young, intelligent, he was learning and he appreciated that she left him alone. Not lots of leg squeezing and sawing of the reins. He picked up a trot, staying a distance from Weevil.

Hounds moved away from the beautifully restored stable and the Carriage House, toward a sturdy hay shed, a toolshed, and an old bunkhouse in surprisingly good shape. The fox snuggled under an old Woolrich blanket woven in 1830. He had hunted most of the night and was tired.

The bunkhouse doors were shut. The fox, a young male, new to Chapel Cross area, noticed a well-concealed den entrance under the back door, protected by a long overhang. He crawled in and popped out under the bunk. The hounds awakened him but he went back to sleep. They couldn't get in. Falling back asleep, he felt this would be a good place to live.

Weevil called his hounds to move along, which they did.

Noses again down, the pack climbed upward, reached the slave graveyard, in which they headed west, weaving through small stones, larger tombstones, and a few bases with carved angels or sheep on top. Now at the edge of the large graveyard, hounds picked up a line. They quickly moved through what was thought to contain some Monacans, people who died long before any European or African landed in North America. Crawford hoped to attend to this search in time. The hounds didn't care a bit about buried humans. A live fox focused their attention.

The scent curled around the possible graveyard then plunged down toward the back of the big estate.

Sister, trotting through, noticed a bit of a gleam. She motioned for Walter to come alongside.

"Walter, take the field, will you?"

He nodded, immediately moving on, as hounds were moving faster.

Kasmir trotted near her and she motioned to him. The amiable man rode over.

"Will you hold my reins?"

"Of course, Master. But please let me dismount. A master's feet should never touch the ground."

She smiled at him. "Well, yes, but mine have often done so involuntarily." She slid off, pulling the reins over the young Thoroughbred's head, handing them to Kasmir.

Alida now drew next to Kasmir and both watched the tall woman bend down, brush earth and leaves as she pulled out something from soft earth. It was an old heavy metal long-shanked bit, surprisingly undamaged, with rust on only parts of it.

She held it up.

Kasmir commented, "An old bit for a driving horse. Maybe a workhorse."

"I think so, too." She handed it up to him as she took Matchplay's reins.

She walked to find a large, felled log, stood on it while Kasmir put his horse alongside of Matchplay. Stepping on the log, she put her foot in the stirrup to hoist herself up. She did this in one motion but the gracefulness of her youth was gone. Then again, were she young, she wouldn't have needed the log.

"Funny this would be close to the graveyard," Alida commented.

Now firm in the tack, Sister took back the bit.

"Who knows what is up here? Over the years I bet Crawford will find all manner of discarded items buried so as not to be unsightly to Miss Sophie."

"She must have been a wonder." Kasmir smiled.

"We know she was beautiful. The painting that Alfred kept in his house proved that."

Alfred was one of Sophie's direct descendants.

The bit, ungainly, bulged under her tweed jacket. The heavy iron felt not so much uncomfortable but strange. The bit had been forged before steel became common and more affordable.

Hounds trotted, ran off and on, but kept moving steadily for another hour. Close to eleven, the mercury was climbing. Weevil lifted the hounds, walking them to a creek so they could drink. The morning had been good, youngsters kept with the pack and there was enough scent to keep them all working.

Walking back to Tattenhall Station, Gray rode up to his wife. She told him of the bit but didn't pull it out from under her coat. She would need to unbutton the coat, and being a perfectionist about turnout she wasn't about to unbutton her tweed.

Once back at the trailers she handed the bit to Gray, happy to be feeling it. Betty put up their horses, having wiped them down, and she joined them.

Betty took the bit from Gray, feeling its weight. "Who knows what else is out there?"

CHAPTER 20

October 4, 2020, Sunday

Sam and Gray, each using a spade, stepped on them, digging into the earth.

"Think we hit it right." Gray smiled at his brother.

"Did. We have until the first frost, which used to arrive at the end of September, now mid-October. Remember how Mom loved her tulips? Every year we'd plant more tulip bulbs, and daffodils, too."

"You know, most everything Mom and Aunt Daniella put in the ground still blooms. The daffodils proliferate. The tulips need more bulbs every year, but it's still Mom's stuff and Aunt Dan's."

Sam knelt next to a row of equal-sized holes, a tulip bulb by each hand, which he placed in then brushed over the rich dirt. "Ever think if Mom and Aunt Dan had been born at a different time they'd be landscape gardeners?"

"Maybe," Gray responded. "Mom loved her family. Aunt Dan would have been the career girl. Well, come to think of it, she was. Her career was men."

They both laughed then Sam said, "We should get Yvonne out here to dig. Can you imagine that?"

"I can actually. That's a lot of woman, buddy." Gray smiled.

Sam nodded, said nothing.

"You can't plant forever. The light's fading. The soup's on." Aunt Daniella had opened the back door to call to her nephews.

They waved at her, indicating they'd wrap it up.

Gray gathered his tools, as Sam did the same. "You know in all the years I've known my wife, this is the first year she has hired a landscaping crew to get the farm ready for winter. She wants to expand the garden to go back to the hound graveyard. That's a stretch and she says she doesn't have time."

Sam dusted himself off, dirt stains on his jeans. "I don't know how Sister gets everything done."

"Organization. She should have been a CEO."

Sam laughed. "Well, being a master, she is."

Gray nodded, a grin on his face. "You're right."

After putting their tools in the tidy outside garden shed painted the same colors as the clapboard house, they walked to the old place, opened the door to the mudroom, oblivious to Uncle Yancy on the shelf over the door to the kitchen. Clever as a fox, this particular fox over time had pushed the towels on the floor exactly so he could fit behind them and get into the mudroom, although if you looked, the tip of his tail peeped out.

As the men came through the door, Sister, dishes in hand, remarked, "Just in time."

"We were going to waste away." Aunt Daniella winked, carrying salad plates, which Sam took from her to set the table.

In the next room the table, covered by a beloved old tablecloth, waited for the dishes and implements, which Sister and Sam placed. Gray, wisely, brought his aunt a lovely Irish crystal glass with two ice cubes and good bourbon. He then pulled out a chair for her.

Sister and Sam retreated to the kitchen to bring in the food. Two trips, yams and snow peas. Aunt Daniella had made a salad, that bowl was already on the table.

Drinks in the glasses, everything set, they bowed their heads and repeated a simple prayer of thanks.

As they ate, chatted, Sister studied the plates. She loved china. "Aunt Daniella, who gave you this china, the twin navy bands on the rim with a tiny outline of gold? I have always adored them."

"I know. But Mother had this china when I was a child and she said her grandmother had it. Being an unruly child, I never asked."

Sam teased his aunt. "You were not an unruly child because of china."

"Well, no." Aunt Daniella took a healthy draught of her Blanton's bourbon.

Laughing, catching up on the doings of friends, groaning and moaning about Congress, arguing about Virginia Tech's football team versus Virginia, Sam argued for Harvard but no one listened.

"Oh, come on, Sam," Sister tormented him. "Smith College could beat Harvard."

"That is so unfair." He bristled but with fun. "We have sent players to the pros."

"Unfortunately, you've sent more to Congress," Gray tweaked him, to everyone's delight.

"You were the one with the big career in D.C., not me," Sam fired back.

"So I was." Gray sipped his drink, scotch also with two large ice cubes. "This pork is wonderful."

Aunt Daniella replied, "Your mother's recipe."

Yvonne listened to all this. "Well, I will put up Northwestern against all of you."

"Loyal, are we?" Sam liked her more than he was willing to admit.

"It's a great school." She paused. "Would any of you want to be in college now?"

In unison, "No."

"Well, that left little to doubt." Aunt Daniella twirled her fork, as she did not go to college.

Few women did of her generation; race may have helped some white girls but in the main an education was believed to be wasted on women.

After dessert, cleanup, the group repaired to the simple living room, Federal style, which was the time period in which the house was built. Hardwoods burned, the light danced around the room, the glow and warmth drew them closer.

"Anyone want anything before I sit down?" Sam asked.

"We're good," Gray answered for them.

A small gust of wind caused a tree branch, denuded now, to scratch a handblown windowpane.

"Gray, what was going on with Arnold's books?" Aunt Daniella asked.

"That's really Freddie's territory."

"You went over them with her. What I wonder is, did his ex-wife bleed him dry? Woman's revenge?"

"Now, Aunt Dan." Yvonne was quick to jump in. "The male version of that is starve the wife to drive down the divorce settlement."

"Ladies." Gray held up his hand. "What I can tell you is he did not starve his wife. He kept the business but she got everything else. The house, the furnishings, the joint savings account, her car, her furs. His business did suffer some because of Covid. He was having a devil of a time finding drivers, as many quit. The good thing is, payroll shrank, but so did profit. Anyway, he kept it together. Nothing unusual, no large borrowings. We couldn't find receipts for his last two weeks before he died. It appeared he took out most of his cash in withdrawals, under ten thousand apiece. Freddie is castigating herself, but she would not have gone over the books until the end of the month unless he needed her. There was no way for her to know. So the short version of this story is, we don't know much. We do know he was under pressure, but so is every other businessperson we know."

"Hmm," was all Aunt Daniella replied.

Yvonne considered this then quietly said, "People leave life for a number of reasons. Sometimes I think people are just tired. It's time to go."

"Yvonne!" Aunt Daniella's eyebrows shot upwards.

Yvonne quickly replied, "Never you. But truly I think some people lose their zest for life. They wear out."

Gray remembered, then asked his aunt, "Mercer was friends with Arnold, wasn't he?"

"Maybe warm acquaintances. But he liked him. Arnold was one of the few men Mercer's age who didn't have a problem with a gay man. People have come around but when he was young, Mercer didn't have many friends."

"He had such energy." Sam recalled his cousin. "Sooner or later even the straightest learned to like him."

"I think Yvonne's thoughts may be the closest to the reason Arnold left. A horrible divorce. Giving up most of his possessions just to stay out of court. He probably would have come out with more, but it's such a grueling process he most likely couldn't face it. He wasn't dating anyone and then Covid struck. Downward business spiral for a while. Oh, I don't know, it could have looked so dismal for him, no future, you know."

"Sad to think that." Gray looked at his wife.

"To change the subject, find out anything about that bit in Old Paradise's graveyard or close to the graveyard?" Sam asked Sister.

"I sat at my husband's gargantuan computer and searched bits through the centuries. It's old. The closest I found to the bit was something similar, a driving bit, from the mid-nineteenth century."

"Makes sense." Yvonne added, "Old Paradise was founded in 1814. Right?"

"That's the date when Sophie built a small house, stable, some outbuildings. So makes sense, as you say," Sister responded. "That's one woman I would have liked to have known."

"I guess she never heard of women oppression." Yvonne smiled.

"Not in our terms." Sister nodded.

"Are you girls kidding?" Sam teased them, especially calling them *girls*, which made Sister almost giggle, as she was in her mid-seventies. "She used all her feminine wiles. You ladies know we are putty in your hands."

"Oh, keep talking, brother." Gray laughed.

"Honey, you mean you aren't putty in my hands?"

Now everyone laughed.

"Maybe over time other items will work their way to the surface at Old Paradise," Yvonne added. "Crawford certainly has a lot on his plate. I doubt the bit is number one."

"That's true." Gray sipped more scotch. "Losing the money the way he did. The blackmail threats. Glad I'm not in Ben Sidell's shoes. Imagine a dog stealing a bag from the Bland Memorial then a drone at Bishop's Court. Crazy stuff."

"My money's on Crawford. He won't rest until he figures this out, nabs the thief." Aunt Daniella listened as a log crackled. "He's incredibly rich and incredibly determined."

"He is." Sam nodded.

"Well, on to happier things. Ryan Stokes is working on our video. He said the next big shoot will be at Opening Hunt."

"Sister, let us hope so. We need to make money off this video.

Haven't done it before." Sam then thought a minute. "He really should get more cubbing footage. What is it they call it in Hollywood?" He thought a moment. "Insurance footage."

"Is that pretty woman with him, Ayanda, is that her name? Is she his girlfriend?" Yvonne wondered.

"Well, I think so, but he doesn't say. He isn't living with her but she helps shoot, she edits, I guess better than he does. Pretty. Better not to let her slip through his fingers." Aunt Daniella believed firmly that men should be guided through life by a smart woman, who never tells him, of course.

Worked for her.

"Back to these threats. The criminal, I think of him as a criminal, isn't asking for huge sums." Sam was puzzled.

"Not now. This could go on." His brother had seen a boatload of political blackmail.

"True," Sam agreed. "But this person is clever. He's not out to make a one-time killing."

"Oh, Sam, don't use that word." Yvonne shivered.

CHAPTER 21

October 5, 2020, Monday

Wearing an expensive alpaca sweater, a heavy lined Levi's jacket over that, Crawford stood with Sister at the site where she picked out her bit. She had piled a little pyramid of stones to find the spot again.

"This it?"

"Yes," she replied. "The ground isn't tore up, but if you look closely it's been probed in spots."

He knelt down, ran the soil through his hands, loose, a bit sticky thanks to the rains.

"Have you ever found the old midden pile?" she asked.

Midden piles were where people tossed broken items, things no longer useful, as there was no garbage as in modern times. Often a hole was dug into the ground and as it filled, dirt was pushed over it and a new dump dug.

"Have not. The graves took precedence."

"Of course," she agreed.

Standing up he exhaled. "Well, I'll bring back the sweepers." This was his term for the radar people. "If there's anything else up here, they'll find it."

"They did wonderful work the last time." She praised the team as they turned and walked back down to the main stables and fence to the house.

"Well, one of the bills was passed today."

She shot him a curious look. "Wasn't the request for unmarked bills?"

He opened the door for her, as she stepped through onto the gleaming walnut wood hallway.

He led her into his office, sat down, pulled a chair next to him. "Here. The number."

"So they were marked?"

"Some. Ben and I discussed if a thief were smart enough to ask for unmarked bills you give them to him. We thought if the money was to be spent, whenever it was spent whoever would pull the bills off the bottom of the pile, assuming if they were marked it would be the top ones because of the first bag I put out."

"Ah. Clever."

He swiveled in his chair. "Could be he didn't think we'd salt the bottom of the piles."

"Big ticket item, the purchase?"

He shook his head in bemusement. "No. A pair of hiking shoes. Maybe three hundred dollars."

"Sure of himself."

"I wonder about that." Crawford grunted. "Impatient or arrogant."

"Maybe this isn't a professional," she offered. "Granted, I wouldn't want to spend one hundred thousand dollars in obvious ways and I especially wouldn't want to give up one hundred thousand dollars."

"I don't know if he's finished yet. Perhaps this is just the beginning. If you're rich you have a bull's-eye on your back."

She murmured, "I'm afraid you're right."

He half smiled. "Glad I went to Indiana University. I worked my way through. I think I understand those who want money but don't want to work hard for it." He pushed back his seat. "Who do you know that needs money?"

"Just about everyone, but I'd hope no one would steal for it."

"Thou shalt not steal," he intoned.

"Thou certainly shalt not. The government hates competition."

This did get a laugh out of him. "Charlotte."

Within a few minutes his Old Paradise historian came into the room. "Yes, Mr. Howard?"

"Call the radar crew and see when they can come back. I have a new area I want to study thanks to Sister. Where the bit was found."

"Yes." Charlotte smiled at Sister. "Is there any time that you wouldn't want them on the grounds?" She had returned to Crawford.

"No. Anytime is fine. Where did you put the bit?"

"In the small safe in my room."

"Good. Thank you." She left on that as he twirled his thumbs. "She's worked out nicely. I wasn't sure at first. But I'm glad I hired her. These younger people have different concerns than we do."

Sister smiled. "They do for now. Eventually, Crawford, life will catch up with them."

"I've been thinking. You have lived here for decades."

"I have." She nodded.

"You know everybody, their kin, even their cats and dogs."

"Well, I used to, but times are changing. The county is filling with new people, and like any group they bring new ways. Some are good. Others not."

"I agree there. But I have been thinking. Greg Wilson shoots himself. Dramatic way to go. No reason to think it a murder. You all who knew him well, and I did hunt with him occasionally, find it hard to believe he would end his life. He had money. Ben said he was flush."

"Actually, Ben did not disclose that to me. The media did, but it's no matter." She wanted to correct a wrong impression of Ben but didn't want to argue.

"Perhaps he had more money than anyone realized." Crawford's voice dropped slightly. "Could he have engaged in a side hustle? Lucrative but not taxable if one is slick?"

Sister took in her breath. "Greg would never do that. Really."

"Oh, Sister, most people are more than willing to compromise to make a buck." As she remained silent he continued, thinking this was agreement. "So perhaps he had a slightly crooked stream of funds. Perhaps he was about to be exposed."

"Anything is possible but I think Risé would have known. She did not run the business with him but she wasn't ignorant of it. I often think wives know a lot more about their husbands than their husbands realize."

He gave her a benevolent smile. "I beg to disagree. How many wives are shocked when they find their husbands have had or are having affairs? Right under their nose?"

"Yes." She did agree. "But don't you think sex is a special category?"

"Sometimes," he replied.

"Actually, I think women can categorize sex, but their responses are different for the most part. It is a subject I keep far from. Greg seemed devoted to Risé and she to him. If he was off the reservation, he fooled everyone." She paused. "If this was local, I swear we'd know the woman. She'd slip or he would."

"Too close to home." He then said, "Arnold, I would be willing to believe infidelity was the cause of his non-public divorce. Men who give everything to the wife usually feel guilty."

"It's possible." She thought anything was possible, but not probable.

"Doesn't it seem peculiar to you, two men roughly in the prime of life, their business lives, kill themselves? And while this is going on there is someone trying to get money out of me. Maybe they had to pay up."

She lifted her chin, breathed deeply. "God, I hope not. What would they pay to hide? Theft, larceny, shoddy products or work. Surely we'd have some clue."

"My point, entirely." He shrugged. "Maybe there was a lot to lose. It will come out. It always does."

"I don't want to meddle, but you know, Crawford, if I can help, I will. You spent millions to preserve this place, you worked with the Virginia Historical Society, with our district's delegate, with the special organizations of slave descendants. You poured in an avalanche of money, time, thought. Anyone interested in history is in your debt."

He beamed. "Thank you. I've learned a lot. And one thing I have learned is you Virginians know more than you're saying."

"Funny you bring that up. It's true, and you know who knows the most? Aunt Daniella."

He sat up straight. "What does she think?"

"She hasn't said, but knowing her as I do I get the distinct, uneasy feeling that this isn't over. It's too upsetting."

He leaned forward, fingers in a steeple. "More death?"

"She has not said this directly. Aunt Dan has seen a lot. Someone or someones have a lot to lose. Maybe you're the cat's paw," Sister said.

"Me?" His voice rose.

"You. The demands on you, clearly blackmail related to a false accusation. But the means of getting the money, the dog, the drone, it's wacky. If Ben is concentrating on that, and of course he must, maybe there's something bigger. Just a thought."

"Millions?"

"That or something emotionally volatile. For instance, evicting tenants who can't pay due to Covid. There's a stay on that. But what about landlords? They have to pay the banks their mortgage. So, hear me out here, I'm hardly the business whiz you are, but when the eviction halt is lifted, what if people take videos and pictures of the landlords evicting? They'll be assaulted. But it isn't really the landlords. It's the banks. Those that are aggrieved either don't know that, or do, but can't get to the bank presidents to expose them. The landlords are sitting ducks, see?"

Silent for a few moments, he finally agreed. "I do. The cat's paw almost always works."

"That or Sun Tzu's 'Uproar in East, Strike in West.' "

"Right." Crawford sighed. "I'm more in the dark than I ever was. Well, I'll let you know when the radar crew comes back."

"Thank you." She left by the massive front door, stared up at the Corinthian columns in the soft mid-afternoon light.

The acanthus leaves appealed to her. Carving them took an experienced hand. Those leaves symbolize immortality, enduring life. She prayed they would cast good spirits onto Old Paradise, which had suffered much in the last half century.

She stepped on the marble steps lightly, hand on the curving rail which led to the bottom. The outside of the steps curved; this added to the visual appeal of them, nothing harsh or straight. Callimachus created the Corinthian column as an alternative to the Ionic Order, considered for the arts. The Doric column represented what some might consider more serious pursuits. She loved the luxury, exuberance of the Corinthian columns.

Reaching her truck, the car was in the shop yet again, she

opened the door, got in, closed it, kept the window up. Wasn't cold but wasn't warm. Staring again at the columns she wished Crawford luck. Then she thought of murder. If she thought about it, suicide was a kind of criminal act against the self. You murdered yourself. It's a crime against nature, too. Self-preservation is deep-rooted. She cut on the motor, listened to the rumble, drove out of the gorgeous estate, the tree-lined main drive lending a sense of permanence but not necessarily peace.

CHAPTER 22

October 6, 2020, Tuesday

Kettle House abutted Foxglove Farm on the east side. The low hills, remnants from the glacier's great pushing of the Canadian soil, could be rough. To reach the fixture you could park at Cindy Chandler's Foxglove, ride due east up the low ridge, through hanging vines, rough territory. Once off the ridge it gave way to undulating pastures, lovely.

Sister chose this fixture, as it was different topographically but close enough to Foxglove and Roughneck Farm. She could keep an eye on her young entry. If anyone became overwhelmed, they weren't far.

"Find your fox." Weevil cast hounds as soon as they emerged from the woods and bracken.

The field, a healthy eighteen for a Tuesday early morning, enjoyed the touch of briskness, the first blush of color on the willows, maples, and oaks. The sycamores mostly showed a bit of yellow then browned out.

Covering ground with a long stride in their walking, hounds quickly descended to lower ground, groups of old farm buildings in various states of disrepair.

"*Hey,*" Audrey spoke.

"*Hmm.*" Dasher joined her. "*Coyote.*"

Dragon, arrogant fellow that he was, opened and took off.

"*Damn him!*" his littermate cursed.

Didn't do a bit of good, as the whole pack tore after Dragon.

Weevil on Gunpowder kept up as they picked up speed.

The field, Kasmir and Alida, Freddie Thomas, Gray and Sam, Ronnie Haslip, his old high school friend Xavier, and others squeezed their horses. Soon the canter turned into a gallop as hounds flew on the coyote scent, heavier than fox.

Sister on Lafayette sat tight. He knew his job and loved it.

The pasture, open, invited speed. If there's one thing a coyote can give you, it's speed.

A strong running creek gave the coyote the idea to leap in. Foiled his scent. He jumped out downstream, turned back to run for Foxglove Farm. Given the height of the grass he couldn't be seen. Humans could see the grass more. Hounds ran through it but it slowed them.

Dragon bulled through the thick grass . . . uncut hay, really. He was in front giving tongue, singing in his deep hound voice, for all he was worth.

Moving at a fast clip, the field stayed at the edge of the hay. They fell behind. The roar of the pack kept Sister on course, as this was tricky territory. You could lose yourself in a small ravine in a minute.

Betty dipped into the rough territory, bushwhacking every step. Tootie and Iota reached the last ridge. The way down was felled trees, branches, thick undergrowth. Miserable.

Both whippers-in finally reached the clear and could watch hounds in a straight line now heading for the thick woods, which left Foxglove.

Both galloped down, leaning far back in the saddle. You learned your balance the hard way in this territory.

Sister, reaching the bank, just shot right down. Lafayette was in his glory. The field straggled out behind her. Within two minutes the freshly cut pasture on the most eastern end of Foxglove beckoned. This was heaven.

The coyote, speedy, eager to rid himself of the pesky hounds, shot into the woods bordering the pasture. In this respect he lacked the fox's wisdom, for a fox would have made use of fallen trees, torn bushes, anything to impede and tear up hounds, humans, horses. Instead the coyote, heavy fellow, stayed on the path. He was running flat out.

Weevil, only in his second year, dove into the woods and got on the path. The foliage, still heavy, soaked up sounds like a rag. Had he known the territory better he would have skirted these woods, as did Betty and Tootie. Weevil hunted by ear as much as by eye.

He finally shot out by the schoolhouse at the top of Cindy's rolling meadow with two ponds. Exactly where, he wasn't sure. Betty and Tootie rode hard way ahead. He could now see them and the pack.

Sister looked behind her. Everyone was still on.

Georgia, a sleek vixen, lived in the schoolhouse. The coyote originally headed straight for it, slowed, walked around it, taking off again on the north side out of sight. Confused, the hounds finally figured it out.

"Why is he picking us up?" Jeeves, a two-year fellow, said, quite peeved.

Dasher, a leader, especially if his sister stayed in the kennel, called out, *"Just do what he says."*

The pack after a moment's hesitation followed their noses as they picked up coyote scent on the far side of the schoolhouse.

Boom, everyone was on again. Weevil caught up. His whippers-in were in perfect position.

Hounds tore across the pasture leading to the farm road. Down the farm road, toward the two ponds, then hooked left back out onto the farm road. A pause.

Sister looked around just as Trident inched forward looking for the line, which he picked up; trotted toward the wildflower fields on the west side of Foxglove, which then tilted in a southwest direction. The pack roared again, plunging onto black-eyed Susans, Queen Anne's lace, all the colors and wildflowers of fall.

Weevil headed to the deer path, much easier.

Both Tootie and Betty charged on their respective sides, since Soldier Road lay at the end of the wildflowers. This two-lane highway, so called as it was paved after World War II, could be dangerous. While not heavily traveled, it only took one car to kill hounds.

Sister, higher up but picking her way down, saw the coyote cross the road only to disappear in the wildflower field on the other side of it, the northernmost part of her property.

She looked around. Everyone on, everyone ready. She kicked on, tall grasses brushing her boots. Soon, she crossed the road with great care. Betty and Tootie were already over, although Tootie hung back to stop traffic, should traffic appear.

Once Sister and the field were over, she blew through the wildflowers, up to the base of Hangman's Ridge. She rode straight up. The ridge, high, had one good path, a narrower one around it. It rested like four huge football fields on an east-west axis. The narrower part of the field up there, flat as a pancake, being north-south.

The enormous hangman's tree, used since before the Revolutionary War, loomed in all its dreadful splendor.

As she raced across, hearing hoofbeats behind her, she heard an odd whirr over her head. Lafayette flicked his ears. The sounds moved away from her. She then heard a horse snort, and a thump. Someone hit the dirt. Her job was to keep up with Huntsman and hounds, but she turned to look anyway. Flying away from Freddie Thomas, on the ground, was a drone. The sound spooked other horses. Gray waved her on as he dismounted to help Freddie.

Sister quickly moved down the side, toward Tootie's cabin, the orchard. Hounds stopped speaking.

A little voice in her head asked, "What the hell?"

CHAPTER 23

"Did anyone see where the drone came from?" Ben asked as he sat inside Sister's kitchen.

Gray answered as Sister was pouring coffee for the sheriff, who'd had a long day. "No. I didn't notice the thing until we were on top of Hangman's Ridge."

Sister placed the coffee in front of Ben then sat down. "Me, too. I heard an odd whirr and Lafayette kept flicking his ears. Heard the thump behind me, Freddie's horse snort. I slowed, turned around, and Freddie was on the ground, her horse running backwards, which sent the field into a bigger tizz. Gray was dismounting to help Freddie."

"Did the drone hover over Freddie?"

"No. It stayed at the same altitude, which was . . . oh, I don't know. What did you think, honey?"

Gray, drink in hand, he needed one, replied, "Fifteen yards overhead. The problem was, Sheriff, the altitude changed, so it was low. The damn thing scared the horses. At first it scared me. I didn't know what it was until I got a good look."

"I see. Spoke to Freddie. She had no idea why or what, and then I drove here. I would have gotten here earlier but there was an accident on Rio Road and Route 29. The underpass, bypass, sort of mixed bag at the intersection, creates more problems than it solves. Fender bender once a month and more when parents are bringing their kids to UVA."

"The curse of every college town." Gray shrugged.

"Did anyone see where the drone went after swooping over Hangman's Ridge?" Ben leaned back in the chair.

"Going down the farm road, at a fast clip, I could still hear it but I couldn't see it. The sounds seemed to be heading east, toward After All. No one else reported seeing it. I did call the Bancrofts' just in case. They hadn't seen or heard anything," Sister replied as Golly hopped on her lap.

"Under most circumstances this would probably be a kid who lost a drone, or a real estate agent who made a mistake, the drone bypassing whatever it was meant to photograph."

Ben picked up his pen again, notebook open. "However, these aren't normal circumstances. Especially given Crawford's ordeal with the drone."

"Whoever this is obviously has skills with this type of technology. It's pretty new, or at least it is to me," Sister mentioned.

"In terms of technology being available to the general public, it is new." Gray leaned forward toward Ben. "The state police use them to track cars, right?"

"Not as much as they would like. The state budget is, well, difficult, and there are some members of the House of Delegates complaining that this is an intrusion on privacy."

"It is," Gray resolutely said. "Who is to say who can be followed and who can't? There isn't legal clarity."

"I'm trying." Ben smiled wanly. "This is not to say this drone is owned by the same person who took Crawford's money. Any one of us can go to Lowe's, any big hardware store, and buy a drone. At some point reasonable legislation has to be framed. Teenaged kids will send drones to photograph or stream pictures of women naked in their backyards, by the pool."

"Ben." Sister shook her head.

Gray laughed. "It's obvious you weren't a teenage boy."

They all laughed a bit.

"Crawford has hired a private firm." Ben leaned back in his chair again. "I don't think this reflects badly on the department. This type of crime is new, in a sense. I can't go out and hire young computer wizards. I have one fellow. That's it. I expect this will be a hot discussion in our legislature." Ben took a breath. "But I can't dismiss this. Now or in the future. How many people are, for lack of a better phrase, drone savvy?"

"Don't look at me." Sister threw up her hands.

"Operating one is fairly easy. For anyone that had or has remote-control toys, planes. This is a snap." Ben's stomach growled.

"Let me warm up some soup. I made a big pot yesterday."

"Sister, I can't have you feed me."

"You're working overtime, all the more reason." She clicked the burner on the stove, as the big pot was still there. "Back to Crawford for a moment. Any motive ideas? Was he singled out?"

"It doesn't look like that. He is not a particularly popular man but this appears to be straightforward; well carried out. And someone who knows him," Ben added.

"What makes you say that?" Sister inquired.

"Made a fool out of him twice. I expect our perp is having a great time."

"Why send a drone here?" Sister asked.

"It may not be for a nefarious purpose. It is strange."

"Is there anything we can or should do?" Gray asked.

"You've given me your view." Ben finished his coffee. "I doubt this drone was specially sent to you or the hunt. But it is possible."

"But why?" Sister looked at Ben, then added as it occurred to her, "Because no one has asked us for money."

Gray interjected, "Yet."

"That appears to be the motive." Ben flipped his reporter's notebook shut. "It's possible Crawford's problem is not related to the Hangman's Ridge incident. Be watchful. Just too many variables," Ben replied.

The phone rang.

Sister walked to the counter to pick up. "Hello."

"Can you get to Risé's now?" Betty's voice was urgent.

Sister immediately replied. "Yes. Ben is here questioning us about the drone incident."

"Bring him. Risé has tried to commit suicide."

"What? Never mind. We are on our way."

Sister hung up the phone, told Gray and Ben.

Ben hit the siren. Gray, driving his Land Cruiser with Sister in the passenger seat, followed.

Sister simply said as she grasped the overhead hand strap, called the Jesus strap, "Maybe Greg really did commit suicide."

CHAPTER 24

October 6, 2020, Tuesday, 7:45 PM

The ambulance sat outside, three attendants prepared Risé to go to the hospital. Betty sat with the distraught woman, who had taken sedatives. Betty ransacked the house to find the bottle. No luck.

Ben stood next to Betty looking at Risé, who was somewhat conscious but not able to talk.

Betty looked up at him. "She called me and said she wanted to die and if I come over would I attend to her things, call the ambulance, make funeral arrangements. I knew she wasn't joking. By the time I got here she was as you see."

"Sheriff." The head ambulance worker looked to the sheriff for direction.

"Get her to the hospital as fast as you can." He turned his attention to Betty, Sister, and Gray. "Gray, take the bathroom. Sister, the bedroom. Betty, the office. I'll take the kitchen. Look for any vial, bottle, even folded tinfoil that could have carried pills. Perhaps still does."

Each person started on their assigned room. Gray carefully inspected every bottle in the medicine cabinet, nothing. Then he lifted up the back of the toilet in case she had hidden anything in the water. Again, nothing. Sister was on her hands and knees searching under the bed. Nothing. Then she opened each drawer of the nightstands. Notebooks, pens, bookmarks, folded linen handkerchiefs. Nothing. She opened the book on the nightstand with the clock, thinking that was probably the side on which Risé slept. Her search was less what the good woman was reading, in this case a book on the Mitford sisters, than to see if the book was hollow. People often hid items in books, pillows, and no one was the wiser for the compartment. She found nothing so she opened the closet. All Risé's clothing was arranged by color. Her sweaters, neatly folded, rested in plastic boxes on shelves. The closet was so well organized, Sister felt a pang of envy. Then she again got down on her hands and knees to look at the shoes, arranged not by color but by function. One could stick a small bottle in the toe of a boot. But Risé had nothing in her boots and shoes, not even a pair of socks that had not yet found the way to the wash basket.

A knock on the door alerted Ben to the fact that Jackie and Jude had arrived. "Come on in."

The two young law enforcement officers stepped inside, closing the door behind them. Ben gave them directions to go downstairs and search the large recreation room, the room next to it holding a giant TV, a small refrigerator, comfortable chairs, and a sofa. This was Greg's football room.

"Sheriff." Betty's voice boomed.

Ben walked in to see Betty sitting with the computer mouse under her right hand. The computer was blank.

"Anything?"

"Yes, but it's not pills." She pointed to a thumb drive, which was placed in the side of the computer.

Ben stood behind her as she started the thumb drive to scan through images now on the screen.

Both remained speechless until the video ran out.

"I noticed her papers were scattered on the floor. Risé is a meticulous person so either she knocked them off or she threw them off. Saw the computer, the thumb drive, out of curiosity I turned it on."

"There's no doubt that's Greg." His voice dropped.

"Should we call in the others?"

"No. Have you called her sons to tell them she tried to commit suicide?"

"Not yet."

"Do so. So that you don't make a misstep or have to juggle the sons and the doctors, give each son the number of the emergency room at UVA University Hospital. Better they speak directly to the staff there, and to be certain I will call the emergency room myself. I'd do it anyway. Don't tell them anything else until they get here."

Betty pulled out the thumb drive, handing it to Ben. "He must have truly committed suicide."

"More than likely, but the department still has a lot of work to do. The real question is, who sent this thumb drive? Was it someone involved? Someone getting even?"

"Maybe you should ask Sister and Gray. They have a lot of sense. Remember the falsified images used to blackmail Crawford? The department has to study this to determine if these images are of the same time, not added."

"I don't think they should see the video until we ascertain that it is legitimate. If it becomes necessary at a later date, I'll bring them down to headquarters." He stepped outside, called for Sister and Gray.

They stepped in, both frustrated at not finding anything.

"Let's sit over here." Ben pointed to the sofa and chairs.

"Risé has to be one of the most organized women in the county." Sister dropped down, Gray beside her.

"Betty has discovered a video that will help us greatly. It is a list of demands, or perhaps a better word is *negotiations* from a beautiful young woman before she will agree to be his mistress. Then there is a photo, not a video, included in the video of him standing with his arm around her. She is unclothed."

"Greg?" Sister was shocked.

Ben nodded. "His suicide may be a suicide. As for Risé discovering this, well, the shock alone . . ." He paused. "Let's just hope the poor woman makes it."

Gray shook his head. "Blackmail, what else can it be? My first thought is whatever the sum demanded, Greg refused to pay and instead killed himself to both escape the shame and to make sure money was left for his wife."

Sister raised an eyebrow. "A photo next to a gorgeous naked woman has to be worth something."

Ben folded his hands together. "He often took trips out of town, right?"

"Yes," Sister answered. "Business was good. He'd go at least once every month. He'd tell me he wouldn't be hunting. He doted on his wife, which makes this video somewhat odd. He took Risé on vacations, oh, at least once a season. Paris. Banff. Always somewhere beautiful. I . . . well, this is hard to believe."

"It goes on every day. People who seem perfectly respectable. Leaders in the community. That's why it's so shocking to others." Ben sighed. "I am not a psychologist. But I do believe sex is very easy to compartmentalize. If the woman was kept by a man, one could believe no harm was done. It's probably best we leave the house; I'll have Jude stand outside."

"Ben, is it possible Arnold Synder is implicated in this, something like this?" Gray asked.

"Well, another suicide. We'll need to go back to his office and rented apartment. We'll need to crawl over everything." He stood up. "Thank you."

In the car, driving home, Sister turned to Gray. "That poor woman."

"How does anyone recover from something like this? How do you trust anyone?" Gray responded. "Let's pray she makes it. She's going to need a lot of help."

"This is a terrible thing to say, but it would have been better had he been murdered."

"Yes," he replied as the Land Cruiser turned onto the farm road, the tires crunching on the stones.

CHAPTER 25

October 8, 2020, Thursday

Standing in the middle of Jerusalem Field, Sister swept her eyes across the vast pasture loaded with yellow Jerusalem artichokes, hence the name of the field. The air smelled like fall, the slight wind rustled leaves beginning to turn; others were beginning to dry out, without much color, thus the rustle. Intently listening, all she and Aztec could hear was the occasional word of encouragement from Weevil.

Prior's Woods, the fixture, like Chapel Cross and Bishop's Gate, recalled that time when religion determined one's outlook, social position, and close friendship circles.

The prior in this case was an Episcopal bishop responsible for the vast territory now known as central Virginia. A solid brick two-story house, painted a soft yellow, had been built for the centuries and had proven the skill of builders. Apart from replacing some slate shingles on the roof, no major work had been necessary; those walls stayed as solid as the day they were laid.

Betty on Magellan quietly sat on the edge of the well-tended field. Tootie also sat in the open, for the pasture proved huge. As cubbing was drawing to a close, the field had swollen to thirty-six people, rather good for a Thursday when the first cast was at seven-thirty.

Walter led Second Flight, giving Bobby a chance to relax and be a member of the field. Long rays of early sunlight slashed across the cut hayfields, good hay. The other pastures or meadows, all fenced, held Polled Herefords. The owners of Prior's Woods kept no horses but welcomed the hunt. They bred excellent cattle.

The hayfield still released the scent of cut hay. Hay had proved spotty this year. Most people got two cuttings, but a few lucky ones managed a good second cutting, even a partial third. For some it was subpar. Prior's Wood had good soil and therefore good hay.

Flashy Giorgio sauntered along the fence line, a three-board fence painted black. He stopped by a coop also painted black. At three six, the obstacle wasn't huge but it was big enough to keep one alert. He paused. Sniffed. Tail started to flip. He walked to the other end of the coop. Sniffed again, dropped his head to look under the coop.

"Why don't you go home." An angry voice and two beady eyes stared at him. *"Go home. I was minding my own business when you idiot hounds blabbed. This is what I get for staying out too late."* The racoon grumbled.

Seeing Giorgio puzzled, Cora joined him, ducked her head under the side of the coop.

"You can get lost, too."

"You're lucky you're not legitimate game," Cora replied.

On the other size of the pasture, Zandy let out a call, quickly joined by Zorro, Angle, and Tinsel, where all had been working.

"Let's go." Giorgio sped away, followed by Cora.

The racoon waddled out to look at the retreating hounds. Satisfied they were going to keep in the opposite direction, she walked into the nearby woods, where she disappeared in the batting of an eye.

Sister, happy to hear hound music, moved along. That pasture gave way to a neatly manicured trail, which passed a small dam, water spilling over. The fox was giving everyone a brisk early-morning run. Soon the lone old stone citadel used as a fire tower came into view, then just as quickly receded. Next Sister cleared three solid logs bound together at the pasture's corner and then into more woods.

Hounds screamed. She passed a large rock outcropping, plus a small aspen patch turning yellow in the middle of the woods.

Bursting out of the woods, Sister jumped into Devil's Chair, a fixture so named after 1800 to bedevil the prior. As they headed east, the land opened into undulating pastures, flying territory.

Hounds stopped at the small old feed store, long closed but with a tobacco ad painted on the one side of the building; while faded, it remained clear. Pretty and nostalgic as it was, it did not provoke Sister to try chewing tobacco.

Young Baker stuck his head into a fox den at the side of the building, complained, *"Come on out."*

Bellhop added his two cents. *"You're chicken."*

The fox, smart enough not to sass back, as she didn't know these young hounds, had jumped onto the old counter and from there up onto a shelf with some boxes still open. This had been the only store for miles. Once roads were built, the population settling more in some areas than others, bigger stores being built, the old country store finally closed. The foxes, racoons, and even a possum made homes in it. Kept the rain out and if one dragged in enough straw or whatever humans threw out, one could stay warm in the winter. The huge old potbelly stove still sat in the middle of the store, the woodpile long used up. With a lot of work and imagination the old store could have been revived or changed into a guest cottage. The owners of Devil's Chair, a well-off couple based in Washington, D.C., considered options. When they retired they would tackle this.

"Good hounds," Weevil praised his crew.

Betty smiled, for the youngsters did quite well this morning.

Weevil hunted them back. A few brief runs filled out a pleasant day. Back at the trailers at a circle of maple trees off the drive, hounds hopped in, happy to be in their trailer with water, cookies, and deep straw. The real feed would be when they reached the kennels.

The humans, once horses were tied at their trailer, tired, sat on collapsible chairs. As always, these mornings brought potluck food. Everyone was hungry.

The news of Risé had not been made public. The breakfast centered on hunting, healthy foxes. Clothing at Horse Country.

Back at Roughneck Farm, Sister and Betty cleaned tack. Sister usually cleaned Gray's tack, as he would often retire to the library to work. He worked harder as a consultant than he had as a partner in Washington.

The phone rang. "Hello." Sister held the cleaning cloth tightly. "Good. I'm so glad the boys will get here. This is going to be dreadful for everyone. Thanks for calling, Ben. Good luck."

"She's alive." Betty breathed a sigh of relief. "Could tell that from your tone of voice."

"They found what she took. The pill bottle was in the glove compartment of her car. Oxycontin. The whole bottle, it would appear."

"You know, a lot of people if they've had an operation will

keep the meds. Those opioid pills really do kill pain. Remember Risé had her shoulder operated on a year ago? Said the rehab was worse than anything."

"Greg doted on her. Betty, I don't understand these things. I really believe he loved her."

Betty swung the saddle up on the saddle rack. "I believe he did, too, but sex is different from love. If what I saw is real, not falsified, I think maybe it's about a man fearing getting old. Maybe Greg, if it is true, thought sleeping with a young woman would keep him young. It can't be just sex."

"I have no idea. I asked Gray. He said he doesn't understand any man wanting to go to bed with someone who doesn't truly want to go to bed with him. He understands being attracted to women, hitting on them, but that stuff about using your position to dominate, like politicians or heads of corporations do, Gray said he doesn't understand the thrill, although he hastened to add he understood the thrill of sex. Men are funny."

"As we are both married to them, yes, I'd have to say they are funny. We both married good men. Plenty don't."

"I *thought* Greg was a good man." Sister was exasperated, confused.

"Well, we will never hear his side of the story."

Having finished their chores, the two women walked outside. As they did so, a drone flew overhead. "What is that damned thing doing here!" Sister threw up her hands.

"Maybe on the way to something else." Betty asked, "Where's the shotgun?"

"In the house. I will shoot that damned thing if it comes back."

"Sister, I can't imagine what or who would send a drone here. What do you have that someone would want?"

"I don't know." She took a deep breath. "Too many crazy things going on, whether it's what you saw, Greg and Arnold's sui-

THRILL OF THE HUNT

cides, and I really believe now that Greg killed himself. And, well, this damned drone."

"There are too many loose ends." Betty shook her head.

"There are. Two men are dead, and one woman just tried to kill herself."

CHAPTER 26

October 9, 2020, Friday

Looking at his cellphone, Crawford followed the image. "It's clear."

Charlotte Abruzza, handy with electronics, tools, nodded. "What would you like to see?"

"The burial grounds?"

She held a small device in her hands, directing the drone with her thumbs. Overhead it circled the two then sped toward the low ridge. The hum of the propeller blades was not loud.

"There."

He stared at the result. She had synched up his phone with the drone's camera. The drone, missing the trees, kept about twenty feet above the ground. From that height, both were surprised at what they could see. Small indentations, odd rock formations.

Crawford directed her. "Go back to the rocks."

The drone turned to hover over the rocks.

"It's possible they were once more pronounced, a small circle, but hard to tell now. They may naturally be that way." Charlotte now moved the drone in a westerly direction, both of them looking for more rock formations, any sign of markings. As there were none, she directed the drone back to the slave graveyard.

"You can see the graves from this height. Not that they are deep. I guess sediment filled the outlines over the decades, the centuries," Crawford murmured.

"Well, it's like excavations in Rome. They dig down for the foundation of a new building or to repair an old building and find Roman buildings underneath, often in decent shape. It seems the earth adds more than it subtracts."

He nodded. "Except by water, I think. Okay. Bring it back."

Within a few minutes the whirr was overhead. The drone stopped in front of them, propellers turning as it sat down. Charlotte turned it off.

Crawford bent over to pick it up, finding it surprisingly light. "Can this knock out another drone?"

"I don't know. If it can catch the other one I would think it could ram it, damage it."

"Well, I'd like to see that. Of course, we will probably never again see the drone that took the money."

"I don't know, but if we could bring it down, the serial number would tell us the manufacturer and from there possibly where it was sold. That's a start."

"Right."

Earl watched from the side of the Carriage House. The early-morning sun felt warm, as the night had been cool. He watched the humans and the drone.

He knew Old Paradise, every inch, every den, most of the other animals. After the plaque was placed, the slave graveyard cleaned, made presentable, he noticed that the other area, the possible Monacan burial, had also been cleaned up. For now, no one was there with equipment. Earl could not have known that these events aroused people in a variety of ways. He knew the people who worked and lived at Old Paradise. He didn't know those who snuck around in the graveyards. He didn't know why, but then again, he was a fox and sensible about things. There's no point digging. Humans would sweep the ground with metal detectors. He watched when Old Paradise was being restored. The two people probing the ridge mystified him. They didn't belong but as long as they weren't disturbing the Carriage House he didn't much care.

But humans were peculiar. He noticed the carvings on the tombstones, such as lambs, staffs, rings. Odd things, he thought, but again, this meant something to the humans. The angels really got him. Humans with wings!

Sister, Betty, Weevil, and Tootie brought hounds back to the kennel after walking.

Sister checked each hound as he or she walked to the draw pen. Weevil and Tootie brought out the food, which they poured into the long trench feeders. The boys ate in the draw pen, the girls had a big square space in their indoor kennel. After eating, everyone could do as they pleased. Many of the hounds wanted to go outside to their condos, especially now that the weather was becoming cooler.

After feeding, Weevil power-washed the feed room. Chores done, the four humans rendezvoused in the office to discuss tomorrow's hunt.

"We're getting close to Opening Hunt," Betty remarked. "Want to stay close to home? We've actually gone to more fixtures this cubbing season than usual."

"Foxglove? After All? I'd like to save Tattenhall Station for after Opening Hunt."

"After All," Weevil suggested.

"Sounds good to me," Tootie agreed.

"Betty?" Sister asked.

"Sure."

After this agreement Weevil and Tootie left to go work their horses, Sister and Betty made their inevitable cup of tea in the kennel office, then they, too, walked to the stable to ride one set each.

Walking across the wildflower field, Sister on Midshipman, Betty on Outlaw, the two friends side by side, thought about Risé.

"The good thing is, the boys are home." Betty inhaled the early fall scent as Outlaw slid through tall black-eyed Susans, the odd Allium, seed dropped by a bird. The colors, amazing in variety, were beautiful to behold.

"Going to be painful for everyone. I assume she is still on suicide watch. She's not home."

"With the boys here, she should be home soon. You know what I think? I think Ben and those young law enforcement officers . . . kids, really, to me . . . will study that video and possibly identify tiny clues, say a type of lamp. Law enforcement now has more tools. Who knows what or who they'll find."

Sister agreed. "Modern technology is amazing but I think law enforcement is still gathering lots of evidence, thinking, and even hunches."

"The woman looked so young." Betty sighed. "I've reached an age where everyone looks young."

"Me, too."

"I wish to God I hadn't seen that video," Betty burst out, saying, "If people cheat on their partners," she paused, "maybe there's a reason. I just don't want to know about it."

"Gray and I were talking about that. He is a sensible man. I asked him did a lot of his friends run around in D.C.? He said he thought some did, but he didn't want to know. How could he look their wives in the face? Sometimes he surprises me."

"Maybe having a gay cousin helped," Betty thought out loud, then asked Outlaw to jump the hog's back, which he did. "Mercer pushed him to think of people's behavior. He wasn't a run-around but he was gay and that was so different when Gray, Sam, and Mercer were young."

Sister, following again, drew alongside Betty as they walked the weed-whacked fence line. Usually they plunged straight into the woods, as that was the decision of the chased fox. Today both were happy to walk along the tidy green path. All the fences at After All, miles of fences, were kept in good order, a big annual expense, if nothing else those fences announced that the Bancrofts had major resources.

"I can't imagine Mercer doing something like that." Sister named Gray's deceased cousin. "He wasn't rigid but he would never use people. Mercer being truthful about being gay upset people, tough people. He was brave."

"He never hid his sexuality, but he also never took a partner. I don't know. Maybe he didn't feel free. Maybe it would have upset Aunt Dan. He loved his mother. Maybe he still paid a price."

"I think she always knew he was different, even when he was a child, but maybe she feared what would happen if he had a true partner. Who is to say. If he did have a partner, a lover, I expect most people would have gotten over it. He was too much fun to push away."

"He really was fun." Betty stopped herself. "Well, Greg could be good company, too. If it's true, I don't get it. It's some kind of weird power play. I don't know." Betty's voice carried an edge.

"You don't know because you're a woman, and neither do I."

The beautiful covered bridge came into view in the distance.

"My wonderful Bobby has an extra pound where his abs used to be. Do I notice a gorgeous twenty-two-year-old boy? Sure," Betty mentioned. "Do I want to sleep with him? No. Both Bobby and I are growing old. But he will always be my handsome Bobby. I love his forearms. I don't think forearms gain weight." She laughed. "He is uncommonly strong."

"So is Gray. Funny. I wouldn't want to be with a man who wasn't stronger than I am."

Betty pondered this. "Maybe it's just the way we're made. Maybe everyone should get over whatever it is they are complaining about and accept we really are different and yet the same. Everyone has a right to their own life, their own form of expression."

"Yes, but what if your form of expression is destructive to others?"

Betty sighed. "Do you think this has something to do with money?"

"You mean keeping a young mistress and finding women for other men? Not exactly prostitution but matching women with men ready to keep them?"

"That is an awful thought."

"Well, everything is about money. Money and me, me, me." Sister's voice rose slightly. "I hate it. I just hate it. I don't care if it's some buffoon on the media bringing attention to themselves or the possibility that someone we thought we knew, we liked, I really liked him, made money off the backs of young women, or just kept one."

"We're getting old, Sister. It's a whole 'nother world."

"It is, but we can still run on a beautiful day. Come on, I'll race you to the bridge."

Midshipman and Outlaw, happy to stretch their legs, galloped to the bridge and two friends forgot their years and their troubles if ever so briefly.

CHAPTER 27

October 10, 2020, Saturday

Alight fog hung over meadows and forests. The first cast was at eight o'clock, the air cool. Hounds left from the kennel, heading across the wildflower field, up and over the hog's back jump.

As Sister and Betty rode this yesterday, both noted where a branch had come down, and a few small rabbit warrens. Fall had arrived. The blaring trumpets, trombones, and brass crescendo of leaves in full flame was ten days to two weeks away. Sister was grateful this fall seemed to be on the schedules she remembered from her youth. These days, the change of the seasons was anybody's guess. You knew they were coming, but when?

Matador, eager to go in the refreshing air, let out a little whinny as Betty, on Rickyroo, moved forward on the right. The two were big pals. Sister loaned Betty Rickyroo, as Betty's "boys" needed a break, she thought.

Given the invigorating briskness, everyone moved along at an awakening trot.

Juno moving next to Taz, stopped to investigate a black gum tree. *"Hmm."*

Taz, nose down, told the younger hound, *"Strong. Look up. See those scratch marks?"*

"Do."

"Bear. We can chase bear, but Sister and the staff really want us on a fox. It's quite a strong scent. My guess is, if Weevil moves along to Broad Creek, we'll pick up fox scent. The air will be cooler by the water and the soil holds scent better. They've all been out. A good night for hunting."

Gray, astride Wolsey, rode alongside Kasmir. Alida rode next to Freddie Thomas. The field expanded with every week. The cool air, the blush of color on some leaves, encouraged people to hunt. Even moving the first cast down a half hour helped. It was as though foxhunters needed convincing each season that it would really start, really get cool, and the runs would pick up. Over forty-five people rode out this Saturday.

Weevil listened as a mockingbird sang in a tree. Mockingbirds like to hear themselves sing. If the fellow was telling him something, he didn't understand it, but he did understand the purple finches, and the gold finches were not in the bushes right now. The nuthatches hung on the trees, but not low. This was a sign a fox had recently passed. Not that a red fox or a gray is out birding, but if a bird should be so clueless as to ignore the omnivorous creature, that could be a foolish move. Foxes and cats possess lightning reflexes. A brief time in the company of either species usually teaches a human how painfully slow we really are.

Betty, hunting for years, also watched the bushes and peered up into the trees, looking for an owl perched on a branch staring below. Hounds moving through would stir up mice, moles. The owl happily took advantage of this. Occasionally Betty might catch sight of the great horned owl, Athena, huge, fearless, and one to study Betty as Betty studied her.

Betty noted not many birds were sitting on branches. She wondered had they risen early and eaten their fill or were they obscured by the leaves? She also checked for tracks; as they neared the Broad Creek, racoon tracks were visible along with rabbit. No fox.

Fox tracks were visible up ahead as Weevil noted large tracks heading to the creek bank. As he saw them, Pookah opened. All rushed toward the site. Everyone opened, splashing into the swift-running creek. The rains lifted it a bit although the water wasn't near the top of the banks.

Pansy, Pookah's littermate, skidded down the bank into the water, swimming across, then clambering up the other side. The entire pack followed suit.

Weevil galloped to an easier crossing for Gunpowder. Down they went, the 16.2 hand horse easily trotting through the water, which was not even up to his knees. Close enough though. With a mighty lunge he hoisted himself up, as the bank proved more vertical on the other side, the eastern side. Sister on Matador easily followed. Most of the field did okay but the farther back in the field you rode, the more torn up the bank was by the time you got to it.

A rumble, distant, announced that Yvonne, Aunt Daniella, and Kathleen Sixt Dunbar crossed the covered bridge, out of sight around a sweeping curve of the creek. Another rumble signaled they were not alone.

Sister paid little attention as hounds opened up, running flat out. She noted to her discomfort that they flew due east where the woods grew thick. The club had not had time to clean up that part of After All. The Bancrofts usually had this done but they were in Santa Fe with their daughter, who had asked them to come hunt with her and Caza Ladron hounds. They so enjoyed themselves that the family also drove to Albuquerque to hunt with Juan Tomas Hounds. As the Jefferson Hunt had a lot of repairs and cleaning up to do, they never got to the east side of After All. It had been a hard winter. Lots to do. Sister wished they had gotten to the east side. Leaning forward, her face next to Matador's neck, she avoided low-hanging branches. Once out of that rough patch, the deer trails opened wide enough for a tractor.

Hounds screamed. Betty fought vines, branches, tree trunks on the path, as did Tootie. Both whippers-in were falling behind. Weevil, too, couldn't keep up. Aunt Daniella, who had grown up at After All, gave Yvonne directions.

"Go back out on the farm road, turn left at the clapboard dependency. There's a farm road there. You'll come out on the easternmost border of the estate."

Yvonne, following directions, emerged at the southeastern corner of After All, abutting an old Westvaco timber tract, the trees not yet harvested. Edward Bancroft bought the acres when Westvaco sold most of their property in central Virginia.

Just as they came out, Ryan behind them, Yvonne stopped the car. The entire pack bolted in front of her into the timber tract. Ryan quickly got out of his truck, camera in hand, videoed the entire thing along with the roaring sound. Then Weevil came out, listened for his hounds, spurred on. Betty shadowed the pack, weaving in and out of debris along the old boundary. Tootie hit a good timber road on the left and thundered along, soon having the pack in her sight. They were all on.

Another creek appeared. It was really Broad Creek, which had been fed by a northern tributary so was now wider and deeper. No crossing in sight.

Hounds charged to the creek. Stopped.

Noses down, they investigated the edge of the running waters.

"He didn't go in. I know he didn't," Dreamboat declared.

Diana, who got along well with this littermate, kept pushing. *"He's turning back!"*

Hounds ran by their huntsman, ran through the field, all standing still as they could, and within seconds disappeared. The sound was pure magic.

Weevil touched his cap with his crop as he, too, blew by Sister. She smiled in return. What a morning.

As the field kept in place so their master could get in the front, Yvonne, with Ribbon, her Norfolk terrier, in her lap, exclaimed, "This is something. How can anyone find their way in a timber tract?"

Kathleen agreed. "All looks the same."

Aunt Daniella added, "Imagine hunting in Southern Pines, nothing but timber. Grand hunting though."

She neglected mentioning that in her youth Southern Pines, North Carolina, filled with quite good-looking men and not a few beautiful women, proved exceptionally exciting. The parties as death-defying as the hunting.

Ryan waved to Yvonne. She stayed put, Ribbon complaining, as Ryan drove around her always clean SUV. Then Yvonne turned around, impressing her passengers, as her country driving skills had vastly improved from when she moved here from Chicago a few short years ago.

Within ten minutes they were rolling back. The fox was determined to make a fool out of everyone. He was new to the area but had met Uncle Yancy, the resident fox.

He swerved northward, again, the damned woods such an impediment. Sister quietly cursed. Betty cursed, too. Not under her breath. Tootie, realizing she was the only one who had a chance to stay with a flying pack, didn't have the time to curse. She tried to remember to breathe. Her horse, Iota, stretched to his full length. The exhilaration was ecstasy.

Betty, the first to realize exactly where they were, waved to Weevil, as he had been slowed by a huge tree across the narrow path. She motioned for him to keep going straight while she, too, curved north.

Trusting his senior whipper-in, Weevil smacked limbs, leaves with his crop as he circumvented what had to be the biggest treetop ever. This did not improve his mood. Hounds hit Mach speed and he was fooling around with a damned tree.

Betty took a coop in an old fence line on the edge of the Lorillard place. She had a ways to go, for the pack had pulled a quarter mile ahead. The music saved her. She knew where they were going.

Once Weevil came out on the farm road between After All and the Lorillard place, he thanked Betty. She put him right. He gave Gunpowder a light tap, not that the experienced Huntsman's horse needed it, but then again it did heighten the fun, so Gunpowder literally leapt forward, four legs in the air.

"Stick, buddy." Gunpowder giggled.

Weevil did, but that moment of excessive spirits did catch him off guard. The earthen far road, soft but not muddy, somewhat muffled the sound of hoofbeats. Sister, who also knew the territory by heart, shot out onto the road. She saw Weevil's red coat in front of her, had a moment of relief, then she, too, surged forward.

If anyone took a notion to slow their horse, it wasn't going to happen. This was the best run of cubbing season. Sister hoped this presaged a fantastic formal season. A few in the field simply wanted to live.

Two riderless horses blasted by Sister.

"Hey, you jerks. Where are you going!" Matador whinnied. *"You don't pass the Master."*

"Screw you." The bright bay actually kicked out as he flew by.

Matador, livid, pulled to get alongside these two but Sister, voice quiet but firm, said, "Steady, buddyboy. We have a job to do."

He listened to his rider, whom he loved, but secretly he plotted revenge.

Walter Lungren, now leading Second Flight, did not stop. Ben Sidell was riding tail. Ben as well as Bobby Franklin would have to pick up the Reverend Sally Taliaferro as well as Cynthia Skiff Kane, riding a green horse of Crawford's, who just lost it. It was he who ran alongside of Matador, trying to kick him. Sam Lorillard stopped to help.

"Bobby, go on. Ben and I have this. You're going to need to push Second Flight up there," Ron Haslip, out today, called out.

"Thanks." Bobby smiled, moving along.

Second Flight, galloping, actually did quite well. Maybe the sight of the reverend hitting the dirt kept their legs tighter. If the good Lord didn't protect the Episcopal priest, well, they'd better protect themselves.

And hounds were screaming, just screaming.

The fog, thin, had been lifting but a few heavier patches remained. Betty reached the graveyard as the pack leapt over the stone enclosure, into the graveyard filled with fog. It looked eerie.

She could hear Weevil trying to reach them. The pack shut up, no scent. At last Weevil arrived, walked to the graveyard as Tootie, now behind him on the road, moved to the other side of the graveyard.

"He's down there." Trinity sat by a den opening next to the grave of Graziella, Aunt Daniella's sister.

Well, he wasn't down there. Uncle Yancy had built a maze of tunnels as well as having an extra den under the front porch, plus his very favorite spot over the mudroom door. The young fox, male, new, proved a quick study. He followed one of the underground paths to the outside of the graveyard, then he made off.

Weevil dismounted as Betty rode over to hold the reins. He opened the small wrought-iron gate to step into the peaceful place. Reaching Graziella's grave, he looked at his pack, trying to figure what had happened. "Good hounds. Good hounds. Come along." He turned to go, the pack following.

"Yvonne, when I am resting therein, leave cookies on my grave for the fox," Aunt Dan requested.

"I will, but don't go anytime soon. I can't find my way without you."

This made them all laugh.

Weevil took the reins, easily swung up onto Gunpowder, breathing heavily but not in distress.

Sister rode up. "Let's give everyone time to catch their breath and," she noted the two horses now standing near the front door of the white clapboard house, "time to catch those horses. One looks like Crawford's new greenie."

"Is. Hope everyone is okay." Betty patted Rickyroo's neck. "He is a trooper, this one."

"Yes, he is. I am so lucky in my horses. There's Ryan shooting the graveyard and walking up. Thought he wasn't going to film any more hunting until Opening Hunt."

Betty shrugged. "Well, glad he did."

The two fields rode up. Everyone was grateful for the breather. Sister rode back to Walter. "Anyone hurt?"

"I don't think so. My God, that was a helluva run."

She grinned. "Was."

As horses, hounds, and humans regained their composure, the flasks were passed. Yvonne had Sally and Skiff in the car. Jamison Metzinger had a horse on each side. His horse, very quiet, calmed down the two bad boys who had lost their riders.

"Thanks," the two women said as they got out of the car.

Ryan was filming the two horses that Jamison walked over to the ladies. Walter nodded to Kasmir, who rode up to help the women and Jamison if so needed. He wisely put his horse alongside

Sally's, who now couldn't move away, as the priest put her foot in the stirrup. She easily mounted. She hadn't been bucked off, but she really did lose her seat in a small stumble in those cursed woods. As to Skiff, this was going to take more effort. Jamison and Kasmir flanked each side of Ranger; fussy, he wouldn't stand still.

Finally, Kasmir, always sensible, said, "He's so green. Perhaps you would allow me to walk him back to the trailers while you ride with Yvonne. He needs time and this was an exceptional run."

She nodded. "You're right. I hate for him to be rewarded for dumping me."

"Yes, and his brain is a little fried." Kasmir took the horse's reins while Skiff, after patting Kasmir's boot in thanks, strode back to Yvonne.

Ryan continued to film all of this. Zoomed in on the hounds, sitting as good children should. He managed close-ups of everyone in the two fields. This would be so useful when he edited the season's video.

"Weevil, I know you have a lot of horse left, as do I," Sister called over to him.

"Yes, Madam."

Sister motioned for Walter to ride next to her as she turned her horse away from the house and the graveyard. "Not everyone is in hunting shape, Walter. How about if we walk back? If we pick up a fox, so be it. If not, everyone will be somewhat restored."

"Fine. We could cut through Pattypan Forge."

"A shortcut that is bound to get us another run. Let's go the longer route. No point starting the second with a lot of involuntary dismounts."

"Okay." He turned Clemson back to the field as he then followed the senior Master.

Ryan continued to film, with many close-ups. The Lorillard home place cast a spell, whether on a video or in person.

With Skiff in the car, four ladies ran their mouths at once. Happy, all of them.

By the time all reached the kennels, a few members thought they might have another run in them, but the clock said eleven; they'd been out three incredible hours. Best not to push it. Hubris isn't just for Greek drama.

Hounds in, horses tied to trailers, staff horses quickly wiped down and put in their stalls until after the breakfast, the house was full, jammed with people thrilled with the day plus their own performance. The hunt did have some tricky moments.

Club members helped with breakfasts, especially since Sister had to organize hounds, horses, select the fixture. She couldn't really host a breakfast, so Cindy Chandler of Foxglove took over. Kasmir and Alida lent their cook, which was a godsend even though people brought wonderful dishes. Tootie surprised everyone by bringing wrapped water chestnuts, bacon around them, a toothpick in the middle. Her mother drove to Tootie's place to pick it up.

Ryan filmed the table, lingered over the early fall centerpiece, black-eyed Susans with zinnias, mums, bright petunias, all set off by deep green evergreen boughs plus thin branches with leaves that had been painted. Some people wore masks, some didn't, but everyone appeared comfortable.

Sister spoke to Ryan as he panned the table. "This table could tempt all the giving saints." She laughed.

He did, too. Then cut the camera for a moment. "Said I wouldn't shoot until Opening Hunt but the morning, that fog, too beautiful. And cubbing is drawing to a close. So I took a chance. Boy, am I glad I did."

"Where's your sidekick?"

"Editing. She's so good at that. Much better than I am. I can get the footage but I need help after that. I think we're going to have an awesome record for you all when the season is over. Hope it brings in money."

"Me, too." Sister smiled then left to check that Skiff was really okay. Reverend Taliaferro was talking to Bobby, so she was in up-beat spirits.

The breakfast lasted one and a half hours. People couldn't shut up or stop eating. Everyone was higher than a kite. Finally all left by the mudroom door.

Gray had bought a drone out of curiosity. He and Sister studied it last night. He left it on the kitchen table, Golliwog guarding it as well as a succulent piece of ham she had stolen off a non-vigilant guest's plate when he put it down on the big sideboard. Golly had no shame.

In the rush of getting ready, deciding whether to wear a neck-tie, a bow tie, or a colorful stock tie, both Gray and Sister had for-gotten to put the drone away.

Some people noticed this as they filed out. Ben asked Gray what provoked him to buy the drone. Gray had responded, many people around, that drones had been prominent lately. He wanted to know how they worked. Then again, maybe a drone could help scope territory and save them by knowing where to clear trails when.

One person listened intently. This sent a slight shiver of fear down his spine. If only Sister and Gray had put the drone away. A few people noticed the device, paying little attention, but did note that Golly was eating good food. This only emboldened her.

As to the fearful person, he, too, was now emboldened.

CHAPTER 28

October 11, 2020, Sunday

Four o'clock, still some sunlight left, soft. Sister didn't notice the retreating light really until October, and then again the gaining light in February. It's odd how the body adjusts.

Sally Taliaferro gave a good sermon in church. The pews, packed, were filled with old friends of decades as well as newcomers. Western Albemarle boomed and many newcomers were Episcopalian. Risé was not in attendance but neither Sister nor Betty nor Bobby thought she would be. They knew she was home and they knew that Sally paid regular calls. Risé needed all the comfort she could get. Her sons remained but they had to get back to work, so Sally, Freddie Thomas, and Betty quietly organized people to watch over Risé, possibly get her out for a hike, if nothing else.

The temperature, now in the mid-sixties, slowly dropped.

Gray, transfixed by his giant computer screen, hummed to himself. He often made Sister laugh by his choices, usually songs his mother would sing around the farm. She thought of it as Arthur

Godfrey music, but kept it to herself. At least they agreed on Duke Ellington . . . but then, who wouldn't.

Studying bloodlines, Thoroughbred bloodlines, Sister used a magnifying glass to look closely at a color photo of Midshipman's sire, also called Midshipman. Her fellow, really learning how to be a master's horse, wasn't meant for the track. He was shunted off to Sister. He may not have wanted to run on a track but he gloried in the hunt field. He was at a local stud farm for a year and no one named him. So Mercer, Gray's late beloved cousin, secured him for a pittance, as well as Matchplay for Sister.

"I am reading Midshipman's breeding papers. He goes back to Roberto. I have always loved Roberto's get, as well as Buckpasser's. Sometimes Buckpasser's kids can start a little hot, same with Damascus." She cited another great stud, especially for steeplechase horses, or so Sister thought.

Turning from his computer Gray remarked, "Mercer really was a terrific bloodstock agent. He made a great many people a lot of money."

"And he found me super hunting horses for so little. If they had been track worthy, they would have cost hundreds of thousands even then. I miss him."

"I do, too. As you're aware, I don't know much about bloodlines. Mercer bubbled with enthusiasm. The two of you were two peas in a pod. I take some comfort in the fact that his killer will never be released from jail. Cold comfort."

"Yes," she soberly responded. "You know, and I have said this before, is it better to think someone was killed or better to know they committed suicide to avoid public shame? I really don't know, but I do know I would hate to be in Risé's shoes. Sally said she is doing as well as can be expected."

"It really is hard to fathom. But Betty viewed the video. I believe Betty and I'm glad she didn't drag us through details."

"Me, too. Sometimes Betty surprises me. Not that I would expect her to wallow in someone else's sorrow, but she has good, solid judgment." Sister looked out the window, her nose being flicked by a cat's tail, which she kept removing and it kept returning. "Golly."

"I'm keeping away the flies," the magnificent calico bragged.

On the floor in front of the sofa, Raleigh and Rooster lifted their heads.

Raleigh couldn't help himself. *"There are no flies."*

"What do dogs know?" Golly flicked her tail again.

"Look outside, honey. The light is magic."

Gray did. "It is." He clicked off his computer. "Let's go outside and test the drone."

"Okay."

Within five minutes they'd thrown on light jackets, the two dogs at their heels, while Golly took this opportunity to double-check the dog dishes. Just in case.

Standing in the drive between the house, the kennels, and the stable, Gray held the drone while he handed the beeper, as he thought of it, to Sister.

"Isn't this a little like those model airplanes that people can fly anywhere?" Sister asked.

"I think so. Same principle. Okay, I'm going to send it up and have it hover over us."

He punched in the buttons and the four small propellers turned, hit the speed asked of them, then lifted straight up, remaining over their heads.

"Weird." Rooster, a true Harrier, was only interested in something on the ground.

"They must have some use for it. You know Mother hates to spend money if it isn't useful." Raleigh watched the drone.

"Oh. Why is a fake sheepskin bed for that big-mouthed cat useful?"

Raleigh considered this. *"Well, if she buys something for Golly, she usually buys something for us. The beds she bought us are huge."*

"Okay." Rooster conceded.

Gray moved the drone toward the stables. "Look."

Sister peered at the small screen on the controls. "Can't believe how clear the picture is."

"Realtors are using these all the time now. People don't want to sit in cars because of Covid so the realtor has them at the office to view the property or even sends it to their computer and they can talk later." He moved the drone toward the boundary with After All. "Don't want to set off the hounds."

"So the drone plays back where it has been?"

"Yes. I don't know if a techie can make it better. You know, so you're not just following property lines or looking at the exterior of a house. There are programs that tell you who owns the property as well as the boundary lines."

Sister bent over the screen. "You could follow people with this."

Gray shrugged. "I'm sure nervous spouses do. Follow the car. That sort of thing. I believe drones will have any number of uses not connected to real estate."

"Weapons."

He agreed. "We know that. What we don't know is where our military falls into place, say considering Russia or China. They have drones, too. Well, what do you want to see?"

"Can you send it as far as the house at After All?"

"Sure." He punched in directions. Within minutes the drone hovered at the front door.

"I'll be!" Sister exclaimed.

"Look at this." He had the drone circle the house then fly down to the dependency, where Weevil used to live before moving in with Tootie. And there, big as life, was Uncle Yancy eating out of an open garbage can, as the Bancrofts had a new live-in worker.

"That devil." Sister smiled, for she knew Uncle Yancy.

You chase a fox over the years and you get to know the fox, the vixen, their offspring. In a sense they become old friends, as they allow you sport. No one forces the fox out of the den.

Gray mentioned, "We can use this to check feeder boxes. We've got cameras at many of them but this would also be a big help."

"The real problem is the bears. They pick up everything, smashing it to bits or ripping the top off. We must have the best fed bears in the county."

Calling the drone back, Gray looked toward the east. "Well, our foxes are well fed, too. See. Here it comes."

The drone came to them; he had it rest on the path then turned it off.

"That's remarkable. I wonder if the drone that was here was a real estate drone on a shortcut."

"I don't know. Too many odd things. What I want to do is call up Crawford. Get him to buy a drone. Then go over there and see what we can do with two."

"Like what?" she puzzled.

"If he sends his drone, say, to the big in-and-out jump toward the chapel, can I program our drone to follow?"

She glanced down at the oddly shaped drone, then up at his handsome face. "How do you think of such things?"

"I'm a man. I like toys."

"You." She punched his arm but she didn't argue.

CHAPTER 29

October 12, 2020, Monday

As Bobby and Betty Franklin owned a printing press, they had some control over their time. Marriage season could be busy, sometimes Christmas, but mid-October they had time. Sam Lorillard worked for Crawford so he couldn't be at Risé Wilson's. Gray, working often as a consultant, could also be flexible. Freddie Thomas, Sister, Betty, Bobby, Gray, as well as Kasmir and Alida, tidied up Risé's house for the fall.

Gray weed-whacked. Bobby ran the riding mower. Kasmir purchased a lovely pair of sugar maples, which he oversaw as they were planted at the entrance, on either side of the driveway. Sister, Betty, and Freddie weeded the flower beds, sticking a tulip or daffodil bulb in here and there.

The members of Jefferson Hunt hoped some sprucing up would help Risé's spirits a bit. Outdoor work had been done by Greg. Until she had time to hire a service, they'd get everything ready. Chances were, keeping her lawn and landscape perfect was not high on her list right now.

Sheila, Risé's daughter-in-law, remained inside with her while her sons, Joe and Carl, helped with the outdoor chores. Joe had taken his mother's Cadillac for its state inspection sticker. Carl worked alongside Gray, weed-whacking the opposite flower bed. Kasmir looked up and waved as Joe returned with the CT5-V. Risé loved the Cadillac Greg had bought her for her birthday. Joe waved while passing the generous Kasmir, one maple, leaves turning a rich red, already in the ground. The flanking trees would lend a lot of visual interest to the driveway. Perhaps in time, Risé would line the driveway.

"She loves that car," Betty mentioned.

"Any man who buys you a car for your birthday is a good man." Freddie smiled. "It's hard to think about this, isn't it?"

"Is," Sister simply replied as she put a pinch of fertilizer in the bottom of the space for the tulip bulbs.

"I love tulips, but I don't love replanting them every fall." Betty yanked out a weed. "I know. They come up, but they don't proliferate like daffodils."

"That's the point, Betty. To get you out working on your hands and knees."

Joe walked through the front door, coming out with his wife and mother. He held his hand under his mother's elbow. She'd lost an alarming amount of weight quite quickly.

"Mom, you'll have the prettiest place in the neighborhood."

Sheila took Risé's other elbow. "Kasmir has given you the maples. They will be perfect."

Risé nodded. "My friends." She swallowed then called out in a louder voice, "Thank you all. You need not be doing all this."

Freddie beamed up at her, as she was still on her knees. "Risé, we want to do this. After all the food you have brought to our tailgates over the years, this is a small thank you."

The group worked for another hour. Many hands make light

work. Finished, they stood together to observe their handiwork. Risé, after her thank you, began to cry, so Joe and Sheila took her back in the house.

"Let's leave her be," Betty suggested. "How about if you all come to my house? I have leftover soup from last night. Bobby and I will never be able to finish it off. Come on. We can catch up. If we go to a food joint, too many prying ears."

Within twenty minutes the foxhunters stepped across the Franklin threshold of Cocked Hat, their small farm, brushing themselves off before entering.

Betty, already at the stove, called out, "Come into the kitchen. You'll have to make do. No good crystal and china," she teased.

Freddie, ever helpful, sliced homemade bread while Sister found the Irish butter, such good butter. Gray and Kasmir poured drinks. Bobby made sure there were enough chairs at the kitchen table, which could be extended and was.

Soon everyone was eating, talking, discussing the virus that had upended so much, complaining about the presidential election. That's all the news carried, and who could trust the news about anything? It wasn't that they were leery of discussing politics. They were all good friends, would speak their piece, but no one really knew what to believe. Statements from the candidates veered from the absurd to the tediously bland.

"Kasmir, those maples are spectacular." Betty meant it. "The color."

"Thanks. Alida picked them out." He looked at Gray. "Went to the same nursery where you bought all those white and pink dogwoods to line the drive into Roughneck Farm."

Sister smiled. "What a wonderful wedding present. Every year I can watch it grow, bloom, then change color for the fall. Gray is full of surprises."

His smile grew larger. "That ETHOS shotgun was my wedding

present. The lines are beautiful. Balance is terrific. You know, fellows, why don't we have a clay contest and invite the other local hunt clubs to shoot? We can come up with some kind of trophy. Say fifty dollars for a round and ten? Cheaper if you buy more rounds. Be a nice little fundraiser."

Bobby enthusiastically agreed, but then Bobby was a crack shot. "Let's do it. You know Farmington will come, Keswick, Bull Run. They've all got good shots. Glenmore. Maybe Bedford. We could raise a bit of money. The old pump is about to wear out in the kennel."

CHAPTER 30

October 12, 2020, Monday

Ben sat in front of Gray's big computer screen while Sister sat to his left, Gray to his right. Golly, Raleigh, and Rooster, on the sofa, behaved themselves. The humans were in no mood for tricks. They stared at a video left in the mailbox.

"If you didn't know our kennels, this would look realistic," Sister said. "As it is, it is the outside of the kennels."

"Anyone could drive down here and look at the outside. Anyone in the hunt club could take videos or photographs of the kennels." Gray pointed to a tree to the right of the kennel, in what could be seen as a front yard. "This is old. That dogwood is a good two feet taller now."

"So they could have picked this from old photographs." Ben rested his chin in his hand. "Of which there are many. Jefferson Hunt has yearbooks, sort of, and now this year we'll have a video. Of course, whoever did this would need to have access to a yearbook."

"In other words, whoever is blackmailing people is one of us." Sister's voice had dropped.

"Not necessarily. Your video, thanks to the dogwood and shots of different seasons, has more information than Crawford's, which was of the cemetery, relatively recent in the last two years. But yes, whoever this is has to know what is going on and who has resources."

"I never knew Arnold had resources," Sister said.

"I don't think a person has to have, say, as much money as Crawford, but they must be vulnerable in some way that they will find the ability to pay the bill. We don't know for certain if Arnold is one of the victims here, but the abruptness of his suicide, no warning to others, is like Greg's. Bear in mind the similarities, but also bear in mind we have nothing at all on Arnold. No letters. No DVDs. No thumb drives. No email or messages on his phone. It is possible that whatever set him off was not blackmail. But I can't rule it out." Ben stared at the chimney.

Gray leaned forward, pointing at the chimney. "See the gap on the third row of bricks? We had that repaired in 2018. You can never take a chance with a chimney. So, this is prior to that."

"The rest of the images could have been taken from anywhere." Sister gritted her teeth for a moment. "Starved dogs. Abused animals. A fox torn to pieces. Old photos, I would think, and perhaps not even American. But they are disgusting images and would set any animal lover right off."

"And you would pay to stop that," Ben calmly replied. "For one thing something like this would hurt all hunt clubs. The only running thread I can find . . . and my crew has tried to search for everything . . . is this is a person who knew his victims, or her victims, and knows what is at stake. So the sums requested are large but not completely damaging. No one is asking you or Crawford for millions."

"No, but to me that means this will be a regular request." Gray handed the mouse back to Ben. "Maybe once a year. Giving us time to replenish our coffers."

"Possible. We all understand why people want money by foul means or fair. There are so many things someone can do. They can send it offshore. They can buy paying cash, whether it's cars, jewelry, real estate. Or they can buy into syndications, or small businesses that are legitimate and generate income. A person with some financial acumen knows how to do these things. Am I right, Gray?"

"You are. Money laundering is a big business. There are so many ways to clean up money and I've seen a lot of them. Our government tries to shut the doors but the truth is, the criminals are smarter than those in government. Administrative people play by the rules, which means they can't truly consider criminal thought until those rules are broken. But the knowledge always comes after the fact. The criminal has the advantage every time."

"Whoever this is knows us. Knows this community, not just fox-hunters. And whoever it is seems to have no desire to spend money." Sister was trying to put two and two together.

"That we know," Gray answered. "Our blackmailer could be investing. Cash deals. Same with building supplies. You can be a silent partner in a construction company or, say, Wilson's lumber mill, procure lumber cheaper or sell it higher, whatever the case. It always looks legal and often it really is. But money is crooked. A business can expand, build an addition or a new car lot. There are so many ways to invest to generate income, if that's the point. And if the company you have given cash doesn't pan out, they would be as easy to destroy as Greg. Someone somewhere always has a foot of clay."

"Gray." Sister's eyebrows raised. "I don't think we have feet of clay."

"No. Not in the sense that Greg was vulnerable, but any of us could be made to look terrible. I could be accused of beating you. See what I mean?"

"Is this the world in which we live?" Sister looked so sad.

"It's never been perfect." Ben smiled. "Take it from your sheriff, but most people are law abiding unless the law makes no sense. Prohibition, for instance. There is always a criminal element or someone pushed to it by needs. Then again, there are so many laws on the books, the three of us sitting here are no doubt guilty of something, and I'm your sheriff."

"What do we do, Ben?"

"Appear to pay. Crawford's first attempt was good bills on stacks of false bills. But that gave him a tiny wedge of time. The next demand, higher, unmarked bills, he complied. I will work morning, noon, and night to get Crawford his money back, or what's left of it. Our perp has skill with equipment. Knows the community and obviously knows some big secrets, hence Greg. It's possible that whoever this is was part of the procuring mistress group. I couldn't really arrest anyone, as a woman willing to sell herself for security is not breaking the law. A streetwalker is. That in itself is wrong, a contradiction. But the video would still destroy a career, especially the career of a well-respected man seemingly in a good marriage."

Gray put his hands behind his head. "It probably was a good marriage. Risé and Greg got along. Two great kids. Participated in so many foundations. He was smart enough to remember anniversaries and birthdays. Her, too. A good marriage from the outside and probably from the inside on her part."

"Well, that's just it, isn't it?" Sister's voice rose.

"Maybe it's a case of what you don't know doesn't hurt you." Ben scrolled through the grim images.

"Oh, I would like to think that, but a man kills himself then later his wife tries suicide. So sooner or later it does hurt you," Gray replied.

Betty gasped. "Crawford?"

"Probably not, but then, who among us would think Greg had an expensive mistress; if we knew who she was, it would help. I doubt she lives here. And Arnold . . . well, does anyone know why Arnold really got divorced? It was acrimonious but without detail. She got almost every penny. Freddie knew the books, obviously."

"Like she caught him cheating?" Gray's eyebrows rose. "Cheating is one thing. But this seems to be a long-term arrangement, no doubt renewed. Rent, cars, spending money. Who knows? This really is something else. Would we all be horrified if the mistress was a male mistress? Don't have a word for it. Worse, better, does it matter?"

Sister put down her spoon. "Male or female or in-between, if you sell yourself you have no legal rights, as near as I can tell. A wife does, so I think the potential for abuse is greater. I'm not saying there was abuse, only that there is no protection for the woman, or whomever."

"Crawford was blackmailed. About desecrating the slave graves. He didn't, of course, he preserved everything." Gray thought Crawford had done a public service. "But what's the truth? With cellphones and the Internet, you name it, you can accuse anyone of anything. It takes years and a fortune to recover from something like that. And even when you win in court, there are doubts among some people. The damage clings to you. It's one way to control people, isn't it?"

"You're saying he was smart to pay the ransom, or whatever it is?" Sister questioned, struggling to really understand this.

"Yes, appeasing whoever this is gives Crawford time to hunt him down, if possible," Ben replied.

"It really is blackmail." Sister sighed.

CHAPTER 31

October 13, 2020, Tuesday

The Carriage House sat on an east-west axis, taking advantage of the winds, which usually came from the west. The breeze cooled the place in the summer. Long before fans, it was harder to cool than to warm. Also the windows allowed in so much light. In the dead of winter, lanterns were used. One needed to be careful. A knocked-over lantern in a bedded stall spelled disaster. Those early slaves, freed men, workers, indentured servants proved intelligent about the way the world worked. So every stall had a high hook on one of the poles. You could hang a lantern there then extinguish it when you left, or take it with you. As there had never been a fire inside the Carriage House, this was testimony to how careful those people were. The carriage rested on the other side of the extra-wide aisle.

A large potbellied stove, expertly placed on thick granite, itself laid on packed-down earth, threw out heat from the tack room when the door was open. The fire would be banked at night, hardwood used. A stable boy slept in the tack room. The quarters allowed one to keep warm. A low cot, blanketed, sat across from the stove. If the night was especially brutal, the stable boy . . . it was always a boy . . . could throw in more hardwood then scamper back to his cot to snuggle in the blankets. The driving horses wore their blankets, too.

All the stall doors were Dutch doors, so the top could be opened in warm weather. Where the carriages themselves were parked, no need for that, but each space did have a full door rarely used that opened to the outside.

On a night like tonight a chill crept up. Blankets, folded in a neat pile, on the end of the cot, which could still be used if needs be, would provide Earl with a cozy bed.

He walked along the top walkway. He could see over the land and up in the graveyards. The view lacked sharpness but he could see. He liked a high view. As he walked along the loft, he noticed two figures up in the graveyard, walking west. They paused once out of there and into the thought-to-be Monacan grounds. Hoods drawn up to ward off rain obscured faces, but he wouldn't have been able to see details. All Earl could see were two people slowly walking, the ground getting wetter. Every few steps they would stop and plunge something into the earth. Given the rain, that was easier than if the ground had been hard. He couldn't see what it was, but it was obviously sharp enough to pierce the earth.

This was the third time Earl had observed humans up there. Curious, he watched the first time when the weather was good. They neither saw nor smelled him. He had no idea why anyone would stick something straight into the earth. They appeared to be listening for something or waiting a bit. And here they were again, protected by the rain. He knew they avoided the buildings. He had watched them walk east until they disappeared last time. They did not go over the mountains.

Earl neither liked nor disliked humans. He found them odd.

He knew the people who worked at Old Paradise. He might be twenty yards from them, obscured by a bush, they never noticed. He knew Sister and her staff well enough because they put out feeder boxes. The food was sprinkled with wormer. He could taste it but he didn't mind. Thanks to the Jefferson Hunt Club neither Earl nor any other fox in the area hosted parasites. His thick coat gleamed.

Silently he sat and observed the care with which the humans walked. Finally, he wearied of it, climbed down the ladder, and retired to the tack room. The sound of the rain, rhythmic, made him happy to have such tight quarters, an old cot, and tidy blankets.

Sooner or later perhaps a human would live in the tack room. Then again, there were many outbuildings, restored, on the huge estate, so perhaps not.

After an hour the rain intensified. The two humans walked back through the graveyard. One carried a rusty buckle in his hand. They passed restored gravestones, not understanding the symbolism of them.

As they reached the edge of the large graveyard, had they'd known the symbolism of the tombstones it might have helped them in their search. The outermost tombstone, the first one they passed slogging east, was a smooth-fronted large simple headstone with a broken pillar carved on it. This meant a life cut short, someone dying in the prime of life, for children's stones were usually small little squares with dates carved on them. Immediately next to the broken pillar stood the last of the tombstones. Tall, a realistic carving of an acorn, faded over the decades yet uncannily realistic, so it was unusual. Once Crawford had the stones stood up and cleaned, the workmanship stood out. The name, Ransom Patrick, born 1790, died 1853, suggested not an early death, for many did live longer but a life whose end did not seem at the time untimely. The acorn was a symbol of wealth, power. Ransom Patrick may have been a

slave, but he knew success in some form and his survivors made
sure the acorn was prominent. No one in centuries had thought
about it.

If the two trespassers had known more about symbolism in
death they might have found what they were looking for in the rain,
on this cold night.

CHAPTER 32

October 15, 2020, Thursday

Rain splashed on the windowpane of Charlotte Abruzza's small but inviting office. Sister sat next to her at the desk, papers organized carefully on top. The thin vellum stood the test of time. Sophie Marquette's handwriting, flourishing in a manner few could reproduce today, filled the pages.

"She kept good records of prices, what and who owed her, that sort of thing." Charlotte pointed to a page dated September 9, 1827. "Careful. All the lines straight. So this is how we could piece together how the farm, managed by her, of course, was doing. She notes the weather in the top right-hand corner, as you can see." Charlotte pointed with her forefinger.

"Was it Sophie who kept the slave records? Births. Deaths."

"Yes. Occasionally she would comment on someone's work or to whom she had lent out the slave. She was paid for her slave but they also received some money. She was an honest person. A person of her time. If slavery disturbed her, she didn't note it."

"Any other hand in the records?" Sister asked.

"No. Her husband appeared to lack her business acumen but he cut hay, harvested corn, kept things going according to the season. He doesn't seem to be . . . or I should say *have been* . . . a lazy man." Charlotte looked up from the paper she was reading. "I've worked with them for almost two years now. I feel that I know them."

"I imagine you do. Did anyone keep a diary?"

"Yes, sort of. Ransom Patrick, Sophie's head helper, scribbled a few notes. He could read and write. The two worked closely together, especially in adding acres to Old Paradise. Sophie believed you could never own enough land. He was enslaved but he had high status. His odd notes were filed with her papers. Not exactly a diary, but he would note a landowner's personality, whether he grew healthy apples, how he treated his slaves, and most of all was the person shrewd financially."

"Did she ever write about her days during the war?"

Charlotte shook her head "No. What a loss. She owned Ransom and his wife as a young woman from just before the war. She was relatively poor then. Many whites struggled. Having a man and wife . . . your people, as was thought . . . you might begin to make a decent living. Ransom in particular accompanied her and sometimes her brother did, too. We only know that because her brother made a list of the places where they ambushed the British. He was especially focused on how many horses, mules, wagons they captured. Oddly enough he never wrote down the sums of money. We know Sophie captured payroll wagons because the British did keep records. Furious, of course, about being bested by rebels."

"Any idea?"

"According to them she made quite a haul in Maryland and as far as South Carolina. Mostly she operated in Virginia, crossing the Potomac according to troop movements. The funds were pounds, some loose coin. Crawford converted the British pounds in, say,

1812 to 1814 to today's funds. He estimated she stole eight million in today's dollars. She wiped out payroll for entire regiments."

Sister smiled. "She must have been an irresistible woman. And a focused one."

"She didn't go out of her way to kill but if she had to she didn't seem to shy away from it. We know, again from British records, that she was beautiful. She had Ransom with her and she said she was traveling, or trying to travel, behind the lines. Ransom appeared to play his part to perfection, as did she; when she wasn't permitted behind lines, she was invited to a spot of tea or an awful army biscuit because the officers or men wanted to be in the company of a woman. Then she would pretend to leave. She didn't. She lay in hiding, waiting for the regiment to pass. Wagons always brought up the rear. I would guess Ransom and her brother would attack. As they knew the territory, especially in Virginia, they could evade the British, who usually didn't know the wagons were missing until too late. The element of surprise compensated for her tiny numbers, three rebels, stealing payroll."

"Well, it was war and they did burn and pillage," Sister remarked. "Did she ever give money to our troops?"

"Yes. Again, we aren't always certain but it seems she would give, say, a percent like twenty, but mostly she gave what they wanted more than anything which were the rifles, ammunition, whatever else was in the supply wagons that the three of them drove. She worked quickly, throwing as much as she could onto three wagons. Over time she attracted more followers. That we know. We also know that once our commanders recovered from these raids being made by a woman, they cooperated when asked. They even lay in wait so the troops marching upriver on the James passed. Then she attacked from the rear, always the rear."

"So often when people age they revisit their youth. They tell things from the past that they've kept to themselves," Sister noted.

Charlotte half smiled. "If only she had that little streak of wanting her sons and daughter to know what she really had done. I expect they heard but not from her and people surmised what they could. Really only her brother and Ransom knew what she did, as well as those American officers who attacked the British lines, and they only knew what she did in that instance."

"I wonder if she kept her beauty."

"Given that men were quite gallant in those days, all said she was a handsome woman even in advanced age. But the women said so, too, those younger meeting her for the first time all marveled at her looks. She was smart enough to keep this big estate going with Ransom's help and her husband's. Obviously Ransom had more brains than her husband."

"Yes." Sister thought a long time. "Until our time, from 1814 to the turn of our century, DuCharmes, Sophie's married last name, kept it going."

"I'm so glad you drove over today. Few people want to examine our past to know the people. I really do feel that in some way I know her, Ransom, her brother. As the generations came, we know much more obviously. Some kept diaries and even her children could afford secretaries for this place, true record keepers. And, of course, many in the county are descended from Old Paradise slaves, proud of their history. I've had a lot of help."

"What happened to Ransom?"

"You've seen his tombstone?"

"I have."

"Well," Charlotte took a breath, "he led an interesting life, as much as we know. Became a moneylender."

"His money?"

"Some people have a knack for money. It's probable that Sophie shared some of the treasure with Ransom. After all, he risked his life along with her. But he kept good records of who owed what to whom. He loaned to slaves on Old Paradise but slaves from other estates as well."

"If he were with us today maybe he'd run Morgan Stanley." Sister wished she had known this remarkable man, as well as Sophie.

Charlotte laughed. "It is a talent. Making money. Crawford has it. I don't. I'm happy doing research, having a nice place to live. What would I do with as much money as he has?"

Sister laughed. "I don't know, Charlotte, but people always seem to find ways to spend their money. I've walked and ridden through the cemetery and I noticed many Patricks. Ransom must have had many mouths to feed. Then again, I didn't notice the dates of who could have been his children. They must have been a fertile family. He obviously had a sense of humor, as one tombstone for a son carried the name *Random*. Probably an unexpected child."

"He liked women." Charlotte lifted her eyebrows then laughed.

"He generously distributed his person?" Sister laughed as well. "So, *Random* makes sense."

The rain fell a bit harder. Charlotte noted it. "We've had weeks without a drop and then days of nonstop rain. I keep a raincoat in my car and one by the door. Now that there's a bit of chill, I hate getting wet."

"Me, too." Sister paused. "Whoever is sneaking around in the graveyard, what could they want?"

"Well, I've wondered, are these the people behind the threat to Crawford? Are they looking for grave disturbances or are they disturbing the graves? We noticed probings, some earth pushed aside in places, but nothing that could start an uproar."

"Maybe looking for the treasure."

Charlotte rested her head in her hand for a moment. "It would make so much more sense for treasure to be in or under the house or under one of the outbuildings. I was sure we'd find something when Crawford tore out the old basement, built a new one, entire floor, new thick walls. The damage was extensive. The house had been open to the elements for way too long. Neither of the brothers wanted to spend the money to save it. A fortune lasted centuries until now. They'd blown what was left of the money but they could have at least put tarps on the roof, fixed a few of the leaks that were already decades old. Of course, you watched this deterioration over decades."

"You'd think they would have looked for treasure." Sister, who knew the brothers well, thought them lazy. "They pretty much deserved what they got."

"If Sophie did bury some of what she stole, I suspect she would have been very clever."

"I really don't think there is a treasure. Every old place in the original thirteen colonies supposedly has buried treasure." Sister grinned.

"She used some of what she had stolen to make more money, to keep this place hopping. The hay alone was so good, people would line up with semis when trucks were used. With all these acres of good soil, the DuCharmes could feed their own stock and other people's, too. They made good money on their hay, corn, and apples." She smiled. "And country waters."

The rain pelted the window now.

This made Charlotte smile, too. "Still a good business, moonshine."

"I'd better head home. Charlotte, I enjoyed you giving me your time. Crawford has worked a miracle. Old Paradise is rising from the ashes, literally."

"I enjoyed it, too."

Sister retrieved her raincoat from where it was hanging in the cloakroom, by the front door. She stepped outside, grabbed the handrail, and hurried down the steps. Happy to slide into her truck, she shook her head, fired up the engine as the droplets sprayed, then slowly drove out of the estate.

She'd needed a break and the time spent here gave her a better idea of how to meet her own blackmailer's designs. She had until Saturday. She would use Old Paradise as her drop. If the blackmailer refused, then she would use Hangman's Ridge. A rough plan was forming in her head. Sophie would be her model.

CHAPTER 33

October 16, 2020, Friday

"Ground's soft, ought to be pretty good for tomorrow. This bit of wind helps," Sister predicted as she rode Midshipman along with Betty on Magellan and Gray on Cardinal Wolsey. Usually when they rode they walked hounds or worked a younger horse. Sometimes, especially before the season, they rode two and three sets a day to get everyone midway to hunting fit. By now, close to Opening Hunt, these horses were almost totally hunting fit. Sister was careful to start the formal season with just a touch of extra weight on her horses and her hounds. They burned it off quickly during formal hunting thanks to the speed of many of the runs as well as the falling temperatures. Like most masters before her, she learned once a bit of fat goes off your horse or hound, it's the devil to put it back on when hunting. She also added some extra fat content to feed with a boost of extra protein. Midshipman, Magellan, and Cardinal Wolsey gleamed in the sunshine.

"You know, I forget what it is to ride," Betty smiled, "with no program. We are lucky."

"That we are," Gray seconded the thought. "Every time I drive into Washington through all those clogged suburbs built in my lifetime, then turn into a city built to slow traffic, I already count the hours until I can drive out."

Betty asked, "Aren't the circles to slow troops? When L'Enfant designed all that, what, around 1791, did it not have a military purpose?"

"Did." Gray patted Cardinal Wolsey's neck. "Well, it didn't do any good in 1814, did it? The British marched right down Bladensburg Pike."

Gray, who liked history, continued, "Came down the Bladensburg Pike, but the circles did slow them in places. By the time they got to the president's mansion, Dolley was out. Not that she wanted to go, but she just made it with two slaves who stayed with her their entire lives even when they didn't need to do so, as well as her major domo, who was a sailor who jumped from his French warship during the Revolution. What a story. But it is true, our capital was not built for ease of transport."

"Well, I think our three horses are." Sister beamed. "What a beautiful morning. After yesterday's nonstop rain this is a scrubbed world. Glistens. The temperature at fifty-eight degrees Fahrenheit helps."

"You would know. You have giant outdoor thermometers everywhere." Betty laughed. "Outside the mudroom, outside the tack room, outside the kennel, outside Tootie's cabin, outside Shaker's former quarters. What are you going to do about Shaker's house? It is small but perfect."

"I don't know. Could we use more paid staff? Sure. I'd put them there but we can't afford another salary. Well, we could afford another salary until you factor in payroll taxes and workers' comp."

"Don't look at me. I'm your accountant but I don't make the

tax rules. But I can tell you with the wisdom of all my years, the power to tax is the power to destroy."

"Why are you looking at me?"

"Because you're the Master." He grinned.

"Oh, well, you can call the shots."

"As your husband I much prefer you be the Master, always," Gray demurred.

"Well, I'll make a decision. Why don't we walk up to Hangman's Ridge? Walking up a grade is good for hindquarters. When we get up there we can decide whether to go down to the north side or wiggle down a deer path and come out near the After All border."

"Sounds like a plan," Sister agreed with Betty as they walked by the kennels.

Hounds outside rushed to the chain-link fence.

"Hey, we want to go," young Juno begged.

Asa, now retired but part of the group, advised, *"You'll hunt tomorrow. Take this chance to rest. You know the light is hanging, the temperature is dropping. Chances improve for long runs."*

"I can do anything," Juno bragged.

"We'll see." The older, kind hound watched the humans. Sister waved to the kids.

"You spoil them," Betty said, then she waved, too.

"Do you all think they care?" Gray teased them.

"They care that they aren't out with us," Sister replied.

Past the kennel they walked faster, then reached the bottom of the high ridge. The path was wide on the farm side, while the steep proved easy. Just keep moving. Once at the top the wind blew harder, but not enough to be problematic. The space, open, had little to block the wind. The great hanging tree stood as always near the end of the flat field. Halfway to the other side, Sister stopped.

"Maybe we should use this ridge."

"For what?" Betty asked her Master.

"We still have not been told where to put our blackmail money. What if I tell whoever that it will be on the ridge in the open?"

"But how can you tell whoever this is? You can't call. You can't text," Betty sensibly replied.

"Well, Ben tracked down the cellphone calls. Each time anyone is contacted it's from a cellphone that is then destroyed. Since our thief hasn't called us, why can't I put another black square on our mailbox? It's worth a try," Sister replied. "He or she knows our mailbox."

"It may be worth a try but I don't think whoever is going to let us determine the drop spot," Gray noted. "The hanging tree is actually not bad. It's open. It's hard to reach but not for a drone. No human would need to climb up. But he would know we expect a drone."

"I don't see how that can be a problem," Sister replied. "We know no one is going to break cover and show themselves. Drones make sense."

"Sister, he has to know we are prepared for a drone and he has to know we are working with Ben," Gray replied.

"Well, so be it, but how is the bag going to be picked up? Someone or something has to get the money." Sister turned toward the eastern deer trail. "What's left?"

"That's what worries me," Gray honestly replied.

Carefully picking their way down the eastern side of the high ground, they reached the bottom. Stepping into the wildflower fields, still spots of color, they walked across then turned back to the stables. While not a long ride, it lifted everyone's spirits.

They chatted, wiping down their horse's tack, commenting on weather, tomorrow's hunt. Risé still stayed at home but Betty felt sure she would be going to church soon. Betty also heard that Arnold Synder's ex-wife inherited his trucking business. It may have been an acrimonious divorce but he never cut her out of his will. What surprised Gray and Sister is she intended to run the business.

"Well, why not?" Betty questioned.

"It's a male dominated business. She'll face some real resistance," Gray commented.

"If she's as smart as she is tough, my money is on her," Sister remarked.

Walking back to the house, Gray was the first to notice the Ziploc bag with a note inside pinned to the mudroom door with a colorful stick pin. He pulled the pin, opened the note.

Sister and Betty looked at each other then Gray as he read the note: *Place the bag tonight at Old Paradise in the slave graveyard's western edge.*

They went inside. Gray called Ben, said he'd touched the Ziploc bag and the note but he was wearing his thin riding gloves.

"I'll get the note later. Can you do as he says?"

"Yes. It's not the amount. It's what Crawford did. Bills on top of fake stacks, but it bought him time. I hope it buys us time."

"I do, too."

Then Gray called Crawford.

Betty listened intently. "Where's a bag or anything?"

Sister walked back into the mudroom and pulled out an old bag into which she used to store her backup clothes in the truck. "Got it."

"Let me help."

The three of them took rubber bands, counted out the fake bills into stacks, which Crawford had helped them get for when they would again be contacted. They placed a one-hundred-dollar bill on top, secured this with a rubber band. Without Crawford, this would have been much harder.

"It's not one hundred thousand dollars, even fake," Betty noted.

"We know; we wait and see."

The sun was low when Sister and Gray reached Old Paradise. Betty had gone home. In the back of the Land Cruiser, Gray brought his drone. Crawford met them at the door.

"Why don't we walk up together?" he suggested.

The three of them climbed the soft rise, moved through the tombstones, finally placing the bag at the last row, which meant it was open after that, flattish, although trees closed in twenty yards away. But it would be easy for a drone to swoop down and pick up the bag.

"I took the liberty of putting up a camera while you all counted bills," Crawford said matter-of-factly. "And I now have a drone, and I know you do, too, Gray. My hunch is whoever this is will come in the middle of the night. We would not see him. We'd hear the drone at the last minute if we could stay awake."

"I'm ready to stay here with our drone," Gray volunteered.

"Where can you hide?" Crawford asked.

"Nowhere up here. Even if I laid flat for hours I could be detected from above or by someone walking. I thought if I stayed in the Carriage House I might be able to see. Might even be able to get my drone up. It's a clear line. A bit far, but no one would see me behind the double doors with the paned glass. What do you think?"

"Worth a try," Crawford replied. "I'll sit in the main stable's loft, with the door open. I can see, and I can send out my drone."

"Both of you fellows will need warm coats and blankets." Sister was hearing the plan for the first time.

"Plenty in both the stable and the Carriage House. I just hope I can stay awake," Crawford informed her.

"Me, too," Gray agreed.

"Why don't you park your car next to mine at the house?"

"All right." Gray then turned to Sister. "I'll drive you home and come back."

She thought and couldn't find a better solution. "Okay."

By the time Gray returned, the light had faded. He walked from the big house to the Carriage House. There was enough light to see. Fortunately, no low clouds. Pushing the big double doors open with both hands, he knelt down, picked up the drone and the control, placing them inside, then closed the doors again. Inside, the temperature was low sixties, that would fall. He brought up two chairs to the side of a stall. He could see more clearly through the windows in the stall door than he could looking through the massive double door windows. This was helpful, or he would have to stand for hours.

Having found some blankets, he sat on one, keeping his coat zipped, placed another blanket next to him for when the mercury dropped even more. He put his feet on the other chair.

He caught the whiff of fox scent but didn't notice Earl watching him from the tack room. Gray didn't frighten him. Earl didn't know why he was there but that was okay. Gray placed the drone next to him, keeping the control in his pocket. All he would need to do would be to open the Dutch door window and he could send the drone up to the graveyard.

It was going to be a long night.

C H A P T E R   3 4

October 17, 2020, Saturday

The new moon signaled the night would be deep and dark. A few stratus clouds inched along in the cold air. Earl woke up, hearing the human snore. It surprised him how loud a human could be sleeping. He nosed out from under his blanket, walked under Gray's feet on the chair. Gray slumped to one side in the chair, two heavy blankets warming him, one around his shoulders, the other over his legs. Earl, ears far better than any human's, heard a screech owl over in the main stables. He walked back to his place. If he hopped up on a small ledge for blankets, folded old work towels, he could see in the night. Dark though it was he saw two figures in the graveyard. The same place where he had seen them before. Whatever continued to draw them back fascinated Earl. He forgot to pay attention, knocking off the towels and a heavy brush on top of them. The clatter awakened Gray.

He jumped up, oblivious about Earl, who quickly ducked back into his blankets. He peeked out because the human opened the door to send up the drone.

Earl couldn't stand it. He had to get to the window again. Although dark, one could see movement. A doe and her growing fawn stepped away from the drone as it lifted in height, moving toward the spot where the humans were once again probing the ground. To Earl's surprise, another drone flew out from the main stables.

The two humans in the graveyard were not yet aware of the drones. However, one of them walked closer to Ransom Patrick's tombstone, over which was draped a large bag like a feed bag. As he did so, or perhaps it was a she, the drones became obvious. The taller human swung his long probe like a long thin blade as the drone came close enough to send a photo of the man's face. In one swoop, that fellow smashed the drone, which fell to the earth. It was Gray's drone.

Heedless, for those two up there could have been armed, Gray started up the rise. Fearing the second drone, which stayed out of reach, the two ran down the other side of the rise. Gray could no longer see them, as it was pitch black. He couldn't run fast either, as he couldn't see where he was stepping. When he finally reached Ransom's tombstone, he saw the bag was gone. He could still hear Crawford's drone as it tracked the men. Knowing it was hopeless, he turned, picking his way down.

Opening the door to the stable, Gray called Crawford.

"Up here," came the voice. "I'm up in the loft."

Gray found the ladder affixed to the wall, climbed up to see Crawford, hay doors open in the loft. He was peering at images on his control screen.

"We've got them!"

"Where are they?" Gray asked.

"Going to the back road. See. It's the old, rutted farm road behind the graveyards. Getting in the truck now. Got the bag."

Gray focused on the images of the two still indistinguishable humans getting into their old truck then lurching down the road. The drone perfectly shadowed them.

"Now comes the good part." Crawford grinned.

Indeed, Ben waited at the end of the old farm road, along with two other county SUVs. When the two thieves saw him, the driver slammed on the brakes, backed off in a hurry, only to discover another squad car hard up on his rear. So he cut the motor, opened the door, as did his passenger; they ran, leaving the bag in the truck. Two shots fired in the air stopped them.

Neither Gray nor Crawford could hear but as the thieves' hands went up, the two men figured someone had fired. They were handcuffed and marched to one of the SUVs.

"Too clever by half." Crawford motioned for Gray to follow him as he walked across the vast loft then climbed back down.

Gray didn't put a foot on a ladder rung. He put his feet on the outside of the ladder and slid down.

"Come on!" Crawford sprinted to his big Tahoe outside.

The two men jumped in, Crawford holding his cell in one hand, the steering wheel in the other. This made Gray send up a prayer that the Lord watch over them as the Tahoe flew on the worsening roads.

"Ben, we're coming to you."

"Okay," came the answer.

Both of Crawford's hands now on the wheel allowed Gray to exhale.

The old back farm roads had some potholes but nothing was as bad as the back country road the two thieves were on. In five minutes Crawford pulled up to the county vehicles, cut his motor, hopped out, as did Gray.

Jude turned the lights on in his county SUV.

Crawford peered at the two faces. "Who the hell are you?"

Neither man, probably in their thirties, said a word.

Gray looked into the old truck. The bag was there.

Ben, sliding on gloves, pulled it out, dropping it in a larger bag. Prints. "Even though we know they picked this up, I can't leave a stone unturned. You know this will hold up in court." Gray, gloves on, took the note he'd saved out of his pocket, giving it to Ben. Ben dropped that in the bag as well.

The two culprits slunk further down in their seats.

"You almost pulled it off." Gray stared at them, not knowing either of them.

"We weren't doing anything," the taller one remarked sourly.

"You were trespassing if nothing else," Crawford challenged, then turned to Ben. "Just to make sure, open the bag. Maybe they hid the money while driving. Just in case."

The two captured men looked at each other, confused.

Ben opened the bag. "All there."

"All what?" the shorter handcuffed man asked.

"What's your name?" Jude asked. "It's easier if you tell us. We'll find out anyways."

Ben opened the glove compartment of the old rust bucket, reached in, pulling out registration papers. "Which one of you is Gardner Thompkins?"

"I am," the shorter man replied.

"And you?" Ben asked the taller man.

"William Odegaard."

"And you want us to believe you don't know what's in this bag?" Ben held it up so they could see.

Both shook their heads. "No."

So Ben pulled it open, revealing the carefully stacked bills.

"Shit," William whispered to Gardner.

"We don't know nothin' about it. We were poking into the earth and as I turned to walk away from that spot to another at the edge of the tombstones, I saw the bag. The next thing I knew, two drones were on us."

"I smashed the one," Odegaard bragged.

"So we ran. Took the bag."

"You two will have plenty of time to reconsider your statements," Ben quietly said then turned to Crawford. "We need to get them in a cell."

"Wait a minute," Crawford asked, then turned to the two in the backseat. "What are you looking for on Old Paradise? I know you've been up there in the night. This isn't the first time. You don't do damage, but what are you looking for?"

The two again looked at each other, then William answered. "The treasure. It's here. We watched sometimes as you restored the buildings. Thought you would find it. Anyways, it's here. We wanted to find it."

"Why? You were doing all right using blackmail." Crawford's voice rang bitter.

"We aren't blackmailers."

"You expect me to believe that?" Crawford drew closer to the opened window and Ben slightly moved that way in case Crawford reached in.

Gray, watching the two intently, voice more soothing, asked, "But you knew about the blackmail?"

"We don't know nothin'," William replied.

Ben ordered Jude, "Take them away."

"Well, Sheriff, guess you'll have to squeeze it out of them. If I'm lucky, they won't have spent all of my one hundred thousand dollars." Crawford pulled up the collar to his jacket.

Crawford and Gray climbed into Crawford's car. As they drove back, Gray, also a bit cold, remarked, "What if they don't know anything?"

"How can they not? You were told to put the money in the graveyard, the last row of tombstones. And they know the territory. Yes, maybe they would find a treasure, but it seems to me that black-mail is sure money."

Gray said nothing but he didn't believe this was open and shut. Something was missing.

Crawford left him off at the Carriage House. Gray picked up his control for the smashed drone, folded the blankets, putting them to the side. He moved the chairs back. He could smell Earl but paid little attention. Earl opened one eye then closed it. Gray walked out of the Carriage House, closing the big double doors tight. He called Sister even though it was four in the morning. He knew she wouldn't be asleep.

He told her everything.

"Are you all right?"

"Yes. I thought we had them. Crawford thinks we do. I'm not sure. I'll be home in about twenty minutes. I suddenly feel ex-hausted."

"I called Betty and told her to lead the field today, that we would miss the hunt. I am totally confused. Did these two look, well, dangerous?"

"You know, they looked like two not very bright white guys hoping luck would substitute for hard work. The idea that they would find a treasure that people have been talking about since Sophie founded Old Paradise, not a good chance. Blackmail is steadier income," he proclaimed.

"Yes it is, but it can be dangerous."

She was right, dangerous to those behind it and those singled out for being a rich victim.

CHAPTER 35

October 18, 2020, Sunday

"Red-handed." Betty smacked her phone down.

"Yes." Gray agreed. "What surprised me is that they were dumb enough to grab the bag with the drone over them."

Betty shrugged. "Money seduces us all, I guess."

Both denied anything to do with blackmail, Gray informed Betty, who again looked at the images on her phone sent from the reporter, an old friend, from the local newspaper.

"I don't recognize them." Betty peered closely. "Don't know which Thompkins and Odegaards they are."

"There's plenty to choose from." Gray smiled.

"They're locked up. Crawford has his lawyers on it. We'll have to do the same, I suppose, if for nothing else than to get our money back, although it wasn't much thanks to the false bills. Until this is resolved, the department keeps anything that can be considered evidence."

"They don't know that," Gray responded. "They never opened

the bag to count the money. They were apprehended before that, which may be a good thing."

"Ben said Gardner can read and write. William is semi-literate, so Gardner had to have authored the letters. They aren't handwritten, obviously," Gray filled Betty in with more detail. "Still, quite clever for local boys."

"That's what worries me." Sister finally got to what was bugging her. "I don't believe these two could come up with blackmail, especially the images on the thumb drive."

"Sister, you don't know that. Maybe they were helpful in some way. Covering for the woman or women. Delivering goods, presents, when the keeper, for lack of a better word, couldn't get away."

Gray nodded. "Ben said they claimed unemployment."

"Do you really think these homeboys would have been mixed up in something like that?" Sister asked. "I really don't believe it. It's too sophisticated."

"Maybe they figured out the shame, the exposure for upstanding well-to-do citizens was worth it." Betty considered the argument. "Money covers many sins."

Gray thought about this. "Sex is sex and love is love. Women or men, it doesn't make much difference, but sex or faked affection for money is upsetting. Creates evasive behavior obviously. How long can you lie to people before it catches up with you? Look at this whole process, the threats, the threats to the hunt club, all bizarre, but it worked. Two men killed themselves rather than be exposed, I think. Ben doesn't know exactly how Arnold fits in but he's certain he does. So William and Gardner were smart enough to figure out they would pay a huge sum. They didn't figure on suicide. As for us, for showing photos that are not of our hounds I suppose they figured the same thing. We'd pay rather than go through the media hell. You are now guilty until proven innocent."

"But Gray, Ben says they swear they know nothing about our

foxhunting. I mean, more than the usual occasional photo in the paper. I know everyone is eager to wrap this up. It looks tight. I don't think it is."

"Do you believe they were looking for Sophie's treasure?" Betty wondered.

"I do. At one time or another over the centuries I think half the county has looked for Sophie's treasure. But that's not blackmail. Why would they be up there poking around if they had this scam going?" Sister asked.

"There's no saying you can't look for money in different places, sort of two income streams," Gray posited but without enthusiasm.

"Before I forget, how was Mousehold Heath?" Sister asked Betty about the hunt she and Gray missed.

"Good. The B line did very well. The J's, too. Our youngsters should be solid by Opening Hunt."

"I won't take a lot but I will throw in a few. Opening Hunt is overwhelming."

"Always."

CHAPTER 36

October 31, 2020, Saturday

The thap thap thap of the giant waterwheel rhythmically smacking the water, dipping down into the mill race and coming up, throwing water off the wide planks. The wheel had been turning since the early eighteenth century as settlers began to venture to the edge of the Blue Ridge Mountains. A few intrepid souls crossed the mountains, finding a place to live in the rich Shenandoah Valley. Others came to the valley from Pennsylvania, hence so many German surnames.

Mill Ruins could still grind grain if Walter rehabilitated the inside a bit. He thought about it but his cardiology practice consumed most of his time, foxhunting the rest. He swore one day he would find someone who wanted to open the mill and they would go into business.

The house, also built around the time of the mill, displayed the usual Virginia patterns of growth. One started out with a center hallway, rooms on either side, usually two, so there were four rooms and a kitchen across the back, with corresponding rooms upstairs.

That's if the money was pretty good to start. Otherwise it was clap-board building with an upstairs, downstairs, and little else, but even then money did come in over time, especially during Monroe's presidency. Additions were added, like an L or the back was ex-tended. In the case of this house it was the typical four over four with the L. The sight of it, simple, pleasing, made one wonder if our ancestors lived better than we do.

All the people gathered there for Opening Hunt were not thinking much of our ancestors at the exact moment. A last-minute brush of a horse neck or one's boots, a double check of tack, espe-cially the girth, and a hoist up by a friend or stepping up on the portable mounting block kept in the trailer tack room. Scarlet daz-zled on the men who had won their colors. The ladies with colors often wore swallowtail coats called shadbellies. Stock ties proved blindingly white; a stickler for correct terms would not call them a stock tie but usually a tie. A few had a subtle white-on-white pattern. Some wore plain white silk. Others had a digital weave, still others a tiny square weave, which if touched had texture. Gold, or silver, or brass stock pins, carefully in place, set it all off.

One hundred and twenty riders showed up for this special day. The horses, as smartly turned out as their riders, also picked up the excitement. A few snorts and whinnies were issued. A nervous rider was made all the more nervous by this.

An old hand, equine, usually said, *"Come on. You've done this before."*

As humans and horses tarted themselves up, the hounds, noses pressed at the slats of the hound truck, could barely contain their excitement. They'd endured a bath for this, now wearing their very best leather collars. Dressing up always raised expecta-tions.

Walter, as a joint master and the host, still on foot, greeted everyone, asking the visiting Masters did they wish to ride up front in First Flight? Many did, but a few elected to ride Second Flight with Bobby Franklin. Took the pressure off of them. Being a master teaches the individual many things about horses, hounds, landowners, land itself, and people. Any master could go into politics if they so wished. Most did not so wish, hence those few deciding to ride Second Flight, which was a bit less pressured. Well, all flights can be pressured if the horses behind you ride up your butt.

Sister, wearing her elegant shadbelly and a top hat, mounted Lafayette. As her oldest boy, a gleaming gray, he earned the honor of carrying his lady up front. Then, too, he hadn't an ounce of stop in him when a formidable obstacle appeared. Horses came in two types, "Giddy up" and "Whoa." Lafayette was a whoa if it came to that, and if it did Sister was smart enough to ride it out. He usually came back to her. He shone and he knew it. His bit a simple broken D bit, a form of snaffle, also shone. Everything was perfect.

Weevil, Betty, and Tootie, mounted, patiently waited by the hound trailer as they nodded and chatted with people until Sister and Walter called them to order.

As the people pulled themselves together the excitement mounted, which it would at any Opening Hunt even if the temperature was in the seventies or if it was a light rain, nothing could truly dampen the excitement.

James, behind the mill, grumbled, *"If they think I am coming out they are mistaken."* As he aged he began to talk to himself. Crabby young, he was much worse now.

As all this was transpiring in front of the mill, Ryan Stokes had driven his Ram out beyond the mill off to the side to get a shot of every single rider as they turned by the mill and rode on the farm road, two still greenish pastures on either side.

Ayanda wasn't there yet. Ryan was getting anxious. He needed two cameras and he needed her hanging out the window when he drove. She was usually reliable but now he had no idea where she was. While they were sort of a couple, he didn't want to live with her. At this moment he wished he did. He would have gotten her out of the house. Usually she texted. He wasn't worried about her. He was worried about not having that second camera.

Aunt Daniella, Yvonne, and Kathleen had taken up their place way in the rear of all the horses. Ben Sidell, riding, had invited Jude, Carson, and Jackie to come, as his three young officers had never seen Opening Hunt. They were crammed in a car with Marty Howard, who drove over to Mill Ruins to support Jefferson Hunt. Crawford was at home tending to business. Marty, a genial and knowledgeable hostess, put the three younger people at ease. Soon all were chatting, ready to roll.

"Thank you all for coming out today to celebrate our one hundred and thirty-third Opening Hunt. We thank all who have gone on before, be they hound, horse, or human, and especially the foxes. We hope to live up to their example and, as always, to show good sport. Afterward the hunt breakfast will be in the house, hosted by my joint master, without whom I could not function, Dr. Walter Lungren."

Sister nodded to him, so he spoke. "Welcome to Mill Ruins, a part of our hunt since 1891. One of the joys of our sport is the riding over lands tended for centuries. They hunted in good companionship and so do we. Welcome, and we will gather at the breakfast."

Sister then in a clear voice called out, "Hounds, please."

Weevil, after a nod from Sister, put on his cap, which was proper. The Huntsman held his cap until instructed to go by the Master. Everyone quieted. Sister rode to the front of the field along with Walter.

Sam dismounted to the ground as Gray held his horse, the one he was making for Crawford, and opened the party wagon door. Twenty-five couples of hounds rushed out, thrilled. Good kids that they were, they rushed to their huntsman, who was walking forward. Tootie and Betty rode on each side. As it got a bit tight going by and around the huge mill race, going over the old stone bridge, one whipper-in rode forward and one stayed back. Jefferson Hunt teamwork was practically flawless, which certainly made for great sport.

All the foxes living at Mill Ruins knew it was a big day. Those few living in the outbuildings by the house peeked out, watching them go.

Hortensia decided to leave a trail when they returned; she had about two hours to do so. She delighted in seeing hounds run around singing at the top of their lungs while she was already back in the shed watching through the cracks.

Ryan, off the road, had driven through the open gate so he could face the hounds, the Huntsman, and the field coming up from the mill. Standing in the back of his truck he put his camera on the tripod. He avoided handheld shots when possible and this would be a long shot, given the size of the field.

"Come along," Weevil called as Dasher and Diana led the hounds, with Zorro right behind. Tattoo, Audrey, and Aero, the hounds in their prime, eager, pushed forward. The youngsters, who had proved themselves during cubbing, rounded out the middle of the pack. Juno and Jingle, Pantyhose and Pilot moved along with Baylor and Barmaid, while the slightly older hounds moved close behind. They were excited but no one spoke. Hounds and horses knew formal kit when they saw it. The shadbellies and weazlebellies gave Opening Hunt away for animals. The horses all knew because they were braided. Eight braids for geldings, nine for mares. The yarn was the color of the mane. Sometimes a color proved hard to match. Kasmir Barbhaiya was on his new chestnut mare, Lucille Ball, and she was the color of the late Miss Ball's hair. No one could find a flaming red so Lucille had a dark brown braid. Looked fine. Lafayette had white, given he was now almost bleached white. The horses knew the drill, except for the first-timers, whose riders had the sense to keep them in the rear. One hoped that sense would prevail them from moving up during a hard run.

Yvonne, Aunt Daniella, and Kathleen, creeping thirty yards behind the last of Second Flight, thought everyone looked smashing. Behind them drove Marty Crawford, telling Jude, Jackie, and Carson about the sartorial rules. She carefully explained that beautiful as the clothing was, the reason one dressed as they did in the hunt field was that everything was practical.

The fabric on the coats, thick, repels water. Of course, there's not much you can do when the water drips into your boots. There is always a bit of a gap in the back or on the side. Wet feet can be miserable on a cold day. Today it was quite good. The mercury in the low fifties, light breeze, low clouds promised sport.

Jackie asked, "You don't want sunshine?"

Marty replied, "Anything that keeps scent on the ground is desirable. A cloud cover pushes air down a bit. Sunshine allows air to rise, but that doesn't mean you can't get a good run. If the scent is fresh, what we call red hot, you can get a run in difficult conditions. But today is pretty good."

As her passengers listened, windows partly down, all they could hear at that point were the hoofbeats and in the distance Weevil's voice telling hounds to "lieu in," which Marty explained was Norman French. The term told the hounds to go in, look for your quarry. This type of hunting came in with William the Conqueror. Those fighting with King Harold hunted, too, but the Normans felt they were uncivilized.

The last time Mill Ruins was hunted, scent was found in the left large pasture under not very ideal conditions. Today Weevil cast his hounds on the right as he jumped the zigzag fence in the middle of the three-board fencing. He did this because where he cast didn't make much difference in the high pastures and because he wanted to give Ryan good footage. The need for club funds was not lost on the young man.

"Get 'em up. Get 'em up."

Young Peanut, excited beyond belief, ran in circles.

Zorro, mature, driven, chided the lean girl, who was still filling out. *"You look like a ninny. Calm down, put your nose down, and inhale. Inhale. Hear!"*

Peanut said nothing but took in such a large amount of air she coughed, which only disgusted Zorro more.

"Zorro, give her a break. She'll calm down. It's her first Opening Hunt," Thimble advised Zorro, a big fellow.

"Damn kids," was all the hound said in return.

Up ahead, moving at a fast clip but moving with care, Angle, a seven-year-old male whose bloodlines went all the way back to Andrew, one of Jefferson Hunt's great hounds from the 1950s, moved a bit faster. Then his stern flipped a bit and he paused.

"Red male."

Given the regard in which Angle was held, there was no need to double-check. Diana and Dreamboat opened. The rest followed with a roar. Yvonne and the girls, along with Marty and the officers, had inched up closer to the rear. The three passengers in Marty's SUV heard the sound that brings the hairs in your neck up. Hearing about it is one thing. Actually hearing it is quite another.

Weevil had no need to ask Kilowatt for speed. The Thoroughbred zipped right up behind the pack, which ran close together.

Betty followed along the right fence line, while Tootie remained in the other pasture but kept up. She as well as the rest of the staff knew this territory. Foxes delighted in crossing the farm road, forcing people to find their way out of the fencing. Each line of fencing did have a jump but you still had to get to it, which could produce amusing results.

Well, this fox produced another result. He was a new fox who made his home near Grenville, at the bottom acres called Shoot-rough. He blasted out of sight . . . just out of sight, given the roll of the pasture . . . crossed the road, and found himself in the left pasture, right under Tootie's nose.

She counted to twenty. "Tally-ho."

That was all hounds, who had turned with the line as well as the Huntsman, high on the music, high on Opening Hunt, needed. Weevil squeezed Kilowatt toward the three-board fencing. Both sailed over in perfect form. That was a bit too formidable for many, even in First Flight. Sister was tempted to do it, partly because she was in her seventies and wearied of hearing how she was old. She could wear their asses out, but perhaps not at Opening Hunt with one hundred and twenty people behind you. Sometimes a girl must throttle her ego.

Lafayette, seeing Kilowatt, was furious that they couldn't do likewise. His jumping, that visible gleaming gray coat, really was spectacular, but he listened, galloped down to the coop, which itself took some courage for others. It was three six but freshly painted, appearing quite stout. Over they flew, only to have the coop right across in the other fence line, so it was jump, four strides, jump. Lafayette was flawless. Sister hoped that she was, too, but there wasn't time to consider was her leg perfect, because another jump loomed ahead at the rear of the left pasture.

Sister heard the pack now in the woods. With some leaves off the trees, sound became magnified compared to cubbing. Her heart raced not from fear but thrill. Nothing in her life could ever compare to a run with hounds in full cry. Not even giving birth, which wasn't exactly a thrill but was a memorable physical experience. Over the three substantial logs they flew. She could hear behind her the occasional rap but as she heard no cries she assumed the field was still on board. Now, that was special, for she almost always lost one or two in the first run when the field was huge.

The landing, soft in the woods, allowed Lafayette to dig in. The path, big enough for an ATV, was clear, quite good, but it began to drop and almost without warning became steep. She knew the territory so she leaned back a bit, asked Lafayette to rate not a lot but enough. You never know about a steep grade. He listened. Hounds screamed.

Grenville also heard hounds scream. He came out of his living quarters in the large old equipment shed down in Shootrough. No longer used for big equipment, some hay bales, big round ones, had been rolled in there to escape the rain. The lesser quality hay bales sat across the road from the shed. Walter usually sold that to his neighbors for their cattle. The hay in the shed he used for Clemson and Clemson's pasture mate, a horse old enough to vote. Grenville was not going to give hounds a chase but he had met his new neighbor and thought he might watch for a bit.

Sure enough, the young red, sleek and bright, shot out of the woods, making for the indoor hay bales.

"Lucifer, here! They'll dig you out over there."

The young fox veered toward Grenville's voice, saw a bushy tail disappear and followed as he, too, slid down then emerged into the shed. Marveling at the vastness of the space, the hay lined up along the one long seventy-foot wall, he breathed the proverbial sigh of relief.

"You need a better den. Those outdoor hay bales will be moved. I know you've dug into them. It seems like a good place but it isn't. Hounds will dig you out and then where will you go?"

Catching his breath, the young fox dropped his eyes a moment then looked up. *"Thank you. Where will I go?"*

"I'll show you once they're out of here. It will take a few hours. We have to wait, for you can never trust the people or the hounds, they go in circles sometimes. I've done it to them, you think they'd be dizzy and fall over." Grenville laughed.

"Does this happen often?"

The gray looked at the flashy red and answered, *"About once a month. They'll come here in a light rain, snow, sun, of course. Usually you can hear them and smell them in enough time to get away."*

"Ah." The young fellow was now listening to hounds carrying on at the den openings. There were two, one he used and then one on the other side.

"Come out," Barrister hollered.

Dasher, next to the young hound, smiled. *"He is sitting in there laughing at us, but hey, we got in a good run. We'll find another. It's a good day for scent."*

"Can he hear me?"

"He can," Dasher replied. *"The longer you hunt, the more you will discover foxes are smart. Here comes the Huntsman."*

Weevil dismounted, blew "Gone to Ground," then praised his hounds, reaching down to pet Dasher and Barrister. The young hounds wiggled in delight.

"You've done well, Barrister. Dasher, you always do. All right, hounds, let's find another fox."

Betty held Kilowatt's reins, the Thoroughbred not even winded, while Weevil swung up into the saddle. All hounds' eyes lifted to him.

"Ready?"

You bet they were.

Weevil looked around. The field stood fifteen yards away in a semicircle so people could see. Sister was at the front of First Flight. Walter was at the back and Bobby Franklin was even farther behind, but everyone could get a bit of a view. Weevil felt a cool wind on his cheek from the north. It was enough to carry scent. He rode onto the rutted farm road. It was deep back there heading north. The territory became rougher, although it was not steep. Hounds cast onto the cutover acres into the wind. On they moved until they reached a tertiary state road at a ninety-degree angle to the Shoot-rough farm road. Stopping, Weevil chose not to cross the road. The territory on the other side, an old timber tract that was let go, had fallen trees, limbs, and choking undergrowth. Turning back he moved one hundred yards from the state road to disappear into Walter's timber abutting the pasture. The climb was steep, one had to climb to reach the upper meadows, where the land again flattened out.

Hitting a deer trail, hounds moved ahead, some fanning out into the woods, which while thick had good trails.

Ryan couldn't shoot anything. There was no way in there, plus if he went on foot and hounds hit, he'd fall far behind, having to run to his truck to drive to catch up.

He could hear Weevil blow a note or two. Frustrated, he climbed back behind the wheel, put the window down to listen intently. Ahead of him, anticipating where hounds would come out, Yvonne and Marty used the steep road by which they came down. Ryan waited about five minutes then decided it was the best way, so he, too, got on that road.

Tootie trotted twenty yards ahead of Weevil on a decent deer trail. Coyote prints and bobcat prints caught her eye. If they hopped a coyote, how would they follow him in this?

She was about to find out.

Parker, a steady hound now ten, was close to the end of his hunting career. He'd live in the kennels when that happened and work with youngsters. Hounds learned more easily from one another than they did from humans. Amazingly, most humans never figured this out.

"*Coyote!*" the handsome boy shouted.

Whoever this coyote was he was far ahead, for scent proved faint and the coyote scent is heavier than fox. Hounds know this, of course, and they could have run faster but Diana, the wisest hound, feared they would overrun the line, which was easy to do in woods. Better to be steady, and then as the line heated up one could always turn up the speed.

Hounds, noses down, walked on then trotted a bit. The steep grade forced everyone to pay attention to the climb. Many riders stood in their stirrups to throw their weight forward. While one always hopes to be over the center of gravity it is easier said than done. One misstep, a slip, a slight hole, and your center of gravity would soon be on the ground.

Sister leaned forward but she didn't stand in her stirrups. These two had been partners for so long she needed only to put her hands forward and almost rest her face on Lafayette's neck. He'd take care of things and he had to reach and push hard from behind. It was a hateful grade.

Hounds came out of the woods in that meadow in which they first encountered scent. They followed the fence line on the far side of the pasture. Scent heated up enough that they could trot.

Weevil now appeared, petting Kilowatt's neck for his hard work climbing the grade. Betty and Tootie, already in place, watched, slowly moving with hounds from their respective positions.

Out of nowhere it seemed, Jeeves, a second year entry, boomed, *"He's heading for the mill."*

He was. His scent seemed to intensify in a flash and the pack roared toward the mill, which was not an easy place to hunt. Then they stopped, turned back, and ran away from that direction only to parallel it farther down, so instead of heading toward the mill they all flew toward the many outbuildings around, as well as from the house.

By now it seemed to be every man for himself, as the field had gotten strung out by that steep climb. Also quite a few riders were still recovering from Lucifer's run. Not everyone starts Opening

Hunt hunting fit. Walter tried to goose them up as Bobby Franklin came up hard behind him. Second Flight had more sense on that run and climb than the rear of First Flight. Bobby slowed. He had no choice but he and his flight could see the entire pack flying again toward a part of the farm they rarely hunted. This was going to be interesting.

A basic coop in the fence line was easy. Hounds jumped over; a few wriggled under the fence, but most jumped. No one wanted to be left behind, as everyone was screaming. Tootie and Betty moved ahead but Betty had to circumvent the mill ride and came around the house. She was not woefully behind but she was behind. Outlaw, a great whip horse, was not a Thoroughbred. He was not going to catch up to Kilowatt, who could blast through a furlong in fourteen seconds, which might seem slow to a racetrack trainer but this was fast enough. In Jefferson Hunt territory you needed balance and handiness as much if not more than speed. Kilowatt had both. Tootie, on her older fellow, Iota, a Thoroughbred, could not get in front of the pack but she stayed close to Weevil.

Lafayette, in his glory, left everyone behind. Sister was a good rider on a beloved mount; however, he was not about to be rated. So you sat there and enjoyed it. He was so happy, his stride, long and fluid, allowed anyone who had ever seen a Thoroughbred at full reach to understand why they are and always will be the greatest of athletes. Cats might disagree . . . but then again, Lafayette could snort and scare the devil out of Golliwog.

Tears fell from Sister's eyes, they flew so fast. The pack roared. Across the western side of Mill Ruins they blasted over a cutover hayfield. The footing was perfect, giving but not sticky. Without warning, in their excitement Juno, Baylor, and Pater disappeared as the entire pack screeched to a halt. So did Weevil, who previously came close to following his young entry now swimming in the mill race. The pace was so intense, the ground covered so fast, Weevil, who didn't know this part of Mill Ruins, was not fully prepared for the mill race.

"Come along," he called to the three swimmers.

"What happened?" Pater whined.

"You overran," Dasher, leaning over, told them.

"I did not overrun the line," Juno fumed.

"You overran the territory." Dasher stifled a laugh.

Weevil called for Juno and Baylor to climb out.

Pater had hauled himself up.

Betty rode up in case she needed to dismount and pull up hounds but everyone made it.

"Is there a bridge?" Weevil, anxious to follow this hot line, asked.

"Yes, follow me. It's almost a mile down the road on the way back. It's a culvert with packed earth, but we can do it."

She took off, Weevil following. Tootie also had to follow, as there was no way to jump the mill race. It had to be twenty yards wide and fast flowing.

Betty relaxed, even as the gallop got them there in good time. She walked over the center of the earth to be the guinea pig. Still held after all these years in this back, relatively unused territory. Weevil followed, then Tootie. They fanned out as Weevil pushed hounds toward where he thought the line might swing back. It certainly wasn't going to conveniently be by the rutted but serviceable road.

Sister shortly came up, stopped. She held up her hand. "One by one. Please one by one, and when you are across make sure to wait for the rider behind you." She stepped across, waited for Kasmir, who was behind on Lucille, a real flyer. He in turn waited for Alida and she waited for Gray. One by one the remaining field, now sixty strong, did cross without incident. And hounds hit the line again, full throttle.

Yvonne stopped, as did Marty. Ryan stopped but ran across the bridge on foot to shoot what he could. If only he could have gotten the shot of the three hounds in the mill race. Ryan was frustrated but doing the best he could. If he had had Ayanda, he might have been able to send her up ahead, but then again, she didn't know the territory, few did back here.

Weevil pressed on. Horses had had two long runs, a hard climb. A few needed to pull up. Staff horses, in good shape, did not, but how long could this go on? The acres, also cutover on this side, undulated just enough to make you tighten your leg. Hounds kept going.

Finally they stopped at a sweet gum tree, that bark so noticeable.

Looking down at the pack was not a coyote but a gray fox.

"What happened to the coyote?" Barmaid wondered.

"He must have crossed the line close to this tree." Trooper put his nose down to backtrack a bit. *"Here. Right here."* The pack followed him as Weevil rode up.

"Did we do wrong?" the young entry asked.

"No," all the older hounds answered. *"This is so close."*

"We were all so hot and so close we didn't notice the change in game, but a few more strides and we would."

Sister came up. The rest of the field filed in one by one. Ryan ran on foot, thrilled to get the shot of the gray in the tree.

"Good hounds. Good hounds." Weevil praised them. He considered blowing "Gone to Ground" but then took his hat off to the gray fox, who looked down.

Sister walked up to Weevil. "I would never have believed we were on a gray. Surely we would have seen this fox."

Weevil smiled. "I don't know. If I could get down on all fours and have a sniff, maybe I would know. It was, well, original."

She laughed. "That it was."

Ryan walked around everyone, videoing the crowd, then he again swung the camera up to the fox, who looked fetching.

"Many people are about out of horse. Let's walk back, cool down and call this one of our best Opening Hunts ever."

"Yes, Madam." He grinned, which only made him more handsome. "Come along, my angels. You were so wonderful."

"He said we were wonderful." Young Pantyhose was the happiest she had ever felt in her young life.

Diana, in the front, replied, *"We were."*

All the hounds murmured their agreement and all walked the two miles back to the big mill. No one realized how exhausted they were until they reached their trailers. Hounds were put up in the party wagon with lots of water and piles of biscuits as treats until they returned to the kennel for a restorative and rewarding hot meal.

People winced as they dismounted. Legs were sore.

The three car followers parked away from the crowd, disembarked to walk through the riders, offer assistance. The young law enforcement officers crowded around Ben Sidell, who glowed. They had never seen their sheriff this happy. Nonni, his beloved mare, gladly accepted a wipe down and some fresh water, which Jude brought her.

"May I untack her, Sheriff?"

Ben, a bit shaky, replied, "Thank you. She's an easy girl."

Jude liked touching the horse. Nonni liked the attention.

Ryan walked around everyone, taking close-ups of horses drinking, hay bags being tied to the sides of trailers, and just wiped-out people dropping on their trailer steps.

Sister dismounted, a twinge of soreness, for it was one helluva ride. She patted Lafayette's neck then walked around to give him a kiss.

"You are the best, Lafayette. The best."

He kissed her back. *"We showed them. Everyone saying we're too old."*

She took off his bridle while Weevil quickly came over to help her take the saddle off. Usually she would leave it on, but the temperature was now a balmy sixty degrees. No need to worry about cold air on a sweaty back. He wiped him down as Sister wiped Lafayette's face. Then a thin cotton dark green sheet was tossed over the lovely fellow. A feed bag with alfalfa mixed with orchard grass, really enticing stuff, hung on the side of the trailer.

"Weevil, you were terrific today."

"All credit to the hounds, Madam. All those glorious American hounds."

Tootie came over. Weevil bent down to give her a kiss. She was not one for public displays but she actually kissed him back.

Betty winked at Sister.

Ryan hollered, "Will everyone line up in front of the mill so I can get a quick shot of all of you after this hunt? Will prove who can still stand."

Everyone laughed.

Sister, who hated photographs, knew it was for the best. She generally cooperated. Everyone filed toward the mill. That big wheel's paddles making a sound familiar for centuries. The mill race turning the paddle had been dug in 1816 as the mill itself was being built. For the first time many of the riders saw how long the mill race was and they still had not seen all of it. The man hours alone for a structure that big and a fast-running race would be hard to fathom. No one knew how to work like that today. Back then it was raw manpower, the owner, his workers, his indentured servants, his slaves, and slaves borrowed from other owners. Everyone pitched in because everyone needed a mill.

As Ryan moved riders in place, Sister, Walter, Weevil, Tootie, and Betty in the center, Ayanda drove up. She hopped out of her car, racing with her camera. In her excitement she didn't close the door tightly.

Her dog followed, carrying her purse. "Get that dog out of here!" Ryan screamed, but it was too late.

Jude squinted.

Jackie wondered but Jude, who had been in the church closest to the memorial statue, called to Ben, "That's the dog."

Ryan pushed Ayanda in the mill race as he turned to run, dropping his camera at his feet. He forgot about her dog, who jumped, grabbing him by the throat. Both fell into the mill race. Ayanda tried to swim to the side but Ryan reached for her with one hand as her dog continued to bite him. Ryan dragging her down, the dog again managed to reach his throat, tearing at it. Slowly swimming with the struggling man toward the water wheel. They were close as Ayanda swam for all she was worth to the side. The dog released Ryan, who reached for his bleeding throat. He drifted in range of the huge water wheel. A paddle came down on his head. People screamed as they heard the crack.

The dog swam to his master, who was being pulled out by Walter, who then pulled up the brave dog.

Ben was immediately there as Gray, Sam, and Kasmir threw a rope. Ryan didn't surface until the wheel came up. He was splayed across it as it climbed. He was dead. Throat bleeding, one arm hanging over the paddle.

Jude said to Ben, "That's the dog."

Ayanda held up her hands but said nothing.

"You are under arrest." Ben read her the Miranda act.

"What in God's name is going on?" Betty said to Sister.

"I'm not sure but I think we may have found our killer. Too late."

CHAPTER 37

November 2, 2020, Monday

The next day's presidential election dominated the airwaves, Facebook, whatever communication device was in use. However it was barely noticed by people who had been at Opening Hunt on Saturday.

The afternoon sun warmed hounds, horses, and people. Staff rode with hounds to walk them. Stretching everyone's legs after being hunted Saturday was a good idea.

Opening Hunt did leave cleanup. Whether it was Walter and his crew, which had most of the house cleaned up at Mill Ruins (people had to eat no matter what) or checking and double-checking hounds and horses once home, as it had been an intense hunt.

The real focus was Ryan's unforgettable death. Seeing his body rise out of the water, paddle holding him, throat and head bloodied would remain in everyone's memory.

Ben sent a diver to search for Ayanda's purse, which he found. Everything and anything that could be used as evidence for that day was searched, eyewitness accounts taken at the breakfast, which proved helpful to the law enforcement officer. Much as officers are accustomed to it, it was tedious work.

The dog, who protected his master, was sent to the SPCA for safekeeping until Ayanda would be released from jail. As she was young, she had no lawyer, no one to post bail. Finally, Freddie Thomas contacted a lawyer from McGuire Woods, who did get Ayanda released. The first thing she did was get her dog but she had to wait while the ladies at the counter phoned Ben Sidell for confirmation that the dog, Doobie, was not dangerous.

Ben cleared Doobie, who had been protecting Ayanda. It was a provoked defense.

Having untacked, washed down the horses, thrown a light sheet over them, Sister and Betty repaired to the house this Monday. Gray, working from the library today, greeted them.

"Ben is coming over. Told him we'd be happy to see him."

"Let me call Weevil and Tootie; they should be here, too," Sister replied as she walked for her phone.

She still preferred her landline; for one thing, a cell so close to the mountains provided erratic service. You could clearly hear the landline most times.

Ben showed up in half an hour. Sister and Betty made sandwiches. Gray brewed his famous Jamaican coffee, reserved for special occasions. Ben could use a lift. Apart from Ryan's death there had been unfortunate incidents of fistfights outside each candidate's headquarters.

"Someone's here," Raleigh announced.

Rooster walked to the mudroom door. Golly stayed on the counter. She could see better.

"Come on in, Ben," Gray called as Betty walked over to open the door.

"Come on. Sit down. You've got to be hungry and tired."

"Well." He didn't answer, but he was.

"What can we do to help?" Betty asked as they all sat in front of fat sandwiches.

"Well, I did call on Risé as well as Arnold Synder's ex-wife to prepare them for what will show up in the news. If they are lucky, the election will bury much of this."

Nobody said anything because they had no details, except that now they knew Ryan was connected to the suicides.

"It might do that but eventually this will grab everyone's attention. Local news is always so much more interesting than national." Betty put more Duke's mayo on her sandwich.

"Betty, just put the whole jar on."

"You know I love mayo." Betty kept at it as Sister opened her own sandwich. She thought she had put on enough mayonnaise. Then again, she took the jar from Betty, dipping in her own knife.

Gray poured Ben coffee as well as for himself. The girls, as he thought of them, stuck to sparkling water this late afternoon.

Ben opened his notebook. "Ayanda, I believe, is telling the truth. Ryan wanted money to advance his career. It was all he thought about. He had shot advertising videos for Arnold, later did one for Greg to send to lumberyards selling to the public. Greg was a wholesaler. He began to cover the market. Over time Greg realized he and Arnold needed an outlet for their energies. A pickup, sort of.

"Ryan lived online. He was prisoner to the screen, especially the porn videos. Ayanda said she asked him to stop. He swore he was trying to learn how to make money off of sex without operating a house of prostitution. He found a series of websites where young women, beautiful, advertised to become your mistress. The videos were alluring and the women were clear about their demands. Sort of sexual HR."

"Like money?" Betty asked.

"That and sexual acts they would perform but that was alluded to in code, really. This way they wouldn't be breaking the law for offering sex. They were offering companionship."

"But the salary was stated?" Gray asked.

Ben nodded. "I've gone on the sites. Most all contain the words *Sugar* or *Honey* on the website. They state salary, working hours, rent or purchase of a condominium or apartment or house she selects. Also a car in her name and a weekly spending account, much of which was preselected as to his benefit. Like her hairstylists, fingernails, wardrobe. These were not cheap girlfriends."

Sister blurted out, "I can't believe it."

"It's part of our lives now," Ben replied.

Tootie said, "This is how some women get through college."

"My God." Betty threw up her hands. "What happened to scholarships?"

"Ayanda was editing hunting footage. Opening Ryan's desk drawer to see if they had more footage, she found three thumb drives. Curious, she put them in her computer and she said she was shocked and devastated. She loved Ryan. Never thought he would blackmail people. She at least found out he wasn't cheating on her, which was her primary concern," Ben continued.

"Do you truly believe she didn't know?" Betty asked.

"Meaning could she have been the person who edited the thumb drives? Could she be lying about how much she knew? Possibly."

Sister, wiping some mayo off her lips, remarked, "Betty, it sounds like she was truly in love with him. Maybe she was beginning to realize how self-centered he was."

Ben added, "She believed once he rented a major studio in Richmond, they would be working together. She would benefit."

"What I don't understand is, was this really a cash cow?" Sister put down her sandwich.

Ben put his cup in the saucer with a little clink. "Neither Greg nor Arnold knew Ryan had tiny cameras set up in the women's apartments. That was his demand for finding the women Johns, so to speak. You can hide cameras behind a piece of tape with a slit big enough to capture images. We will never know how much he did film. Given the extreme reaction, I believe Ryan sent a series of thumb drives, all explicit. Humiliating."

"Ah," was all Betty said.

Weevil, who had been silent, said, "A sex scandal is worse than forgery, larceny, crimes like that. Yes, a few men will kill themselves over money, but more would end their life over something this ruinous and ultimately ridiculous. People will laugh as well as judge."

Sister looked at Tootie then Betty. "He's right. I'll bet this is why Arnold's wife settled out of court for everything but the business, which she got when he died. She must have found evidence, Ryan's videos."

Ben bit into his sandwich then swallowed. "Years ago there was a place in New York called Plato's Retreat, where people could go to hook up with one another. And even as we speak there are women seeking a high-life with high-living men. If you're young, good-looking, have good manners, and you're promised money, access to the rich and possibly famous, maybe you don't know what you're getting into but it sounds good."

"That is true." Gray nodded. "So much of what you do when you are young comes back to haunt you when you realize what it was. Is it immoral? Human beings can justify anything. If you can handle money, it is very easy to justify sex with a married man. If you're the man, you probably feel young again. Plus you are in control. You pay her rent, her car, her jewelry. She'll do whatever you want once she gets used to living well."

"How in the hell do you know what you're doing if you're a

twenty-two-year-old beauty linked up with a fifty-two-year-old man whose wallet is huge? Women who are kept or an ordinary sex worker, you know, five guys a night, at fifty to a hundred dollars a pop. They all say this is what they want to do. They are in control?" Sister's voice questioned the premise.

Tootie quietly agreed. "I think many people feel that way. They don't express it."

"Well, have you ever been approached?" Betty blurted out.

"I have, but I never fell for it, and I thank Mom for that."

"Doobie," Ben replied. "Ayanda said her dog was trained to carry packages, to fetch slippers and most anything. Ryan wanted to blackmail Crawford, more on that later, and he thought Doobie could do it. He was smart enough to know Crawford wouldn't initially comply with the sum and would play him for a sucker. That's why he wanted the bag at the Bland graveyard monument. Hang it there, which Crawford did. Jude, Jackie, Carson, and I waited and waited.

"After hours you get fatigued trying to stay alert. It was dark. Jude, in the church, looked out, as the rest of us were hidden in other places, and saw a motion, then saw Doobie streak across the graveyard, grab the bag strap, and run off. When he saw Doobie running after Ayanda with her purse, he called out that it was the dog, as Ryan was yelling at Ayanda to put up her dog."

"You have to admire that he was clever about the money and the church. But who would ever think of a dog as a thief?" Sister looked down at Rooster.

Rooster replied, *"Another dog with a bone."*

"Do you really believe Ayanda?" Gray asked, echoing Betty.

"She's no doubt left out details or anything that would further implicate her as an accessory, but she swears she knew nothing about Greg or Arnold's blackmail until she found thumb drives with compromising material. She did know about Crawford and later the threat to Jefferson Hunt. That money demand. It was all about money now."

"This is a lot worse than I thought," Gray admitted.

"But Ryan?" Betty pushed. "Who would have thought he'd do something like this."

"It's hard to believe this was going on in our community." Sister was stunned.

"Betty." Gray looked at her. "Greed. One of the seven deadly sins."

"It isn't something one would think about," Weevil responded. "It's not that we all don't know there is a lot of sex everywhere, but this is so planned. Almost corporate in a way."

"It's gross," was all Tootie could say.

"What was the point of Crawford?" Tootie asked as she had spent some time with Crawford, as her mother was over there taking riding lessons from Sam, who worked with Crawford.

She had come to like him.

"Well, Ryan hoped for money, but basically blackmailing Crawford was to throw us off. His motivation with Greg and Arnold was money. Given the cameras in the apartments, he must have considered this a long-term source of income."

"If it had gone on, say, for a year or two, who is to say that either Greg or Arnold wouldn't have killed Ryan."

"Good Lord, we've been through some unconventional things at the hunt club, but I doubt we will ever see anything like this Opening Hunt." Sister finished her sandwich.

"Honey, don't say that." Gray reached for her hand. "My mother always said, 'Talk of old troubles may bring on new.' "

Sister squeezed his hand.

Betty asked, "Does Crawford know?"

"Yes," Ben replied. "He also offered to drop any charges

against William and Gardner, including trespassing, which is all we have against them now."

"That's decent," Tootie said.

Weevil smiled at her. "What were they doing? Really."

"Looking for the treasure. They said they thought if they pierced the earth they might hit a big box or something. You know they aren't the brightest bulbs on the Christmas tree." Ben shrugged. "They didn't mean any harm."

"How did Risé and Paula take the news?" Betty asked of the wife and ex-wife.

"With resignation," Ben answered.

"Ben, does it have to be public knowledge about the kept women? After all, Ryan is dead. Only Ayanda and we know, and the wife and ex-wife."

"Let's put it this way, I will cite that Crawford was blackmailed. But as Greg and Arnold committed suicide, there was no crime reported at that time, but even though I might be able to keep all this out of the news I had to warn the wives. You never know what the media might dig up, or if Ayanda is charged what will happen in the courtroom."

"We'll do what we can." Betty meant that. "One can only hope people won't prod. As to the media, they'll wallow in it until people tire of it, I guess."

They all sat silently, sandwiches finished.

Finally Weevil inquired, "There were no letters to Greg and Arnold?"

"None found. All we have is that thumb drive, which once Ayanda told me where the footage was shot, I am pretty sure Arnold received a thumb drive, too. When and where is the evidence. He may have destroyed it. It may show up years from now in a crack in the floor of his office. You never know."

"How is Doobie?" Betty thought the dog incredible.

"Okay, I guess, now that he's home with Ayanda and she's out on bail. Will she be found guilty? Who knows? She participated in a criminal activity. Blackmailing Crawford is a crime. One can hope she repents."

"If she goes up the river, I'll take the dog." Betty surprised everyone. "Bobby and I haven't had a dog in years. If he's that smart, maybe I can teach him to do the books."

"Dogs are too dumb to do the books," Golly announced.

"Shut up," Rooster shot back.

"Well, Ben, I hope this is over," Sister quietly said.

One can always hope.

CHAPTER 38

November 27, 2020, Friday

A semicircle of Crawford, Sister, and Charlotte stood around a hole being dug by three stout men. The air, chilly, did not keep the men from sweating. Digging is hard work.

Another clink was heard. This energized the men in the dirt. Ransom Patrick's tombstone stood guard over this intense activity.

Two men bent over to wiggle a large chest. Another chest could just be viewed next to it at the same level. "One. Two. Heave," Whitney, the head worker, chanted.

Up wiggled a large, heavy chest. No one could lift it out.

"Bring up Brutus." Crawford was already on the phone. "And for good measure, how about Rufus, too. The chest is hundreds of pounds."

The three men climbed out of the hole, sat down to rest. Charlotte offered them bottled water. She usually had a bottle near her. They politely refused. Sunlight sliced through the denuded trees as well as illuminated the lush evergreens.

Twenty minutes later, up came two stunning Clydesdales, Brutus and Rufus. Hitched, groomed, ready for the work for which they were bred. No fancy pants, these two.

The men back down in the rectangular hole wrapped chains around the first chest.

Whitney counseled, "Tight. You all stand back. If one of these chains snaps, it could take your head off with it."

Everyone did as they were told.

Sam drove the team. The driving stable manager was accustomed to fine harness horses. Hitching up the big boys he could do, but not quickly. Luckily, Sam was there, as he had brought over a young hunt horse to work at Old Paradise, since that's where the beautiful blood bay would be riding most times. Sam whipped together the harness quickly.

"Okay, boys," Sam gently urged the two.

Straining, Brutus and Rufus pulled, pulled, and finally the chest pitched upwards until freed from its earthly grave. The team dragged the enormous chest about twenty feet away.

"Okay. Let's unhook this and the boys can cinch up the next chest." Sam worked quickly, soon throwing the chains to the men in the hole.

"Power. Raw horsepower." Sister smiled, for she loved heavy horses, having grown up with them.

Crawford grunted. "Easy to forget what life was like before the internal combustion engine."

Five minutes later, Whitney tossed the chains out of the hole. Sam picked them up, hooked back to the equipment behind the horses, a metal horizontal bar attached by a crossbar.

"Okay, boys."

Again, the two obedient horses strained, pulled, dug into the earth with the front hooves, finally sliding the chest over the top, dragging it maybe ten feet away to near the first chest.

"Anything else down there?" Crawford asked.

"Hard to tell. We can keep digging. My advice is, if you brought up a backhoe, you would find out faster." Whitney wiped his brow.

Looking at the fatigued man, the horses calmly standing, Crawford nodded. "I should have thought of that in the first place. The backhoe is at the farm."

He meant his living quarters, Beasley Hall, another big estate but everything brand new.

"Okay. Let's break the lock." Whitney climbed up.

Sam wanted to watch, so he asked his boss, "Do you mind if I watch, then I'll take Brutus and Rufus back? These are great horses. You have a good eye." Sam wisely praised Crawford, who reveled in praise, accurate or not.

"Sure."

Using a crowbar and a large hammer, Whitney at the first chest and the other two at the second one, struck as hard as they could. Finally, both locks broke. Sister, Charlotte, and Sam moved behind Crawford.

"Oh my God!" Charlotte exclaimed.

A huge grin crossed Crawford's cleanly shaven face. "Sophie's treasure."

Inside both chests, stacked, were gold florins. The value of these coins varied over the centuries. At the time of the War of 1812, they ranged from two shillings to perhaps four. Hard to say because currency varies. Even then people invested in currency and took their chances.

Crawford put his hands into the coins, lifting them, coins spilling through his fingers. "A fortune. A fortune then and worth far more today."

Crawford, thrilled, scooped up a handful, which he gave to Sister. "Happy hunting."

Then he repeated the process, giving a handful to Sam, Charlotte, Whitney, and the two men.

"Boss, this is so generous." Sam had an idea each florin today was worth about $150 apiece, if not more. There was real gold in the coins.

"Here!" Laughing, Crawford again gave everyone a handful. "Finders. Keepers. Here's to Sophie Marquette." He nodded to the sky above.

Driving home in the afternoon light, Sister reached over to poke the old horse cookie bucket in which she put her coins. Sam, stables full of hard plastic cookie baskets, had given everyone a bucket. The euphoria grew instead of wearing off.

Sister wanted to show Gray in person. She thought a phone call would spoil it.

As she drove by the main house at Old Paradise, the sun reached the top of the columns, turning the acanthus leaves gold.

She thought to herself how Callimachus intended the Corinthian capital to represent immortality, enduring life. Not a woman given to flights of fancy, she nonetheless wondered if Sophie could see her home now. Without a doubt, Sister believed, Ransom and Sophie had buried much of the treasure. Sophie'd had much more or she never would have built Old Paradise, underwritten Custis Hall, the girls' school. The woman stole millions. The two of them were a formidable team. Was Ransom Sophie's Potemkin minus the sex? Were they two people who could mesh their energies?

One was a slave, the other free. Both were discounted. A woman and a slave. Sister thought that helped them get the better of their enemies.

She slowed, staring at the majestic columns.

"Are we not a summation of all that has gone before? The savage brutality, the blinding intellectual brilliance, the magic of the arts, the love between partners and between friends? Perhaps we have moved onward. Perhaps we have simply changed clothes." She didn't know but in her mind she saw a line of great hounds, great horses, clever foxes, marvelous people she knew and loved who had gone on. How she wished she had known Sophie and Ransom.

The light shifted, even more intense gold than before. She wished her son could see this and then she allowed herself the wish we all wish, that he was with Sophie, Ransom, his father, the hounds, and all were looking down laughing at this absolutely rapturous moment, a moment filled with hope and treasure.

She believed you honor the dead by living, living at a full gallop. Grab mane and kick on.

ACKNOWLEDGMENTS

Richard Roberts, Huntsman at Middleburg Hunt, est. 1906, Matthew Van Der Woude, Huntsman at Warrenton Hunt, est. 1887, and Stephen "Reg" Spreadborough, Huntsman at Orange County Hounds, est. 1900, have endured my questions, visits for years. They have helped me breed good hounds.

Special thanks to Suzy Reingold, ex-MFH of Plum Run Hunt, and to her co-author, Emily Latimer, for their book, *English Foxhound*. I refer to this often as I do to Robert and Polly Smith's, *The American Foxhound*.

The doorstopper in my reference reading is Alexander Mackay-Smith's *The American Foxhound, 1747–1967*. Mine is tattered.

I try not to inflict my breeding passion onto you readers. Yet Sister Jane is a master and breeds hounds. I try to be brief but accurate.

And, of course, I think my hounds are wonderful. Parental love!

Rita Mae Brown is the bestselling author of the Sneaky Pie Brown mysteries; the Sister Jane series; the Runnymede novels, including *Six of One* and *Cakewalk; A Nose for Justice* and *Murder Unleashed; Rubyfruit Jungle* and *In Her Day;* as well as many other books. An Emmy-nominated screenwriter and a poet, Brown lives in Afton, Virginia, and is a Master of Foxhounds and the huntsman.

ritamaebrownbooks.com

To inquire about booking Rita Mae Brown for a speaking engagement, please contact the Penguin Random House Speakers Bureau at speakers@penguinrandomhouse.com.

A B O U T   T H E   T Y P E

This book was set in Baskerville, a typeface designed by
John Baskerville (1706–75), an amateur printer and
typefounder, and cut for him by John Handy in 1750.
The type became popular again when the Lanston
Monotype Corporation of London revived the classic
roman face in 1923. The Mergenthaler Linotype Company in England and the United States cut a version of
Baskerville in 1931, making it one of the most widely
used typefaces today.